HEIRESS OF ARDARA

HEIRESS
OF
ARDARA

MARGARET EVANS PORTER

Doubleday

NEW YORK

1988

LIBRARY OF CONGRESS
Library of Congress Cataloging-in-Publication Data
Porter, Margaret Evans.
    Heiress of Ardara/Margaret Evans Porter.
        p.   cm.
    "Starlight romance."
    I. Title.
PS3566.0653H4   1988
813'.54—dc19   87-21928
            ISBN 0-385-24491-6

For Chris, with love and gratitude
for his forbearance and faithful
support.

HEIRESS OF ARDARA

CHAPTER I

The Dublin streets were dampened by the thin March drizzle, and most of the fashionable pedestrians on Grafton Street had rushed into the nearest shop at the onset of the rain. But two female figures continued on their way, unhurried and apparently unconcerned by the inclement weather. The younger lady's sigh of resignation attested to the fact that the circumstance of a shower was neither unusual nor unexpected; her barely quickened pace indicated that she was in no way discommoded by the damp, despite possible damage to the pelisse of fine brown cloth and straw bonnet trimmed with fur. Her every step disclosed a white muslin dress beneath the brown fabric of her wrap, and her stride was both graceful and yet decisive. The lady was followed by a neatly dressed maidservant wearing a long-suffering expression, carrying several parcels of various sizes, which indicated that a lengthy shopping expedition had taken place that afternoon.

The young lady crossed the street. As she walked along the outskirts of Trinity College campus, she kept her eyes demurely lowered to avoid the admiring glances of the several students whom she passed along the way. Two of them nodded at her in a friendly fashion, and at this pair she directed a warm smile, betokening some measure of familiarity, but she did not speak. It could be supposed from the lack of surprise these gentlemen exhibited at her appearance that she was not entirely unknown to them. Nor did it seem that the university grounds were at all alien to the lady as she wove her way along a walk, circling the imposing buildings, although there were no other females strolling the premises.

Beyond the college she turned onto Merrion Square, a handsome residential district surrounded by rows of red brick terrace houses. The patch of open land bordered by the houses was the gray-green color that heralded the advent of spring, but on this rainy day no children played on the broad expanse of new grass. The south side of the square was the young lady's destination; she must have been expected, for the white door to one of the houses was opened at her approach. Each of the four levels of this house possessed three neat, white-framed windows; those on the second tier looked onto a small balcony enclosed by a delicate iron railing. Over the front door, which glistened with a coat of fresh paint, there was an elaborately leaded fanlight. On first glance it appeared to be identical to those above each of the many similar front doors in Merrion Square; closer inspection revealed that it, like the others, was unique in its design. The half-moon of its window was dissected by lead tracery as intricate as a spider's web.

The young lady skipped up the five front steps carelessly, not even taking hold of the rail to prevent herself from slipping. She smiled up at the butler who stood patiently holding the door for her; the maidservant ascended the steps more slowly and gloomily than had her mistress.

"Had you quite given me up, Worsely?" the young lady asked roguishly, untying the ribbons of her damp bonnet and handing it and the pelisse to the maid. "Mary feared that I would never leave off shopping!" This was accompanied by a sparkling look of mischief in the direction of the abigail's back; Mary was already climbing the wooden staircase on her way to the upper regions, her burden of parcels augmented by her mistress's discarded garments.

"Nivver you mind about Mary, Miss Rora. The post and a fire are waiting for you in the library," the butler informed the girl. "I've had James to poke it up, for the master sent a message earlier, speaking of how he'd be home in time for tea."

"For once! Poor Papa!" the lady said, already on her way to the chamber where the inviting fire awaited her. There, on a small embossed silver tray she found some letters, most of which were addressed to Mr. Jasper Donellan. The young lady sorted through these and at the bottom of the pile she found one bearing the direction: "Miss Aurora Catherine Donellan, care of Jas. Donellan, Merrion Square, Dublin." She took this one up and broke the wafer eagerly, having at once recognized the flourishing writing as her grandmother's hand.

Miss Aurora Donellan settled herself in a comfortable chair; she read the letter once, then once again before folding it up. On the second reading her eyes crinkled at the corners in evident appreciation of the heading this letter bore: "Ardara Castle, County Kilkenny, 15 March a.d. 1812." When she had refolded the letter and set it aside, the girl suddenly jumped out of her chair in one fluid movement, and upon rising, she began the lively steps of a jig and hummed the tune to the dance merrily. This quick change in her heretofore sedate demeanor was occasioned by a fit of glee that could no longer be contained, and this was obvious to the gentleman who had entered the room, unnoticed by the girl.

He stood in the doorway for several seconds, watching the young lady with amusement and pride mingled on his handsome face. She was undeniably a creature of beauty, with her rich russet hair tumbling loose from its moorings atop her head; her complexion was clear and creamy, her pink mouth full and inviting, and her eyes sparkled with the green fire of emeralds. They were set beneath dark, arched brows, which lifted in surprise when she spotted the gentleman in the doorway.

"Papa!" she cried, and stopped dancing. Running to him, she kissed his cheek and pulled him into the room. "How long were you standing there?"

"Long enough to realize that you're in transports over something, lass," the dark-haired gentleman replied. His voice was cultured, yet it contained a hint of the Irish lilt. Nothing in his appearance suggested his near relationship to the girl save the color of his eyes and the humorous twist to his broad mouth. A tall man, he towered over the lively young woman; looking down at her, he pressed one of his hands to his graying temple. "Can this hoyden be that charmer Miss Donellan, courted by all the bucks in Dublin, and praised for her elegance and grace?"

"Oh, Papa, you know as well as I do that's fustian! But do come sit down in your chair, for I've something of a very important nature to discuss with you—after Worsely brings our tea. You must bear with his displeasure at your being on time, however; you know how he hates routine to be disrupted!"

Jasper Donellan, a revered professor and scholar of medieval history at Trinity College, allowed himself to be pulled across the room and pushed into a leather wing chair whose high back sported a depression created from years of the pressure of that gentleman's head. In a very little while the tea tray was brought in by the butler, and Miss Donellan poured out the cups.

"How was your day?" Rora asked pleasantly as she performed her duties at the tea table with all the ease of one to whom they were routine.

"Fair enough. The young Englishman Percy Shelley called upon me again today, full of questions about universal suffrage and the

Catholic Emancipation issue. He has written a Declaration of Rights similar to the American and French examples and means to have it published here in Dublin. While I agree with some of his political views, his religious ones are an anathema to me—the pup is an avowed agnostic." He stirred his cup with a tiny spoon. "And young MacSweeney is continuing to be a disappointment as a scholar. He persists in associating Thomas à Becket with Henry the Eighth. Can it be Wolsey of whom he is thinking? You must stop flirting with that lad, Rora. His understanding lacks enough as it is!"

The young lady frowned at her parent. "You know I don't flirt with Mr. MacSweeney—or anyone! That sort of behavior is quite beneath me!"

"Oh, aye, and so would your mother have said, for all it's perfectly true! It took a man like me to take the lass at her word and make off with her at dead of night." Mr. Donellan's greenish eyes kindled reminiscently.

"The two of you ought to have died of shame, eloping as you did!" his daughter reproved him with mock primness. Her parents' elopement, shocking as it had been to those of the previous generation, had been a family joke for years. Over twenty years before, during a visit to the town of Kilkenny, the studious yet fun-loving Jasper Donellan had met and fallen in love with Lady Alanna Morres, the only child and heir of the Earl of Liscarrol. He had, most unfortunately, met her within days of the lady's betrothal to the much older Lord Briavel, a viscount who already had a young son from a previous marriage. But she had preferred the handsome scholar to the wealthy nobleman and allowed young Mr. Donellan to spirit her away from her family and her home, Ardara Castle. The couple had journeyed to Dublin, where the bridegroom had been granted a fellowship at Trinity College, and there they remained. Ten months after the elopement, the union was blessed with a daughter; on this occasion Lady Alanna's parents accepted her shocking misalliance and bestowed their largesse upon the small family. The only blemish on the Donellans' life was the lack of a son and the failure of any other children to make an appearance in Merrion Square. But the little daughter was well loved by her parents, and she grew up in a happy, lively home. The only sadnesses Rora had suffered in her life were of fairly recent date: the death of her mother four years previously, and the passing of her grandfather, Lord Liscarrol, in the year following his daughter's demise.

"What is your news, Rora?" Mr. Donellan prompted his daughter, marveling anew at the girl's resemblance to her bright-haired mother, particularly when her face was in thoughtful repose. This in itself was odd, for Lady Alanna had never been of thoughtful mein, but more typically had presented a charmingly animated countenance to the world.

"I had a letter from my grandmother, sir. Can you guess what she has to say?" Rora smiled mischievously at her father as she dropped two lumps of sugar into her teacup. She expected him to make his usual comment, begging her to add a third lump, that she might be three times as sweet, but he was momentarily diverted by her announcement.

"I suppose she wishes you to join her at Ardara," he murmured, a twinkle appearing in his eyes. "What is her reason this time?"

"One that I cannot ignore, Papa—she claims to be suffering from a putrid sore throat, and is hardly able to rise from her bed, besides! Is that not clever? If I refuse to go to her, I must be thought the greatest beast in nature! You must admit she is *most* inventive!"

"Aye, and most conniving, too, is Hester Liscarrol!" he added with a wink. "And was that display of terpsichorean glee signaling your willingness to go—to leave your poor old papa all alone?"

She laughed at his assumption of grief. "Poor old papa, indeed! You'll be so absorbed with your fusty old books within five minutes of my departure that you'll scarce know I've left you."

"I fear 'tis true," Mr. Donellan admitted ruefully, eyes still twinkling. "For the past twenty years I've been praying that you'd be gone one day. How often I've pictured it: myself alone, the house silent and peaceful as befits the household of a man of my age and pursuits. No more young bucks wearing out the door knocker, no more of Worsely staggering about with floral tributes on the day of a ball. No more fear that my daughter's name will figure in an affair of honor held at Phoenix Park at daylight. Yes, I have longed for this day, indeed!"

Miss Donellan's warm laugh was the only sympathy elicited by his plaint. "I've always said you ought to have been an actor, Papa—it's not for nothing you're related to Mr. Sheridan the playwright! So, 'tis settled, then. I'm to go to Ardara to live and thereby satisfy my increasingly importunate grandmama."

"Aye, you'd best go to her. Ardara Castle is your birthright, and if you put her ladyship's nose out of joint, she might have her revenge by leaving it to that repellent nephew of Lord Liscarrol's. I met him once and am convinced it would be only the rent roll that would interest him—at least you love that preposterous old place, with its follies and its ruins!"

Rora shook her head, serious for the first time since he had joined her. "You know that Grandfather's nephew can never possess the castle under terms of the will. Grandmother merely holds Ardara and the lands in trust for me during her lifetime: the bequest to me is unalterable. Nor would she want to alter it even if she could; she wrote that she longs to see me as mistress of Ardara while she lives, and vows that she'll wind up the trust as soon as I'm wed. Not that there's any prospect of that!"

"Come now, lass—you're not telling me that young Mac-Sweeney's life is about to be blighted? Nor those of the twenty or so young gentlemen who haunt our doorstep?"

"Oh, Papa," she remonstrated with her teasing parent in like manner, "you know that none of those—those lads is worthy of Jasper Donellan's daughter. But as you yourself would tell poor Tommy MacSweeney: we digress, sir! The fact at hand is that I'm about to wholly abandon you to your books and your medieval manuscripts to take up residence at Ardara Castle in County Kilkenny. I shan't send word to Grandmother by post, for my Mary and I will arrive on the castle doorstep before the letter itself. I fancy a day is all the preparation time I'll need, and I can easily hire a suitable housekeeper for you if I go to the Registry Office early tomorrow."

His reaction to this suggestion was violent in the extreme. "No!" he thundered, so forcefully that the teapot and teaspoons seemed to rattle on their silver tray. "I'll not be having some strange woman getting in my way! Cook can keep to the usual schedule and Worsely shall have the ordering of the staff as usual. I want no woman, Rora," Mr. Donellan maintained with a darkling glance at his daughter.

"Very well, Papa," she agreed meekly, but with an amused light in her eyes. "Will you be escorting me to the assembly tonight at the rotunda? Or are you too exhausted from last night's St. Patrick's Day revels to lend me your arm this even?" Rora rose from her chair, and going around to her father, put her arms around his neck; her display of affection did considerable damage to the arrangement of his neckcloth.

Mr. Donellan disengaged himself from her embrace, but with a fond smile at his sportive daughter. "As you wish, lass. I'm not fortified enough against your cajolery—you and your fair mother could ever twist me around to your will!"

Rora knew this to be not entirely true, but she dimpled in pleased fashion at what she deemed a compliment to her wiles.

An observer might have believed Rora little more than a frivolous young lady of fashion, so great was the care that she and her maid took during the process of dressing her for the assembly ball, but her father could have set anyone straight as to the truth of his daughter's character. Miss Donellan, though a beauty, had a sharp mind and a well-trained one. Not for Jasper Donellan's daughter the prim and proper, spirit-crushing governesses of other genteel establishments; no less a scholar than her own father had been responsible for Rora's education. She had pleased him and herself by proving clever in all subjects save mathematics; since her mother had deplored her exposure to such an unladylike subject on the grounds that it would turn her pretty daughter into a bluestocking, this could be considered no fault. From each of her parents she had received liveliness and spirit, and more than a fair share of temper, although her disposition was in the main so sunny that she was seldom angry.

As Mr. Donellan's carriage conveyed father and daughter to the Rotunda on Drogheda Street, the young lady discussed her probable future at Ardara Castle; it was clear to both that from now on she would make the castle her home. This was the wish of Lady Liscarrol, and that imperious dame must have her way at last. Neither believed the tale of the putrid sore throat, and they well knew that in refusing the old lady's previous requests to send her granddaughter to Ardara, they had merely been delaying the inevitable. Moreover, Rora truly wanted to join her grandmother; she had always loved the Ardara property and was proud that it would someday belong to her, from the crumbling ruins of the original fortress castle to the beautiful house that had been built by the Morres family during the seventeenth century. As difficult as it was for Rora to leave her papa and the happy, comfortable life they shared, she longed to go to the castle, for she had long known that it was her heritage and her destiny.

The life of a fashionable young lady had begun to pall, and ever since the reading of the late Lord Liscarrol's will three years previously, Rora had known that one day she would leave Dublin for the castle. Just as her mother had left the castle for an unknown life in what had, twenty years before, been Ireland's capital, so must Lady Alanna's daughter leave that same city to live at Ardara. Rora rather like the symmetry of it all.

There was a glittering company at Dublin's handsome assembly rooms that evening, for the six-week social season was still in full swing, despite the fact that St. Patrick's Day, its climax, was twenty-four hours gone. Rora was solicited for numerous dances by the young gentlemen, for she was a prime favorite. One and all knew that she was the heiress to Ardara Castle, a large and estimable property in Kilkenny; moreover, she was the daughter of the renowned scholar, Mr. Donellan, who had made most of the young men's lives miserable during their university days. The gentleman was forgiven for past sins, however, because he had given the world a daughter with much beauty and wit. Miss Donellan was universally admired, and when she hinted that she would soon be leaving Dublin, more than one youth wondered if he should screw up his courage and make her an offer of marriage. Somehow, none of them found the opportunity to do so, for the young lady was taking great pains to keep her suitors at arm's length. She flirted most deliciously behind her silk fan, and danced indefatigably, but when she departed that evening in her father's company, she had received no proposals, only innumerable compliments.

"Well, Papa, I rather think 'tis glad I am that I'll attend no more assemblies this season!" she uttered, leaning back against the squabs as the coachman directed the vehicle out of the crush of carriages around the rotunda.

"Had enough of reels and jigs, my love?" Mr. Donellan asked her in mildly shocked accents.

" 'Tis true—I have had. At least, until I'm dancing them at the assembly in Kilkenny-town! Oh, Papa, tonight half the young men were angling to get me into a quiet corner, alone, and parrying their attempts was quite wearing, I assure you." She smoothed the white silk of her gown with an injured air. "How glad I shall be to escape them all!"

"And you're thinking that there are no single gentlemen in the county of Kilkenny, parish of St. Canice? Fie on you, Miss Donellan!"

"None to signify, Papa."

"There'll always be lads to admire the trim ankle and slender waist of Miss Rora Donellan! And if your graceful dancing doesn't win the hearts of the gentlemen of Kilkenny, then your horsemanship must recommend you to their notice, my girl. You'll be taking Falstaff?" he asked, although he knew it was a foregone conclusion. Rora's chestnut stallion was her proudest possession.

"Of course. I may be able to live quite easily without my old papa, but I cannot do without my darling Falstaff!"

"You must take Slaney with you to the Castle—he's the only one who can manage that beast besides yourself, and the only one who can manage you at all! I'll have little need for an undergroom in your absence, and if Slaney can keep you from breaking your pretty neck, I'll be glad enough to raise his wages and see him off with you."

They were crossing the bridge over the River Liffey, and Rora gazed through the window, straining to see the water, but the dim glow of the carriage lamps afforded little illumination in the darkness. She sighed deeply and turned her shadowed eyes upon her handsome father once more. "I shall miss you more than you can guess," she informed him pensively.

"Nonsense!" was his bracing reply. "You'll have the whole parish in your pocket and in an uproar besides, at all of your doings. Besides, the Newburghs will keep you merry," Mr. Donellan reminded her.

"Yes, I was forgetting my cousins." Rora's grandmother had been wed to a Sir Hugh Newburgh before her marriage to the Earl of Liscarrol, and she had borne him four sons. The children of Sir Brendan, the baronet's heir, were close to Rora's age and lived in the neighborhood of Ardara Castle. "Louisa's been married these several years, and Joan is all of twenty-one now. I wonder if she has a suitor?"

"No doubt, my dear. But so, too, will you find one in the country, I'll be bound."

"Oh, Papa, what a funny one you are! Why, the only suitors to be found in the country are boys, or old widowers—like that Lord Briavel who wanted to marry Mama. None of the English gentry will be found on their Irish estates at this time of year, not with their London season just beginning."

"So, 'tis an Englishman you're fancying, is it, Rora? I'd no idea."

"Of course I don't! How can you suggest such a thing? I'm a daughter of one of Wolfe Tone's cronies—how could I wed a true-born Englishman when my own papa supported the '98 Rebellion!"

"The aims of the Rebellion, daughter, not the violent means used in the attempt to achieve them," Mr. Donellan reminded her soberly. "Besides, child, we are all of us as much Englishmen as Irish, including poor Wolfe Tone, patriot that he was. 'Twas the sins of our fathers against Erin that we were trying to redress." Mr. Donellan's tone grew reflective whenever he spoke of the ill-fated Rebellion of fourteen years before.

The carriage moved more quickly once it had crossed the Liffey, and soon pulled up in front of the house in Merrion Square. Mr. Donellan assisted his daughter out of the vehicle, the door of which was held open by a footman; Worsely stood on the top step, a branch of candles in one hand. At the foot of the hall stairs, Rora bid her father goodnight, and before taking her bedroom candle from him, she stood on tiptoe to kiss his lean cheek. She went slowly up the stairs, for her feet were tired, both from standing all night and from a surfeit of dancing.

When she was in bed, Rora closed her eyes and conjured up that favorite vision, the one of herself at Ardara. The childhood visits had been too few, too many years apart, for her to have ever had enough of the castle. It had assumed mythic proportions in her mind as a child, but these dreams had not been too far off the mark to be totally dispelled by her more recent visits. Unfortunate indeed that her latest trips to Ardara had been for funerals: once to bury her mother, and then the following year for the reading of her grandfather's will. Jasper Donellan liked and admired his imposing mother-in-law, but he could spare little time from his own work to make the seventy-mile journey very often, and his daughter had been too enthralled by town life until lately to wish for an extended stay in the country.

Now, two years after her come-out in Dublin, she was almost longing to be gone from the city of her birth. Ardara beckoned to her now, offering peace and solitude and country diversions. She had come to the conclusion that there was nothing she needed that could not be had in the fine shops of Kilkenny, and an occasional assembly would no doubt come to be more of a treat than the nightly round of parties in Dublin. The truth of the matter was that Rora was a little bored with her life. At the same time, she knew that had there been no alternative, no Ardara to flee to, she would be happy enough to remain in the city. But Ardara was there, and her grandmother needed her—or believed that she did. Rora was skeptical; Lady Liscarrol had never struck her as the sort of person to need anyone. For some reason she wanted Rora at her side, and such force of will could not forever be denied. It had been one year since the first summons from her ladyship. Surely no one but the Donellans had ever managed to refuse the imperious Lady Liscarrol for so long as that.

Rora spent the next day busily giving orders to the staff on how to look after Mr. Donellan during her absence. The packing of the young lady's clothes was undertaken by Mary, and within twenty-four hours of the receipt of Lady Liscarrol's letter, Miss Donellan was prepared for her journey. A post chaise had been bespoken for early the following morning. It would be a fatiguing day, one spent closed up in a carriage, but if Rora made good time, she would arrive at the castle just before nightfall.

She and her father enjoyed a quiet evening together in Merrion Square, dining at their usual hour then amusing themselves at cards; the cosy, book-lined library rang with their laughter and their jokes. Rora well knew that her future evenings would be different, that they would lack the stimulation of the male company which had always been present in her home. Since her mother's death, she had acted as her father's hostess, and she knew the value of masculine conversation. The older gentlemen at the university were better company, thought Rora, than were the callow students who frequently called upon her father and dined at his board, and who had tried to impress her by aping the airs of the fashionable bucks who could be seen daily in Dublin, strolling along Beaux Walk on St. Stephen's Green. Had the lads but known it, she had little use for fashionable gentlemen, or for students. None of her suitors was as entertaining or as witty as her own beloved father, and Jasper Donellan was the measure against which any gentleman desirous of pleasing her must compare favorably. So far she had met very few who were up to her exacting standards; this, she knew, was the only reason she was still unwed.

"What are you thinking, Rora?" the aforementioned gentleman asked his unusually thoughtful daughter on the eve of her departure.

"That it will be difficult to accustom myself to more feminine pursuits!" she answered readily, dimpling at her parent. "Can you imagine me sitting sedately, embroidering or tatting lace all day, or reading out loud to Grandmother every evening? I have not done such things since Mama died—I have been used to entertaining dons and professors, or dancing holes in my slippers at balls! It will be quite a change."

"The picture you paint of Hester Liscarrol sitting about so idly makes me wonder if she is more ill than I suspected. Your grandmother would scorn such paltry pursuits for herself or her granddaughter, for the tale around Dublin was that she gave up hunting a scant five years ago! Not bad for a woman of sixty, which she was at the time."

Rora laughed at this. "True enough, and riding is one pursuit that I intend to enjoy to the fullest in the country—gardening is another." In a moment she laid down her cards with a tragic air. "I'm bested, sir, and I consider you most ungallant for beating me so roundly, and I your own daughter!"

They spoke no more of their impending separation, but both Rora and her father promised to write to each other faithfully.

"And I'll count upon you to come down to Ardara during the long vacation," Rora said before going up to bed. "A few weeks of rustication will do you so much good after suffering through those horrid examinations and all those papers! You can even bring your own texts and manuscripts with you and hole up in the castle library. How would you like that?"

Mr. Donellan kissed the top of his daughter's auburn head; the curls on her forehead tickled his chin. "Aye, 'tis a lovely plan. And I fancy Brendan Newburgh could tempt me with some of his horses. You'll be needing a new hunter this autumn, Rora—don't purchase one for yourself unless from your uncle. He drives a hard bargain, but he'll see to it you're well mounted, you may be sure." After giving this fatherly advice, he added, "Now, off to bed with you, for it's a long journey you'll have on the morrow, my girl."

CHAPTER II

Early the next morning when Rora made her farewells, father and daughter remained jocular till the last. Jasper Donellan teased her about the enormous muff she carried and the dashing feather in her bonnet, while she returned a scathing denunciation of his good spirits in the face of his only child's departure. But the final embrace they exchanged was warm and hearty, and as the post chaise pulled out of sleepy Merrion Square, each face was shadowed by a tinge of sorrow.

Rora put her hands in her muff and her sober countenance brightened as the carriage continued in its southwesterly direction on its way out of Dublin. In hardly any time at all the buildings and streets were behind her and had given way to the greening, rolling landscape on the outskirts of the city, and twisting roads. She settled back in her place, wishing that the day had dawned sunnier for her journey, and drier. The chaise sloshed through the ruts and puddles, and as Rora pulled the lap robe more closely about her legs, she was glad of the warm brick beneath her booted feet and replaced it with another when she made the change at Sallygap. Mary, seated across from her mistress, tried to sleep, but was jolted awake by the bumps in the road.

As the day dragged on, Rora passed through County Wicklow and into Carlow, finally crossing the River Barrow into County Kilkenny. From the river it was under ten miles to the town of Kilkenny, where the last change was made and Lady Liscarrol's own horses were put to for the final few miles of the journey. Rora was road-weary and excessively hungry, and her thoughts were centered as much on the dinner that she hoped to enjoy at the castle as upon the approaching reunion with her grandmother. But she exhibited some interest in Kilkenny, with its narrow streets and sixteenth-century stone houses; there were some promising-looking shop fronts as well. Soon the chaise left the town and was rolling past meadows, woods, and the thatched cottages of the locals.

Rora's flagging energies revived as the vehicle turned off the main road and into the long drive leading to Ardara Castle. The impressive stone lodge was just as she remembered it, and Drennan the gatekeeper smiled and bowed as the post chaise clattered through the heavy iron gates: he knew the identity of the traveler. Rora sat upright as the mile-long approach to the house neared its end; the driver slackened the pace and the postilions straightened perceptibly.

Ardara Castle came into view, an immense building in the classic Palladian style. It stood white and pristine among huge trees, resting on a rise of ground overlooking a small ornamental lake upon which swans were gliding gracefully. The facade of the house was two generations old, but it glowed in the light of the fading sun as though it had been newly fashioned. The central portion of the house was linked to twin pavilions on either side by means of colonnaded walls. The remains of the original fourteenth-century fortress could be seen from the drive, looming above massive oak trees; it had been abandoned two hundred years before, when the Morres family had obtained the earldom of Liscarrol and decided to build a residence more suited to that high estate. The ruins were on a hill, some distance from the newer building, but this was deceiving; when one approached the house from the front, its Palladian grace seemed to rest in the shadow of the ancient castle. Yew hedges and topiary bordered the front of Ardara, and the rear of the house opened onto formal ornamental gardens that had been preserved for generations. In keeping with the tradition set by Capability Brown, the substantial park was artfully natural; the landscape possessed the pleasing vista of trees, meadow, and lake.

The chaise pulled up in front of the imposing edifice, and the large door was flung open. An elderly butler, from whose eyes copious tears could be seen to flow, came down to the vehicle and handed Miss Donellan from the carriage, refusing to allow his subordinates this privilege.

"Ah, Miss Rora, we're that glad to see you, we are! Her ladyship wasn't expecting you till the morrow at the soonest!" After directing the coachman to drive around to the rear, where her ladyship's horses would be removed along with the young lady's baggage, he followed her up the two shallow flights of steps.

" 'Tis good to be here, Purdon," Rora said, drawing off her Limerick gloves in the spacious hall. "Where shall I find my grand-mother?"

"You've but to follow me, miss. Her ladyship is in the Great Parlor."

Rora followed the butler to the designated room, smiling to herself as she remembered her grandmother's tale of a putrid sore throat. Surely if the old lady were suffering such an affliction, she would be abed.

At Rora's entrance the only occupant of the Great Parlor rose and came forward, a tall, handsome woman of sixty-five years. Her fine-boned face was wrinkled, it was true, but her black eyes were bright and snapping, and her step was still brisk. The pale gray hair still retained a hint of copper, and was piled high, covered with a delicate bit of lace. Her ladyship's mulberry-colored gown followed no particular mode and could have been fashioned anytime during the past twenty years. The neck and sleeves were embellished with lace, and a woolen shawl was flung over her shoulders, its ends hanging down more on one side than the other.

"Rora—my dearest girl!" Lady Liscarrol said in a hearty tone. "Come here and kiss me."

"Grandmother! You look positively blooming, for one so ill," Rora replied roguishly, obediently kissing the withered cheek. "Pray forgive me for arriving so late in the day, but I made all possible haste from Dublin."

A sniff from the doorway recalled them to Purdon's presence. Her ladyship somewhat snappishly requested that he make sure the covers for dinner had been laid. "I'm sure you're quite famished, child—and I must eat to keep up my strength. You mustn't worry about changing your dress. You are in the country now, and I don't stand on ceremony." Returning to her armchair, the old lady announced pettishly, "After the excitement of your arrival, I shall find myself laid up the rest of the week!"

"Poor Grandmother," Rora sympathized, a dimple not quite suppressed as she cast a pitying glance upon the formidable figure in mulberry satin. "Shall I have my Mary prepare a tisane for you at bedtime?"

"Of course not, girl. My woman does so every night, you may be sure." The sharp black eyes wandered critically over the young lady. "You're looking well enough, miss! Fine as a fivepence in your town clothes! And more like your mother every day. You've filled out since your last visit—grown quite a womanly little figure. At the reading of your grandfather's will you were naught but a scraggly, pert adolescent. You've improved past all recognition."

"Your ladyship is too kind," Rora murmured, untying the ribbons of her bonnet.

"I'm not being kind," Lady Liscarrol contradicted. "You've grown into something of a beauty—Alanna would be proud to see it, as would your grandfather." She changed the subject abruptly. "How does Jasper? Still has his nose between the covers of a book, no doubt!"

"Yes, when he's not lecturing at Trinity. I took the liberty of inviting him down to visit during his so-called vacation."

"Ah, treating Ardara as your own already?" the old lady quizzed her, but she did not sound at all displeased.

"Dinner is served, my lady, Miss Rora," Purdon informed them in sepulchral tones. "In the small dining room," he added, for Rora's edification.

"Rora, give me your arm," Lady Liscarrol demanded, but as she had risen abruptly at the butler's words, Rora was in doubt that her assistance was really required. As they walked toward the dining room together, Rora's arm was held in a grip that was not at all feeble. She wondered to herself for how many days her grandparent could keep up this far from deceptive assumption of ill health.

Lady Liscarrol did not exhibit any signs of being invalidish during dinner. She made a good meal, partaking of more of the dishes than even her granddaughter. The pair of women exchanged commonplace at table, but when they returned to the Great Parlor, conversation turned toward country news.

"Tomorrow I shall send word over to Brendan that I wish Joan to make us a visit. You'll be bored to death here without company of your own age, Rora," the old lady said, her face giving no clue to her thoughts as she continued to look the young woman over, as though judging the fine points of a mare she might purchase if the price was right.

"But, Grandmother, I have never been used to female companionship, not since Mama died."

"Well, miss, it's time you did get used to it! And Joan deserves a holiday from housekeeping for her father. Brendan will rue the day he—well, never mind that now. Newburgh Hall will continue on without her, whatever my pinch-purse son says to the contrary."

"I shall be very happy to see Joan again, but I would have expected her to be wed by now—or affianced, at the very least."

"Joan will marry in her own good time, and a husband of her choosing, or mine—but not her father's. He's already broken up her attachment to a perfectly acceptable young Englishman, out of his own selfishness, no less, but he'll catch cold if he tries to do so again!" Lady Liscarrol gripped the arms of her chair with a ferocity that matched that in her voice.

"Poor Uncle Brendan! And poor Joan. But try as I might, I can't imagine her wearing the willow for some Englishman—or anyone. She is too practical and sensible for that."

"She's not pining!" her grandmother snapped. "And what of you, miss? How many offers has Jasper Donellan received for your hand?" The sharp eyes took on a sudden intensity, revealing a depth of interest that surprised Rora.

"Oh, dozens!" she jested, with an unconcerned toss of her head. "The truth of it is that I don't fancy marriage to a university student or a scholarly bore—or to any one of the numerous Dublin beaux who have more of an eye to Ardara Castle than Aurora Catherine Donellan!"

"I'm glad to see you're no fool," her ladyship approved, in a softer tone than she had employed all evening. "Not but what I don't believe you entirely—not with that face and figure. The gentlemen must have been following you like hounds after a scent since the day you emerged from the schoolroom. But I don't believe in complimenting young girls—they are silly and vain enough as it is!"

"Why, how could I be vain, ma'am, when I have the memory of Mama, who was far, far lovelier than I could ever hope to be—and when I have seen the portraits of you." As she spoke, Rora looked to the opposite wall where a Titian-haired beauty smiled enigmatically from within the confines of a gilt frame. The lady in the picture was fine-boned and fashionably dressed according to the style of forty years before.

"Hmph!" was the old lady's reply. "Well, I'll agree that you can't hold a candle to what I was in my heyday, miss, but you would shine down Alanna, had she lived. You have a livelier countenance and twice as much charm—you get it from both parents. Jasper Donellan could coax the birds from the trees; I always understood perfectly why Alanna eloped with him. Your grandfather was furious, of course, but even he couldn't hold a grudge against your father."

Silence fell as both women recalled Lord Liscarrol, a man who had waited for his Hester for six long years, remaining single until she was made a widow by his own friend, Sir Hugh Newburgh; he'd waited yet another year until her period of mourning had passed before making her his countess. Lady Newburgh became Lady Liscarrol and exchanged nearby Newburgh Hall for the castle, bringing with her her four Newburgh sons. Within two years, Lady Alanna had been born, the only child of the union and the sole heiress to her father's vast estate. It was popularly believed that her untimely death had precipitated the decline and eventual passing of her father the following year.

The lull in conversation was broken when Lady Liscarrol suddenly announced, "Lord Briavel has come to stay at Hargrave House."

This intelligence surprised Rora greatly, and even her ready tongue was stilled. Then, "Has he indeed? How very odd, to be sure—he has not done so since Mama and Papa eloped—since Mama jilted him all of twenty years ago!"

"Nay, 'tis not the same man. The gentleman Alanna jilted is now the Earl of Rothmore—and you are right, he has never returned to Ireland in twenty years. His son, Gavin Hargrave, is the present Viscount Briavel. He was a child when your mama became engaged to his papa, and a very taking little fellow he was, too. We had quite an understanding, he and I, and what's more, he remembers it."

"Good God, Grandmother—have you seen him?"

"Of course, and why shouldn't I have, miss? He's called here twice already, once alone and once with the gentleman who is visiting him at Hargrave House. Both are as fine as they can stare—young Corinthians, from the look of 'em."

"But I thought the friendship between the Hargraves and the Morres families ended when Mama jilted the old gentleman!"

"Aye, that it did, and for far too long a time. Gavin's father left Hargrave House immediately after his disappointment, and has leased it to the Hamptons ever since—they were some sort of cousins. But in recent years the earl has corresponded with me. He sent a kind letter of condolence when he heard of Alanna's death, and then again when your grandfather died. They were once close."

"He never married again, did he? Lord Briavel, I mean," Rora murmured ruminatively.

"No."

"He must have loved Mama a great deal."

"Mayhap, though he was not the sort to spend his life grieving for a lost love. We must suppose it did not suit him to remarry—he had his heir, after all. For myself, I'm glad to see a Hargrave in that house again. It's a jewel of a place, as perfect in its own way as Ardara is, though they're so different to each other."

"Yes, it is a pretty residence," Rora said evenly, dismissing Hargrave House. "Now, ma'am, I believe you ought to go upstairs to bed. I am here to look after you, remember!"

Lady Liscarrol acquiesced, but once again expected Rora's assistance to her chamber. There they found Clodagh, her ladyship's maid, who greeted the young lady with pleasure.

"Yes, I'm here to see to it that my grandmother's precarious health does not worsen," said the irrepressible Miss Donellan.

The maidservant cast a wary glance at her mistress, whose discarded gown she was in the process of smoothing out. After a pause, she replied, "Poor, dear lady—she's been so bad—why, 'tis a great shame she took to leave her bed this day!" But the cheerful tone Clodagh used did not lend any particular credence to her words, and Rora doubted the veracity of the last remark.

"That will be all, Clodagh," said Lady Liscarrol severely.

When they were alone and the old lady was tucked up in bed, Rora pulled up a chair. "Come now, Grandmother, you must be plain with me! You cannot be ill—I vow you are unchanged from the last time I saw you."

A smile twisted the thin mouth, and her ladyship shook her head. "You are an impertinent, uncaring lass—and no, I'm not the slightest bit ill! I did suffer a rawness of the throat a few days past, but that is not why I wrote to you. You belong here, Rora. Ardara Castle will be yours one day, and high time it became your home. You are not angry with me, I hope, for luring you here under false pretenses?"

Rora took up one wrinkled hand and pressed it warmly. "Never! And I knew all along that you weren't really sick—it was the *smokiest* excuse you've come up with all year! I came here because I wanted to, and Papa and I both knew that it was time I did so. You dear old thing, how could I be angry?"

"Let me tell you, miss, I should never have addressed *my* grandmother in such a way as that!" her ladyship declared, but she did not sound at all displeased.

"Stuff—you said you don't care to stand on ceremony! Now, I mean for you to leave as much of the running of Ardara to me as you wish, and in time the bailiff's reports will cease to be a thing of mystery to me, I'm sure!"

"We'll discuss those matters tomorrow, my girl. I didn't bring you here to make an estate manageress of you, or to supplant me as mistress of my own house! But you're no guest either," the old lady added more gently, "so from this day forward, you had best consider Ardara as much yours as mine."

"Yes, ma'am," Rora agreed meekly, before rising from the bedside. Leaning over her progenitrix, she whispered, "Good night, *poor* Grandmother!" Both ladies laughed, each in perfect charity with the other, and eagerly anticipating the morrow.

Within a few days of her arrival, Rora's liking for town life had been entirely eclipsed by her new love for life at Ardara, one wholly different but every bit as delightful as her existence in Dublin. The routine of her days was leavened by the many small trials and domestic catastrophes that were part and parcel of life in a country house in Ireland. Before she had been at Ardara a week, Rora had been called upon to settle a quarrel between the butler and the steward, followed by another between her own groom Slaney and her ladyship's undergroom, and a particularly violent squabble over which laundress was responsible for scorching one of Rora's own lace-trimmed nightcaps. The damage to her cap was far less a concern to her than it was to the two antagonists, and it took a considerable time, days in fact, to mend relations in the laundry, owing to what seemed to Rora the strong desire of the participants in the quarrel to keep the dispute alive. The arrival of the young lady had incited a propensity among the servants to air their grievances in her direction, as though Rora's status as a newcomer afforded her a certain measure of impartiality, particularly toward the younger servants. Lady Liscarrol was more likely to side with the senior members of the staff in any dispute, and Rora was viewed as a potential champion of the underservants.

When she was not busy soothing troubled waters, Rora's days were devoted to many of the pursuits she had been too busy for in Dublin: reading, writing letters, practicing on the pianoforte, and taking long walks. She had a great love for flowers, and each day saw her leave the house with a basket over her arm; her destination was generally the hothouses that her grandfather had erected, where she gleaned many fine specimens with which to decorate the front rooms of the castle. Spring was not yet in its full flowering, but the daffodils were beginning to make their appearance on the grounds, and other early bloomers were forming their buds in the elaborate gardens behind the house. Rora's favorite walk took her through the labyrinth of shrubbery, where the tall hedges on either side of the walkway made her feel strangely small and insignificant a being, despite the fact that one day she would be mistress of all she surveyed. The gardeners could be found constantly attending to the extensive yew hedges and topiary, and Rora could always expect a warm nod and a friendly greeting from those persons in whose care the beauty of Ardara had become renowned.

She enjoyed visiting the tenants with her grandmother and took great interest in their affairs—more than was entirely necessary, said Lady Liscarrol, who was innured to their many complaints. Nor would collecting the annual rents ever be an easy matter, although Crosbie, the present estate agent, had grown old in the office of doing so for upwards of twenty years. But Rora had lived her whole life in Ireland and declared that she was not unable to accept the facts before her, though she might act like an absentee Englishman and try to make a few changes. Lady Liscarrol laughed at this, for the old lady was wont to tease her granddaughter for displaying a high degree of Irishness, saying that in marrying Jasper Donellan, Alanna had effectively diluted the family's Anglo blood to the point that Rora would be hard put to claim any at all.

But this was not entirely true, for Rora's father, like the countess's Newburgh sons, their children, and the lady herself, was descended from the English landholders who had settled in Ireland during the seventeenth century and had intermarried with the existing nobility of the conquered land. When Rora reminded her grandmother of this, Lady Liscarrol replied tartly that the problem with Jasper Donellan was that he had been educated at Dublin's Trinity, rather than having been sent to and eventually sent down from Oxford, as most of her own sons had been. Miss Donellan let this remark pass, but saved it up to tell her father in one of her letters, for she knew he would be amused by it.

When her groom Slaney arrived at Ardara with Falstaff, the beloved and restive stallion, Rora had been overjoyed at the prospect of a leisurely gallop about the estate, but she was forced by circumstances to snatch quick rides, for her mornings were occupied with household and estate matters, and her afternoons in paying calls on the neighbors. The day Joan Newburgh was expected was the fairest since Rora's arrival at the Castle, but she had to consign herself to another afternoon spent indoors. She did not much mind, for she was eager to see her cousin.

It was nearly teatime when carriage wheels were heard on the drive, and on hearing them, Rora jumped up from her chair and ran to the long window of the saloon. A mud-spattered vehicle and pair had drawn up before the house, and the usual bustle attendant upon such arrivals was taking place on the front steps. In but a moment Purdon ushered a lady into the saloon, beaming happily in response to some gay remark Miss Newburgh had just made.

She was slightly taller than Rora, neat as wax, and quite comely, with black hair pulled back from her round, catlike face. She had bright blue eyes, which were creased at the corners as she smiled in greeting.

"Joan!" Rora cried, going to embrace her cousin. "You dear thing, you haven't changed one whit since last I saw you—was it really as long as three years ago?"

The dark-haired lady disengaged herself and removed her bonnet and pelisse, casting them carelessly onto a chair. "That is less than I can say for you, Rora! I'd hardly have recognized the skinny, bran-faced creature from Dublin who used to visit us in the country," she teased.

"I never had the slightest suspicion of freckle!" Rora protested with a laugh, and the two sat down to enjoy the tea which Purdon was even now carrying into the room.

Miss Newburgh pulled off her gloves and turned her pleasant face upon the other young lady. "Didn't you? I must be thinking of my brother Peyton then. Poor thing, he has dozens still, and they are the sorest trial to him, but otherwise he has grown into quite a handsome fellow, if I do say so myself. But just look at you! Such an air of fashion—and grown into a beauty besides! It somehow seems quite natural to see you sitting here in the saloon, dispensing tea with every speck of Grandmama's aplomb. Where is she, by the by?"

"Resting, as I urge her to do every afternoon. I knew you wouldn't mind my receiving you in her stead." Rora passed a heavily laden plate to her cousin.

"Why should I, for Ardara is now your home. Is Gran recovered from her sore throat?" Joan's wide brow creased slightly as she tried to choose between a cake and a tart.

"She only suffered a trifling indisposition. When I told her I knew she was shamming—and using the *paltriest* of illnesses to get me to come here to live—she could not deny it, and we had a good laugh. Even Papa suspected as much, but he was as willing for me to come as I was eager to do so!"

The two girls fell to exchanging news of their respective families, and Rora learned of her cousin Louisa's confinement, and Symon's betrothal. "Only think, I'm an aunt now!" Joan crowed. "It makes me feel hideously ancient, and I suppose I am. Twenty-one!" She made a comical moue.

"When will I have the pleasure of seeing Uncle Brendan and the rest of the Newburghs?"

"Soon, I should imagine—at least, my father and Peyton are looking forward to visiting you, but Louisa and Symon aren't at home at present. Peyton would have escorted me today, but there was some cockfight or other, so he backed out of his offer—I beg you won't be offended: he's sporting-mad, you see. Papa's brothers are all well, or so we hear. Uncle Matthew has been shipped off with his regiment to Canada; he predicts that there will be a conflict with the former American colonies before the end of the year, and is eager to see some action! Uncle Richard and his stodgy wife are doing whatever it is that they do in Galway—but Gran must have told you all this. And I'm sure you know more about Uncle Samuel, since he is in Dublin. What have you been doing with yourself since coming to Ardara?" Joan posed this question as she speared a piece of cake with a tiny fork and lifted it to her plate.

"Keeping Grandmother company, paying calls—settling servants' disputes!" Rora laughed.

"Ah, can you be hankering for the fleshpots of Dublin already?"

"Never! Despite the fact that the only thing of interest in the neighborhood is the presence of one Lord Briavel at Hargrave House."

"Oh? I'm not sure I've heard that news." Joan sounded interested, but her whole attention appeared to be directed toward her slice of cake.

"Yes, he's the son of the very Lord Briavel whom my mother jilted. Grandmother says that his father is now the Earl of

Rothmore. Only fancy, the old gentleman has never set foot at Hargrave House—nor in Ireland, for that matter—since Mama and Papa eloped! He must have been heartbroken indeed!"

"Pooh!" Joan shook her head at her cousin's sympathy for the former Lord Briavel, before saying, "You are a romantic, Rora, just like your parents. Do you know, you were singularly fortunate in having so dashing and notorious a mother. Why, if she ever scolded you for unladylike behavior, all you had to do was bring up her own youthful indiscretion, and all argument would be at an end!"

"Oh, no, Joan, for I would never have done so—not for anything! Mama was most sensitive about her elopement and didn't even like Papa to tease her about it, which he did anyway, being Papa— he's such a jokesmith. I truly believe that it was his happy nature that enabled him to get over Mama's death. In fact, 'twas he who comforted me at the time, rather than the other way 'round. He misses her dreadfully, of course, but he has his studies and writing to console him, and I've always been thankful for it."

"So the present Lord Briavel has taken up residence at Hargrave House! A pity—the Hamptons were delightful people. I daresay Gran will miss them, as they were her nearest neighbors for at least a decade."

"Who can ever tell with her?" Rora replied gaily. "She doesn't seem at all displeased that Lord Briavel is come. Nor am I—I suppose there will be more entertaining in the neighborhood with a viscount come to live here! Grandmother even speaks of giving parties again!"

"Has Lord Briavel brought some lady to entertain for him? It was my belief that he's unwed." Joan blushed suddenly as though aware that her knowledge of Lord Briavel might be considered excessive. Her blue eyes flew to a painting on the wall and remained there as she waited for an answer.

Rora did not appear to have noticed. "You are correct, he is a single gentleman, and has only his friend to stay with him. Both have called on Grandmother, although not since I've been at Ardara, more's the pity. I should greatly like to meet the son of Mama's old suitor!"

Joan released a long-pent-up sigh and returned her gaze to the lovely face across the tea table. "Would you? Well, I'm sure you will get your wish in time. Only think, his lordship could have been your half-brother, had Alanna wed his father!"

"True, but then I wouldn't have been Aurora Donellan—I'd be an earl's daughter now and probably living in London. I much prefer my life as it is, thank you!"

"Rora, there is something I must ask you," Joan said intently, interrupting the other girl's merry laugh. "Why exactly did Gran invite me to stay at Ardara?"

Rora stared in surprise at this odd question. "Well, it must be perfectly obvious! She wished for me to have a companion my own age, and for you to be freed from your duties at Newburgh Hall for a time. What other reason could she have?"

"I wonder." Joan paused and looked down at the stuff of her dress thoughtfully. "It is not so far from Ardara to the Hall—you and I could easily have visited back and forth, and with less trouble than it takes to tell. Yet she bade me come, and in such terms that even Papa couldn't refuse, and he hates to be ordered about by Gran, or to have her meddle in our affairs. All of this makes me wonder what she has up her sleeve."

"Joan, how can you suggest that Grandmother is the least bit—conniving!" But Rora's eyes danced as she said this.

"She told a whisker to get you to come here—why should she not do so to ensure that I was under her roof as well? There is a reason for my suspicion that I—that I cannot divulge at present. But does it not seem odd to you that Gran should invite her two unmarried granddaughters to the castle at a time when there are two bachelors in the neighborhood?" Joan's blue gaze turned from the opposite wall to meet her cousin's green one.

Rora shook her head and said with a smile, "I see why our grandmother threw us together—she hoped that I would infect you with my own good sense, Joan, for you are being foolish beyond permission! Bachelors, indeed! Sir Nicholas Tobin is probably the father of a large and healthy progeny, and Lord Briavel could be engaged to some London lady, for all we know!"

"But he's not," the other girl replied swiftly. She colored, then modulated her tone slightly as she clarified her outburst: "I mean, Lord Briavel cannot be engaged; I'm sure Gran would know if it were so. And you are probably correct, I'm only being foolish, but oh, how I *wish* I knew what is going on in Gran's mind right now—and how much she knows!"

Rora looked mystified by Miss Newburgh's wishes, but politely said nothing. She asked her cousin whether she would like to go to her room, and when the response was affirmative, escorted that damsel to the guest bedchamber, the one nearest her own. Joan did not enjoy the benefit of an abigail in her own home, and when upon learning that she was to share Mary's services, she was overjoyed. She declared that she had every reason to look her best in Rora's company adding, "Otherwise, not a soul in the parish will notice me!"

CHAPTER III

Dinner that evening was a cheerful meal, for between the two of them, Joan and Rora kept Lady Liscarrol amused with their eager chatter and ready laughter. As she leaned back in her chair and watched the play of candlelight on the fair young faces, the old lady reflected that no one in Ireland—or England either—had such fine granddaughters. Joan's older sister Louisa was absent from her thoughts, for her ladyship had little use for a creature who was so paltry as to require three years to produce a single son; Lady Liscarrol had presented her first husband with four strong lads in five years' time. She suspected that neither Rora nor Joan would be so deficient in their duties as Louisa had been, but first one must find husbands worthy of such girls.

Rora was by far the most likely to make a good match; she was heiress to Ardara, besides being extremely lovely. But Joan was a pretty enough female and had much to recommend her: her birth was good, and if she had no dowry worth mentioning, at least she had learned to hold household and was familiar with the practice of economy, for a greater nipcheese than Sir Brendan Newburgh could not be found, his mother thought to herself. He'd settled Louisa well enough, and by all accounts his Symon was about to contract an alliance to an heiress from Cork. Lady Liscarrol chuckled inwardly as she imagined her eldest son's probable delight upon learning that Rora was installed at Ardara, and she wondered how long it would be before he sent his young Peyton over to call upon the girl. Joan did not figure in Sir Brendan's schemes for the advancement of his children, however; he intended to keep her at Newburgh Hall to wait upon him in his old age, and to this end had chased away her only suitor with threats of violence, or so it was said in the neighborhood—her ladyship and her eldest son were on the barest of speaking terms. Lady Liscarrol wished better things for her granddaughter, whom she valued as a sensible, warm-hearted girl, one who had every right to a home of her own, a husband, and a family.

The next morning when Rora asked her cousin whether or not she would like to come along on a long ramble around the estate on horseback, Joan only laughed and said that she much preferred to while away her time with a novel, especially since the day was so gray. So Rora went riding along, haughtily ignoring her groom Slaney's displeasure at not being allowed to accompany her.

He chose to disregard her assumption of hauteur, addressing her in the tones he had used since the day he had set her on the back of her first pony. "Faith, Miss Rora, the master would fair discharge me did he know ye were after riding out alone and by yerself! It's watched ye should be, and if ye wasn't as stubborn a young lady as might be found in all Ireland, I'd march right up there to the castle and tell the poor ladyship what ye're doin'. But I know did I do so, ye'd gallop off soon's I was away—and in the divil's own time!"

Rora nodded mischievously from her superior position atop Falstaff. "So I would, Slaney, but don't trouble yourself about me. All my life I've longed to gallop away and leave you behind, you old shadow, and here I have my chance! What harm can come to me within the bounds of Ardara? Let loose my bridle and don't waste another thought on me—busy yourself with shining the harnesses."

The Irishman glowered back at her, his bushy brows meeting in the center of his forehead. "And who's to open a gate, miss, if ye come upon one? Ye ain't so high and mighty as to be able to climb back into the saddle all on yer own, pardon me for sayin'!"

"If I come to a gate, I'll jump it, you horrid thing! Now stand aside!"

There was an implacable note in the young lady's voice that the groom could not but take notice of, and he knew the unwisdom of further complaint. Rora cast a saucy smile upon him, wheeled her horse around, and trotted away. Slaney stumped off on his bowed legs and continued his arguments to himself, muttering dire predictions of broken necks and sprained hocks under his breath, interspersed with several choice Gaelic oaths.

Rora's eventual destination was the castle ruins, but she cut across the fields and meadows first. As she rode past the flocks of Ardara, she admired the thick wool that cloaked each sheep, and was further enchanted by the green and growing hay fields. An intense pride filled her heart as she surveyed her birthright; the estate was even now beginning to reveal the rich promise of spring, and nothing, she thought, could be more beautiful. As

Falstaff cantered easily over the springy turf, Rora wondered if her mother had ever felt so strong an affinity for this dear land, and came to the conclusion that she must have, for Alanna had always spoken of Ardara as some rare and cherished jewel. Whenever Rora was in a reflective mood, she rather missed her mother; it would have been so agreeable to have known Alanna in a woman-to-woman fashion. Rora was now old enough to have done with most of the rebelliousness that had characterized her adolescence, and she would have appreciated the kind of guidance that only another female could give. But since coming to Ardara she had been pleased to discover that her grandmother, who had been an alarming and commanding force during her childhood, was in truth wry and amusing, a female of strength and one who certainly must be admired. Rora was grateful for the opportunity to come under her sphere of influence; she esteemed the old lady, however much she might be exasperated by her. She had begun to realize that Lady Liscarrol might even be a superior example to a young woman than Alanna would have been, for Rora's beautiful mother had frequently exhibited a tendency toward excess of sensibility and an overfondness for fashion.

These thoughts led her to a pleasant contemplation of how the romance must have been, twenty years before, between an idealistic young scholar and the spirited Alanna, darling of her family. Rora had a theory that marriage to Jasper Donellan had improved her mother greatly, and decided that if Alanna had wed Lord Briavel, she would have turned into one of those bored London ladies, the sort who cared more for the cut of a new gown or her latest flirtation than for her own offspring. During the years of her marriage, Lady Alanna had been an admirable and attentive wife and a loving mother; she had been an elegant and popular hostess, as much with the dons and students of Trinity College as among the lights of Dublin society. The truth of the marriage, Rora reflected, had been that her parents had loved and supported each other through many trials: the condemnation of the bride's family during the first difficult year of wedlock, the straitened circumstances resulting from that disapproval, and the disappointment when no other children followed their daughter.

In the end, the Donellans had gained the goodwill of the Liscarrols, a respected position in Dublin, and an elegant residence in Merrion Square, a belated bride-gift from Lord Liscarrol, who could not bear the thought of his precious daughter eking out an existence in the shabby lodgings of a university professor. Jasper Donellan had accepted the largesse with the same ease that he accepted everything, but he'd remained enough his own man to become involved in the planning of the 1798 Rebellion, much to the despair of his in-laws, who feared Alanna would be widowed young and the six-year-old Rora left fatherless. Fortunately for everyone, and Jasper most of all, he'd had a falling out with the conspirators over the violent means by which Irish freedoms should be won, and long before the unsuccessful May uprising his attentions had returned to his medieval studies and his writings. A fateful decision indeed, since many of the conspirators active in the Rebellion had died violently. The leader, Theobald Wolfe Tone, had been captured, tried, and sentenced to death, but had died by his own hand before his execution could be carried out.

But on this gray Kilkenny day, Rora's thoughts didn't linger on the sad failures of the Rebellion, for through the trees she spied the ruined tower of the Old Castle, as Ardara's first foundations had been known since the building of the present house. She put her heels to Falstaff in her impatience to reach her favorite part of the estate.

In keeping with the previous century's tenets of architecture and landscape design, a folly had been erected cheek by jowl, as it were, beside the original site of the castle. This edifice was a miniature rotunda with Doric columns; it commanded an impressive view of the crumbling and ivy-covered tower and walls, but it had always seemed quite out of place to Rora in its marble whiteness, and she resented its intrusive attempts to overshadow the weathered gray stones of the first Ardara. As she reached the clearing and pulled Falstaff up short, she wondered anew what had possessed her great-grandfather to place the small and foolish temple in such hallowed surroundings, but absolved him on the grounds that he'd done so near the end of his life, when the rage for such things had been at its height. The folly had at one time been used as the site of al fresco parties, but it had been kept locked since the discovery some five years earlier of an itinerant poacher living within its circular walls.

Rora, unaware of this circumstance, remembered the happy days when she and the young Newburghs had tumbled about among the ruins, using the summerhouse as their own miniature palace. She and the boys had often stormed the folly, brandishing long sticks in the place of swords, to rescue Louisa and Joan, who obligingly assumed the guise of captive princesses. Rora laughed aloud at the memory, for as a child she had fancied herself Joan of Arc, and had sometimes envied her dearest cousin not only her raven hair and blue eyes, but the romance of her name as well.

A sudden, nostalgic desire to explore the ruins and to enter the folly prompted her to unhook her leg from the pommel and slide to the ground. Only then, when it was too late, did she recall that she couldn't easily mount Falstaff again without assistance. A swift glance at the folly reassured her that she could lead the stallion to its edge and use it as a mounting block—she would have a three-foot advantage over her present situation. Having determined this, she loosed the horse, who immediately began cropping at the tender young blades of grass.

Walking briskly and impetuously toward the columned monstrosity, Rora failed to spy a rabbit hole in her path and thus put her foot into it. Stumbling, she fell awkwardly to the ground. She sat up and clutched her ankle, more in surprise than in pain. She had wrenched it, of that she was certain, but she was equally sure that it was not a serious injury. Not a sprain, at all events, and if she but stayed still, no doubt the slight pain would go off in a moment.

So she sat there, gripping her kid-shod foot and blaming herself aloud for her stupidity. Slaney's inflated opinion of his usefulness seemed to have been corroborated by the accident, and she let fly a string of Gaelic curses culled from that worthy's extensive vocabulary.

Suddenly a male voice called from the vicinity of the dense wood nearby: "Have you suffered some hurt, ma'am?"

Rora looked up to see a black horse and its rider bearing down upon her, and she wished more than ever that she had brought her groom along on this particular ride. To be found in so lowering a position by a complete stranger was frustrating, and she colored as the horseman came closer. While he dismounted, she rejected the thought of making an attempt to rise, fearing that she would be tripped up by her skirts and fall at his feet, which would be even more undignified and embarrassing.

"I am perfectly all right, sir," she said calmly, looking up at the gentleman as he strode purposefully to her side. She turned her face upon him, and was somewhat taken aback when the stranger stopped short and stared back in what she considered a most rude and ungentlemanly fashion.

"Good God!" he uttered in a low voice, in apparent disbelief. "It cannot be possible!"

"I wish you would not look at me as though I'm a ghost—I should much prefer to rise, sir, if you would give me a hand up!" Rora replied with considerable acerbity. The sharpness of her tone had its effect: his blank look of astonishment was replaced by one of distaste.

The gentleman tucked his whip under his arm and offered her both of his hands, pulling her to her feet with an infuriating lack of effort. He released her at once and gave her a glance that Rora could only bristle at, for she had the feeling he'd like to wipe his hands after touching her, but was too polite to pull out his handkerchief. And when he continued to look down his nose at her, she felt like some insignificant bit of lint he had picked up on his well-cut riding coat and was too lazy to brush off.

"Can I assist you in mounting your horse?" he asked with a considerably more appreciative glance in Falstaff's direction. "He looks to be too much for a lady to handle, so I am not surprised at finding you sprawled upon the grass, Miss—"

"Donellan," she snapped, sticking a strand of auburn hair under her riding hat. Her green eyes sparkled dangerously as she added, "And Falstaff did *not* throw me, whatever you may think, sir. I was already on the ground—walking—when I stumbled and fell—" She broke off as she realized, too late, how clumsy this made her sound.

"I see." He seemed to accept her disjointed explanation, but was clearly amused by it, for the firm mouth twitched and the gray eyes glinted. Rora had never felt so foolish, nor at such a disadvantage.

The gentleman was dressed appropriately for the country, but he wore his clothes with a certain air, and her city-bred eyes had no trouble detecting that his attire was of the first stare and had been fashioned by a master. The fact that he set it off to advantage could not be denied either. He was a tall, well-built man, and his overpowering masculinity exerted an attraction so strong that it left her feeling unaccountably flustered, until she thought of a way to squash his self-important air.

"What are you doing on this property?" she wanted to know, glaring at him; she had abandoned all pretense of civility. "I believe you are trespassing, sir."

"As to that, your name is not Morres, or Liscarrol, and it's my belief that Lady Liscarrol is the mistress of Ardara."

"She is my grandmother."

"So I imagine, but she is also the only person who has any right to question my intrusion upon her property, Miss Donellan," the gentleman said easily, but with a smile that caused Rora's hackles to rise.

"You can be sure that I'll tell her of it, Mr. —Mr. —sir," she finished, angered further by the fact that he seemed unwilling to supply his name. "Besides, a few hundred yards into that wood is the property of Lord Briavel, through which you clearly passed, and he shall be informed of your trespass as well!"

"Oh, he is perfectly well aware of it," was the stranger's reply, which took the wind out of her sails. He appeared to enjoy this effect, for he crossed his arms and looked down at her triumphantly, his eyes the color of the sky above and faintly mocking.

"Are—are you visiting at Hargrave House?" Rora asked, puckering up her forehead. Lady Liscarrol had mentioned that another Englishman was staying there with Lord Briavel. This must be he.

"I am."

Rora had the good grace to apologize to the gentleman, saying that she had not meant to be rude, which was politic, if not entirely true. "If you are a guest of his lordship, then I'm sure it is not to be wondered at, your straying onto our—onto my grandmother's property. Forgive me!" She held out her hand with a sunny smile. He seemed reluctant to take it, but did so after a long enough time that she felt foolish in having offered it; he let it go immediately.

"Can I help you to mount?" he asked again, his eyes running up and down her figure in a familiar manner that caused Rora's face to flame. "Or do you have a groom hiding about in the ruins?"

She was suddenly shy of admitting her unprotected state, for this man was looking quite ruthless—an ugly customer, as her father would say. And he was one of those London gentlemen she had heard of, the sort who made a career of debauchery. If this was Briavel's friend, God alone knew what his lordship must be like! But whatever the dangers of her plight, Rora couldn't repress a giggle on thinking of the flattering portrait her grandmother had painted of the two young bucks at Hargrave House. This man was hardly young—Rora judged him to be in his late twenties—but she could easily believe him one of the Corinthian set. He was evidently something of a rake as well, and she realized that she ought to be more nervous than she was.

"What is so amusing, Miss Donellan?" the stranger wanted to know.

"Nothing that would interest you," she answered tartly. "I have no need of your assistance, and bid you good day." She was afraid to permit him to lift her into her saddle; she could imagine what liberties those strong hands might take—he would probably squeeze her waist or pinch her, she supposed, uncertain of which would be worse. Clearly he had only one use for her sex. She could tell that he disliked her intensely, yet he persisted in looking at her in that horrid way. Damn Slaney—she ought to have brought him along, but how was she to know that there were libertines roaming the neighborhood?

Without another word, Rora stalked away, trying to ignore the wicked chuckle that issued from the rakish gentleman. The skin on the back of her neck prickled, and she fought the desire to turn to see if he followed her. But this was unnecessary, for in a moment she could hear the unmistakable sounds of a horse thundering across the turf.

She breathed a sigh of relief, so thankful to be rid of his presence that she cared not at all that he treated the lands of Ardara as a public highway. She went back to the folly, returning to her original mission, and found the building locked. She strolled instead through the castle ruins, heedless of the rain that had begun to fall and the brambles that pulled viciously at her habit.

When she was ready to return to the stables, climbing onto Falstaff proved to be a simple matter. Her plan to use the foundation of the folly as a mounting block was a happy one, and as she turned her horse's head in the direction from which she had come, she felt a high degree of triumph. She had managed one thing perfectly without Slaney, as she would be sure to inform him, and had even escaped molestation at the hands of an obvious rake without the slightest assistance. Her earlier trepidation was all but forgotten as she wondered for how long that beastly man would be fixed at Hargrave House. She had no intention of speaking to anyone of their brief encounter, and she hoped that he wouldn't cross her path again. Such a pity that so handsome a man, with his black hair and fine, lean face was such a monster. She had even apologized to him for her rudeness, once she had learned that he was Briavel's guest, but he'd barely accepted her civility.

Upon her arrival at the stables, Slaney frowned as he helped her to dismount, and said grudgingly that he was glad to see that she was in one piece. The groom led Falstaff away and Rora strolled toward the house, quickening her pace as she skipped lightly up the terrace steps. A footman opened the door for her and, at a question, informed her that her ladyship and Miss Newburgh could be found in the Great Parlor. Rora went at once to this chamber, pausing only to leave her hat, gloves, and whip with the footman; she feared that she was late for luncheon and hoped that her grandmother wouldn't be put out by her tardiness.

She dashed headlong into the parlor, apologies spilling from her lips, and then stopped short. She wished she'd been forewarned: there was a gentleman sitting with Joan and Lady Liscarrol. As he rose lazily from his chair, she noted with barely concealed surprise that it was the stranger she had met by the folly.

"Rora, my dear, come and join us," her ladyship said, beaming upon her reluctant granddaughter in a pleased fashion. "No, never mind your dirt—Gavin won't care a jot, for he rode over here himself from Hargrave House. Lord Briavel, this is my other granddaughter, Aurora Donellan."

"Miss Donellan," his lordship said with a neat bow, his gray eyes narrowing as he regarded the discomfited Rora. He gave no hint of ever having laid eyes on her before that moment, and he was duly appreciative of the young lady's assumption of unconcern as she inclined her russet head gracefully and murmured all that was proper.

Inside, Rora was seething with anger. What a dreadful person he was, although she had to be grateful that he hadn't given away their previous meeting. She felt the veriest fool for having accused him of trespassing on his own property; and on Ardara, too, for Lady Liscarrol was even now saying how she had given dear Gavin *carte blanche* to ride her acres as freely as he did his own. Dear Gavin, indeed! Her grandmother wouldn't say so if she knew of that slyly insinuating glance Lord Briavel had given Rora before they'd parted. Rora wasn't unused to being ogled by young bucks, but something about his lordship's manner hinted that he might actually follow the look with an act, and the memory made her uncomfortable. Furthermore, she would have preferred to meet his lordship again dressed in garb other than her now dirty and burr-covered habit. For the second time that day she felt at a disadvantage and resolved not to let it show.

"For how long are you fixed at Hargrave House?" she asked him conversationally, in an attempt at masking the true purpose of this question, which was to find out how long the neighborhood would be burdened with his presence.

He looked at her over his glass of wine, a glimmer of understanding lighting his eyes. "I'm not certain, Miss Donellan. Did I not find my neighbors so congenial, I daresay I should be off immediately." This remark was accompanied by a warm glance directed somewhere in the vicinity of the region between Rora's neck and her waist.

How dare he look at her so, and in the presence of her own grandmother and cousin! But Lady Liscarrol hadn't noticed, and Joan, who was pouring out a glass of Madeira for her cousin, was also unconscious of what had passed. Looking up, she said with a smile, "Lord Briavel is invited to the Whitneys' party on Thursday next, Rora, and so is his guest, Sir Nicholas. Won't that be delightful?"

"Yes—delightful," Rora responded mechanically, but with a peculiar lack of enthusiasm.

"I shall hope to have the pleasure of partnering both of your granddaughters, Cousin Hester," Briavel said, not taking his eyes off Rora.

"Good God—never say that we are related!" Rora cried, her surprise jolting her out of her assumed calm.

Lady Liscarrol laughed, but it was Lord Briavel who replied, "No, not actually, but her ladyship gave me the right to call her so many years before you were born, Miss Donellan."

"Indeed I did! When Gavin was a grubby brat he was always to be found here at Ardara among my brood, for all they were much older than he."

While Rora was busy digesting this news, Purdon announced the arrival of Sir Nicholas Tobin. The caller was a pleasant-faced gentleman of no more than middle height; he was much the same age as Lord Briavel, and if less handsome, he was more outgoing. He, too, had an air of fashion about him and as he was introduced to the young ladies, Rora could not help but smile back at his infectious grin.

"Miss Donellan! How happy I am to make your acquaintance—I have heard your praises sung by all of Gavin's neighbors, and was in despair that I would never meet you," the baronet declared.

"And Miss Newburgh—how nice to see you again! We met at Newburgh Hall last year, but I daresay you don't recall it."

"You may be sure she does," Lady Liscarrol answered as Joan nodded her smooth dark head in Sir Nicholas's direction. "Not but what there must be a score of gentlemen in and out of the hall in a year's time. I never thought to see my son Brendan setting up for a horse coper, not but what he breeds the finest in the kingdom, I'll give him that! *And* makes a fair profit, I'll be bound!" she added knowingly.

Joan and her ladyship sat down with the new visitor and they were soon absorbed in a discussion of the Whitneys' party. This left Rora with no one to talk to save Lord Briavel, who shamelessly took the empty chair beside hers and sat patiently as though waiting for her to inaugurate conversation. She sipped at her wine and wished that it were she and not Joan who was engaged in a dialogue with Sir Nicholas Tobin.

Lord Briavel watched as the young lady swallowed her wine, and her action called to mind a story he had often heard of a famously beautiful Irish girl. His father, Lord Rothmore, had repeatedly told him that when the younger Miss Gunning drank claret at regiment parties, all the officers would look to see if they might trace the red liquid as it flowed down the white column of her throat. The Donellan girl had an alabaster skin that must be very like that of the noted beauty, he mused appreciatively. Arrogant she might be, but what a face and figure!

"Allow me to congratulate you on your calm acceptance of my presence in your grandmother's parlor," he said after a moment or two of continued silence from his companion. "When you entered the room, I rather feared that you would give way to curses, as you did earlier today."

Rora hadn't realized that he had heard her frustrated oaths when she was on the ground by the folly, and she turned to stare at him. "How did you know I was cursing?" she asked impatiently. "I wasn't even speaking in English!"

"Your tone, Miss Donellan, left no doubt as to the intent of your words!"

Oh, he was odious! Rora could think of nothing to say to him; it must make her seem very stupid and dull. But she had another question for the monster of depravity at her side. "And why did you look at me in such a way, when we were down at the folly?"

Startled, he gazed back at her for a moment, then gave a reminiscent chuckle. "Oh, that! My purpose was merely to infuriate you, ma'am, and you rose to the bait admirably. Just as you did a moment ago."

She colored faintly, for she had not meant the particular look to which he referred and which she also remembered well. "No, you misunderstand—I was speaking of the way you looked at me at first—with such distaste. I am not so unperceptive as to have missed it."

Suddenly Briavel's face was back in its inscrutable mask. "You do deal in plain speaking, don't you? Well, I shall deal in the same coin: in the instant I first saw you, I was reminded of your mother, Lady Alanna. The memory, as you might imagine, is somewhat distasteful to one of my family."

Understanding dawned, and she exclaimed, "But of course— how foolish of me not to have realized it! People say I am very much like her. So you *were* seeing a ghost when you came upon me, after all, or thought you were."

"For a moment. Probably my fears were increased by the mystery and gloom of our surroundings, the mossy ruins and all that!" he jested. "Foolish of me, but I hope you will accept my hand in apology more readily than I did yours." As he said this, his lordship proffered his right hand, adorned by a heavy gold signet ring.

Rora saw a slight softening of his features, and it pleased her inordinately. She had the upper hand now, and a devil prompted her to make him squirm. She clasped his hand and replied gaily, "How can I help but do so—if only to prove that I am far more charitable than you, sir! What a ridiculous misunderstanding— here I was abusing you roundly for your behavior to me, when you couldn't *help* but take me into dislike. It is perfectly clear to me now: *I* am the one who is at fault, for resembling Mama so closely. No wonder you were cross as briars with me!" There was an underlying irony to her words that was impossible to mistake. "You probably fear that the sins of the mother will be visited upon the daughter."

Briavel regarded her with amusement. "Perhaps they will. But it makes no difference to me, for I doubt greatly that I shall be the one to put you to the test. You may jilt as many men as you please, Miss Donellan, and with my goodwill. Your behavior is no concern of mine."

"Oh, dear, you really did dislike Mama, didn't you? Then how comes it about that you are on such terms with Grandmother?"

"As her ladyship just informed you, our friendship predates Lady Alanna's elopement. When I was a lad, my father came every year to Hargrave House."

"I see. So you knew Mama even before she—before she married Papa?"

Lady Liscarrol interrupted their conversation before the viscount could form his reply. "Dear me, Rora, are you and Gavin discussing ancient history? You would be much better occupied in discussing horseflesh, which is the only thing the two of you have in common, I daresay."

This was not a happy suggestion; Rora recalled only too well the gentleman's disapproval of Falstaff as a lady's mount, and her eyes flashed. "I should dearly love to discuss horses with his lordship, but I simply *must* hurry upstairs to change; I am quite damp. Therefore I'm afraid I must bid our visitors farewell." Rising and turning to his lordship, she said with false sweetness, "I trust you will be gone before I come downstairs again, so I will say goodbye now, sir."

Surprisingly, Briavel grinned down at her and murmured outrageously, "You mean you *hope* I'll be gone. But we will meet again, Miss Donellan—many times!"

If he had hoped to elicit a response, he was disappointed. Rora turned her back on him and said her proper goodbyes to Sir Nicholas, most cordially. Before leaving the Great Parlor, she had the pleasure of seeing that her own exit was causing the breakup of the party. By the time she reached the upper landing, she heard the sound of voices in the hall, followed by the closing of the great front door. She smiled her relief and continued up the staircase, glad that Lord Briavel was no longer under the same roof as she.

CHAPTER IV

The next visitor of note to present himself at Ardara Castle was Peyton Newburgh, Joan's brother and her senior by a year. The young gentleman arrived on horseback one rare sunny afternoon with the intelligence that his father, Sir Brendan, had left Newburgh Hall to embark upon a journey to Galway.

"Galway!" Joan cried in surprise, although there was a certain amount of pleasure in her tone. "Why ever did he take it into his head to do so, Peyton? He made no mention of the journey when I left the hall."

The young man grinned back at his sister and uttered a single word: "Horses!"

"But of course! There is some sort of horse fair, then?" At her brother's nod, she said to Rora, "In that case we can be sure of his being away for some time. Papa won't cut his trip short, because he won't have the expense of lodgings: our Uncle Richard and his wife will put him up!" Miss Newburgh was not the least cast down by the thought of her father's absence from the neighborhood and fell into a smiling reverie, leaving it to Rora to entertain Peyton.

Peyton's hair was carrot-colored and his pleasant face was as freckled as a turkey's egg, but neither of these regrettable circumstances marred his good looks. He was two-and-twenty and possessed all the healthy good spirits of a young gentleman of sporting proclivities. Dressed in buckskins and riding coat, with a Belcher neckerchief tied carelessly about his neck in lieu of a cravat, he appeared out of place and uncomfortable in the imposing parlor. Sensing this, Rora begged him to join her for a gallop around the estate, that he might judge the points of Falstaff. He agreed to the plan, and she hurried away to change into her habit.

When she had gone, Peyton looked at his sister and said, "Hi there, Jo, are you daydreaming again? Lord, you were never used to do so till but lately! Cousin Rora and I are going for a ride—do you join us?"

"Thank you, no. I believe I should go upstairs to acquaint Gran with the news of Papa's removal from the neighborhood."

"Pooh, why should she care what Papa does—except be glad he's gone."

"Peyton!" his sister cried, quite shocked. "You oughtn't to say such things, however true they may be. Someone might overhear —you would be thought frightfully unfilial!"

"Gran says as much to his face—you know she don't like him much, Jo."

"Why didn't Papa take you with him?" Joan wanted to know.

Peyton ran his thin fingers through his cropped red thatch distractedly. "He fancied someone should be at hand to keep you out of mischief, as though Gran isn't enough of a chaperone. He seems to think the presence of Englishmen in the district might prove tempting to you, after that business last autumn. Not but what he said in the same breath that Lord Briavel was a regular Croesus, besides being a viscount and heir to an earldom, and he might do for you, Jo—don't that beat all?" He went into whoops; his sister did not join in. She sat calmly, an odd little smile on her round face. Finally Peyton gained enough control of himself to add, "But I daresay even Papa couldn't bring his lordship up to scratch. Those London fellows are devilish hard to catch, and when they do marry, 'tis to some fubsy-faced filly with a fortune at her back, I'll be bound!"

"Oh, Peyton, no matter what he says about Lord Briavel, you know Papa means to keep us tied to him always: you to help with the horses and the stud farm, and me to hold household. And then someday Symon will inherit, and where will we be? Naught but poor relations, living on his bounty. Caroline will be so glad to have *poor* Joan to help with the children she and our brother will inevitably produce, and Symon will probably turn out to be twice as clutch-fisted as Papa! What a dismal prospect we have before us." Her bitter voice trailed off into silence.

Peyton's cheerfulness was unimpaired, although he went to his sister to put an arm around her shoulders. "There, now, you mustn't speak so! Gran will come through for you somehow, even provide more dowry, if the right fellow happens along. As for me, well, it doesn't much matter. I've no ambitions, outside the horse business, and have no intention of offering for Cousin Rora, no matter how much Papa pushes me to do so."

The young lady of whom he spoke had returned to the parlor at that very moment, unbeknownst to Peyton, and she paused on the threshold. In response to her cousin's last remark she said brightly, "Thank you very much, Peyton—I should much prefer that you did not offer for me!"

Peyton turned and saw Rora standing there, a twinkle in her green eyes. He flushed to the roots of his hair and stammered an apology while his sister apostrophized him as a positive booberkin.

"Never mind, Cousin," Rora consoled him with a laugh. "I have no thought of marriage at present, and so you may tell Uncle Brendan, if he chances to bring up the subject with you again."

He looked at her with abject relief and remarked to Joan that he knew all along Cousin Rora was a right one. "Not that you aren't monstrously pretty, but I'm not in the petticoat line, myself," he acknowledged, his flush receding.

"I should hope not!" Rora cried. "Especially since I left Dublin to escape from gentlemen who haven't a thought in their heads besides flirting. Are you ready for our ride?"

He was, and they strolled to the stables together in a state of perfect amity. Peyton was most enthusiastic about Falstaff, telling Rora that not a single Newburgh horse could cast the stallion in the shade. She in turn admired his mount, a long-tailed gray of which he was enormously proud. After allowing their horses to walk a bit, Rora challenged her cousin to a race along the drive, with the main road to Kilkenny their finish point. They started at the lodge gates, with Peyton maintaining a strong lead in the beginning. But Admiral was already slightly worn down by the ride over from Newburgh Hall, and Falstaff inched ahead.

Rora was caught up in the moment, in the race: she crouched forward, her eyes on the roadway looming ahead tantalizingly, just beyond the trees. "Come, Falstaff, let's give them our best," she encouraged her horse, using her heels to urge him to even greater speed. The wind raced past her ears and stirred the tall oaks and larches that formed a canopy over the drive. She bounded into the main road, holding her whip aloft in victory.

But the test of her mettle was not yet at an end, for there was a curricle and pair in her path, not moving at a fast enough speed to ensure that she would miss colliding with them. She quickly and forcefully tugged at the reins, causing Falstaff to swerve sharply; in his surprise, the stallion reared. As she tried to calm him, Rora heard the driver of the curricle utter a sharp oath, while he in turn tried to control his restive cattle. By the time Admiral came thundering into the road, all danger was past, although Falstaff was still stamping and snorting with indignation at having been stopped short at his moment of victory. Peyton drew up sharply beside Rora, who was looking rather pale. The curricle driver had pulled his chestnuts up and sat glaring at her ferociously, fury darkening his eyes. It was Lord Briavel.

"Good God, Rora, but you're a hard goer!" Peyton praised her breathlessly. "And the way you missed the curricle was beyond anything great!"

"Miss Donellan's horsemanship is exceeded solely by her apparent lack of sense," said a cold voice, and Peyton turned to glare at the stranger.

Before Mr. Newburgh could take the gentleman to task for his rudeness, Rora said shakily, "Forgive me for not being omniscient, sir, but I was wholly unaware that you were on this road." She gestured with her riding whip. "Your approach was blocked by the trees."

"Naturally, but you were foolish beyond permission to go racing into the road so heedlessly." His lordship gathered up his reins, addressing a remark to Peyton as he did so: "Young sir, you would be best advised not to follow where this female leads, or you will probably end in being carried home on a hurdle!"

"Sir, what gives you the right to speak so to my cousin?" Peyton blustered.

"I'm Briavel—ah—an old family friend," his lordship informed the angry youth with cocked eyebrow. "And you, I take it, are one of the Newburghs. I'm sure we shall meet again in future—under happier circumstances, we must hope! Till then I shall strive to forget this near-catastrophe. Good day, sir—Miss Donellan!" With a flick of his whip, Briavel drove off at a smart trot, leaving the riders staring at his retreating vehicle.

"So that was Briavel? Too toplofty by half," Peyton said feelingly. "I'm not at all sure that he would ever do for Joan, no matter how rich he is!"

"Yes, perfectly odious," Rora agreed.

"But did you see those blood chestnuts of his, Rora? Such sweet steppers—good forward action. I wonder where he came by them."

"I neither know nor care!" his cousin said heatedly as she gathered up her reins.

"And did you see his driving coat? It must have had fifteen capes at least—and his way with the thong—'twas beyond anything great!" Peyton urged Admiral into a walk, and Rora followed his example, shaking her head over his abrupt change from disgust to raptures.

"Well, if you are disposed to admire his lordship, be my guest," she told him, "but you will never hear me hymning his praises! Lord Briavel took me into dislike the moment he laid eyes upon me, and I assure you it was a mutual antipathy." She ground her teeth in reminiscence.

"Whyever should he do so?" Peyton asked, somewhat taken aback by the ferocity of her tone.

"Because of Mama! His father was the Lord Briavel she jilted, you see, and everyone was celebrating her engagement to him the very night she ran off with Papa! So his son has taken it upon himself to hold *me* personally responsible." But she feared that it had been her own clumsy and impulsive actions on the occasions of their meeting, as much as her resemblance to Alanna, that were the true reasons for Briavel's dislike of her.

Enlightenment lit her companion's freckled face. "That's it! I knew the name was familiar, I just couldn't come up with the why of it. Of course, I was still in leading strings at the time, but I have heard about Alanna's indiscretion all my life. So that was the present Viscount Briavel!" Peyton sighed his envy and added, "He looks to be a Corinthian—you know, one of those fashionable, sporting fellows."

Rora did know, but she hastened to change the subject; she did not wish to indulge Peyton's great interest in his lordship any longer. She had suffered a shock from nearly colliding with the curricle and pair. In the instant before she pulled Falstaff up, she had nearly panicked, but fortunately (for her own sake and his lordship's) she'd managed to act with what she considered to have been great presence of mind, and little thanks had she received. Nor had he evinced the slightest bit of solicitude for her welfare, which infuriated her even further. Perhaps she and Peyton had selected an unwise finish line for their race, but it was not Briavel's place to upbraid her. She knew herself to be somewhat at fault, but this knowledge only made her even more angry at the gentleman who had happened into her path. And to think that she had once been disposed to think him handsome! His manners certainly didn't match his looks, she thought viciously, although it was impossible not to recall that moment the other day when he had offered her his beringed hand as though he wanted to cry a truce. But any goodwill she had been inclined to feel had evaporated a few moments ago in the face of his cold disapproval. He was a horrid person again, and the sooner he removed himself from the neighborhood, the better pleased she would be.

On the evening of the Whitneys' party, Rora took great pains with her appearance, for she had a strong desire to prove to Lord Briavel that she was not the thoughtless hoyden he considered her. With this in mind she selected one of her most elegant gowns, too fine a gown for a simple country assembly, perhaps, but she was determined to present an appearance that would have done justice to a ball at Dublin Castle.

Joan was concerned with her own toilette, taking special care to arrange a spray of flowers in her black tresses, placing it just so. Although she was pleased with her own lilac sarcenet gown, she was lavish in her praise of Rora's white embroidered crepe, worn with pearls and a scarf of gossamer net draped around the creamy shoulders.

"But, Joan, it is I who must envy your ability to wear lilac!" Rora protested with a laugh as they and Lady Liscarrol were borne to the Whitney residence. "It is one of my favorite colors, and one which does nothing for my coloring—it makes me quite hideous!"

"As if anything could," Joan murmured.

" 'Tis perfectly true!"

Lady Liscarrol announced that both girls were in high beauty that evening, but agreed that lilacs and lavenders were colors that neither she nor her daughter had worn to advantage, and therefore Rora must take after them, even though her hair was marginally darker.

The company that evening was made up of nearly all the families in the neighborhood, and even a few from Kilkenny. Rora was surprised by the number of guests assembled under the Whitneys' roof, especially those of her own age or thereabouts. There were young gentlemen in abundance, eager to make the acquaintance of the Dublin beauty. Bored with partnering girls with whom they had played as children, they welcomed the sight of a new face. This circumstance did not sit well with the young ladies themselves, however, most notably those who had a partiality for Mr. Peyton Newburgh, who could be heard to praise his cousin to the skies. But Miss Donellan, although quite distractingly lovely and well dressed, did not put herself forward nor did she flirt outrageously as the other girls had feared she might. So they, like their brothers and male friends, had to admire the newcomer. Among the company, more than one mother and father of a hopeful son looked upon Miss Donellan as a provident angel sent from above, for the girl would be a considerable heiress once her grandmother went to her reward, and Ardara was the finest property in the parish, perhaps in the county.

Another surprise for Rora was the early arrival of the gentlemen from Hargrave House; she had expected that they would be the last to arrive and the first to leave the party. When they met, Lord Briavel bowed and coolly uttered the merest commonplace, before engaging Joan for the first country dance. Rora was disappointed, for she had hoped that he would solicit her for one of the early dances. Not that she wanted him as partner, only the satisfaction of informing him that he was too late, since the majority of the dances had already been taken by the young men who formed her enthusiastic and constant court. It was Sir Nicholas Tobin who put his name down for the cotillion and quite took Rora's breath away when he sheepishly requested that she save one of the final dances for his friend.

"For I know Gavin would roast me endlessly if I asked for two myself, Miss Donellan, so I shall take one and let him have the other!" Sir Nicholas explained with his ready smile.

It was on the tip of her tongue to reply that Lord Briavel was hardly worth such thoughtfulness on his part, but she bit back her retort and said instead that his lordship might have the reel that would close the evening's dancing. She well knew, although she left it unsaid, that conversation during a reel was virtually impossible.

She was amazed to find that Lord Briavel did not hold himself aloof from the company, for, based upon her experience of him, she had rather thought that he might. He showed all the signs of enjoying himself immensely, and somehow this marred her own pleasure in the assembly. Apparently all the guests were known to him, and she realized with a certain measure of surprise that he must have been making the rounds of the neighborhood since his arrival, calling upon the local gentry and becoming acquainted with them. Did that mean he intended to settle at Hargrave House? Oh, no, that could not be possible! She looked away briefly from her partner of the moment, a young Mr. Whitney whose shirt points were wilting most pitiably in the hot, crowded room, to see that black head towering over the others of similar and varied color. His lordship was speaking to Peyton at present, and from the way her cousin's bright head was bobbing up and down eagerly, she supposed that his original aversion to the Viscount had been forgotten in a discussion of either horses or shooting. Rora mentally shook her head over Peyton's defection from the ranks of those persons who found Briavel insupportable. The nobleman had hardly spoken to her all evening, and she did not know whether to be glad or sorry. The subsequent realization that she felt pique more than anything else was most unwelcome.

When the creature finally deigned to claim his dance with her, it was not the reel for which she had accepted him by proxy, but for the dance she had given Sir Nicholas.

"I'm quite afraid you are mistaken," Rora said to Briavel, her eyes blazing with anticipation of the joy she would have in setting him straight. "This dance belongs to Sir Nicholas Tobin!"

"He begged me most straitly to secure his release, Miss Donellan, and to dance with you in his stead. As you can see, he seems to be engrossed in conversation with Miss Newburgh."

"Oh." It was true, she discovered upon shifting her gaze in that direction: Sir Nicholas and Joan were earnestly talking to one another in an alcove. "Very well, I suppose I must accept you in his place," she agreed with poor grace. The musicians had taken up their instruments and were striking the tune, but it was not the one she had expected: surely this was a waltz tune. "What on earth —" she began.

"You do waltz, Miss Donellan?" Briavel asked in a bored tone. "I had thought that in Dublin . . ." His voice trailed off and the gray eyes looked into hers, twin devils of mischief dancing in them as he waited for her answer.

"Well, yes, I do—I have—at waltzing parties in Dublin, in the morning, but never at an evening assembly. Did you *request* a waltz, sir?" she asked him suddenly.

His only reply was to lead her out onto the floor, although no other couples were yet to be found there.

"This is preposterous!" Rora sputtered under her breath, aware that all eyes were upon them and trying to keep a bland and smiling expression on her face for the benefit of the company. Let them think that she was accustomed to dancing the shocking new dance, but inwardly she was fuming. How could he do such a thing to her, she wondered, for everyone present would think her fast, lost to all propriety, to be waltzing at a simple country assembly with a gentleman she had known scarcely a week. Nonetheless, she responded to the firm pressure of his hand on her waist as he turned her about, and she spun obediently. In a few moments she was caught up in the dance itself, but not so much that she failed to notice that others were joining them. She was greatly relieved to see it, although the watchful parents were all wondering where their offspring had learned the steps.

Rora could hardly bring herself to lift her eyes to the face of her partner, who was holding her so closely.

He was looking down at her with amusement. "Nothing to say to me, Miss Donellan? I do hope that you won't hold my, ah—transgression—against me. It's just that I yearned to find out whether your ability as a dancer matched your admirable skill in handling a horse."

Rora flushed at this reminder of their most recent encounter. "I do hope that you are satisfied," she replied through gritted teeth, "for I know you must be congratulating yourself upon making me an object of contempt among our neighbors."

"I have done no such thing! Quite the opposite, I have bestowed a signal honor upon you, foolish girl. The waltz is occasionally danced at private balls in England now, not just at your morning parties, and you, Miss Donellan, are the first female in Ireland with whom I have engaged in this pleasurable pastime. So you see, I have done you a great favor, and you will be an object of envy rather than contempt!"

She glared at him. "You are insufferable, and I never heard of anything so conceited in all my life! You are not in London, where you can make reputations, although I doubt very much that a girl could be anything other than ruined through association with you! Moreover, you ought to have asked my grandmother's permission before soliciting me to take part in so improper an exercise as this."

"Now why did that not occur to me, I wonder? Perhaps it was because I doubted the possibility that Cousin Hester would concern herself with such a stuffy notion of respectability—as you yourself said, Miss Donellan, this is not London! You know, I am surprised that you would take such nonsense into your head—you are Alanna's daughter, after all, and she had little regard for appearances when she was your age."

"My mother was perfectly respectable!" she flung at him in a low voice. "And why must we forever come to cuffs about such—such ancient history, as Grandmother calls it? I am nothing like my mama, so it is useless to—"

"So you aren't respectable? I admit, I wondered when I first met you, wandering about alone and unattended by a groom, as a well-brought-up young lady should be. But then again—"

"Do stop!" Rora begged, but she could not help but smile at his teasing. "And please do not squeeze my waist so tightly. It is most unfair of you, sir, for while we are in so public a spot, I can have no recourse."

He slackened his hold somewhat. "True, I am at an advantage. But if it will make you feel better, when the dance is done I can take you outdoors for a breath of fresh air, and you may abuse me to your heart's content. I'll allow you to seek any satisfaction you wish—you may even strike me. I should be only too happy to offer further provocation!" His eyes glinted and he squeezed her waist again.

"I would not go half a yard in your company!" Rora declared, grateful that the music was drawing to a close and her ordeal was nearly over. "You are the most ungentlemanlike person I have ever known, and I do wish you will leave me alone." The dance ended and she curtsied to him with a brilliantly wicked smile. "Pray tell Sir Nicholas that I look forward to our reel." She turned on her heel and left him standing there. Her way was impeded by the young gentlemen who flocked to her side, clamoring for future waltzes.

Lord Briavel looked after her retreating figure with an expression of appreciation before turning his attention to the room set aside for the card tables. Miss Donellan was proving to be an intriguing creature, even more so than he had imagined at the outset. He wondered how long it would be before she grew tired of sparring with him, and whether or not he would become bored with her when she did. He had left London before the start of the season for the sole purpose of avoiding young damsels like Miss Aurora Donellan, pampered beauties with nothing but an eye to a title and a fortune. But he had to give this girl her due: she did not fawn over him or flirt with him, and she showed spirit in having taken him into dislike and owning it to his face. Neither was she cast into agonies of shyness at his overly friendly advances—she ripped up at him instead. And she beat most of the London beauties into flinders with her auburn curls and emerald eyes. His lordship was no longer sorry that Sir Nicholas had prevailed upon him to visit Ireland; it was late for hunting and early for shooting, but Miss Donellan was providing him with admirable sport.

As he and the baronet drove home that evening, each man was busy with his own thoughts. Briavel was fairly certain in what direction his quiet friend's thoughts lay. As for himself, he was remembering another reddish head and a pair of laughing eyes—those of Alanna, who had preferred to run off with Jasper Donellan than to marry his father and become Lady Briavel, and his own stepmother. He had been eight years old on the night of Lord and Lady Liscarrol's ball, the one at which the betrothal was to be announced. He had even been present that fateful evening, because the announcement was to have taken place early, well before he would be sent up to bed.

But sometime between dinner and the start of the ball, the lovely Lady Alanna had disappeared from Ardara altogether and a hastily penned note explaining her sudden absence had been found by her maid. It had been a dark night, with no moon to speak of, and Alanna and young Donellan had laid their plans well. They were married in Waterford that very evening by special license, from a cousin's house, the bride still dressed in her ball gown. These details, of course, had been discovered later, after an unsuccessful attempt to trace the couple to Dublin.

Gavin had adored Alanna. An impressionable lad, he had thought her a lovely fairy princess who had the power to transform his lonely, motherless world into one of happiness and light and had wholeheartedly approved his father's intention to marry. As a consequence, he had felt as much betrayed as his father had by the perfidy of one who had previously treated him with a special sort of kindness accompanied by her glorious smiles. The older man's loss became young Gavin's as well, and the boy could only be glad when his father immediately shut up Hargrave House and returned with his son to England. Upon their return to those shores, Gavin had dedicated himself to his studies, although some years later, at Oxford, he allowed himself to be tempted away from his books by sports and petticoats. But he had never again trusted a woman with his confidences or his heart, and he had no intention of ever doing so. Oddly, it had been the son who had taken Alanna's betrayal to heart, more so than the father, who had suffered from wounded pride but had recovered from the loss of the laughing girl he had loved. Gavin had more or less forgotten the incident until his return to the scene where it had taken place; in his case the effects, stemming from his childhood, had been more firmly ingrained. Now the past had been brought back to him, and meeting Alanna's daughter had initially reminded him even more of her mother's actions. Now that the sudden shock of her resemblance to Alanna had worn off, he could admit to himself that Miss Donellan attracted him greatly in her own right.

As the carriage transported the two gentlemen to Hargrave House, Briavel began to toy with the idea of making the beauty fall in love with him. Probably, having been exposed to none but prosy bores like Jasper Donellan and Trinity students, she could be beguiled by a man of the world, one with polish and address—and the lascivious proclivities that she clearly imputed to him. And, he thought bitterly, the chit needed a measure by which to judge her future loves. Heaven knew she was pretty and spirited enough to make such sport enjoyable. Certainly by the time she was head over ears for him, and if he did not tire of her by then (which he was beginning to think entirely possible), she might have proven to be the ideal match, for she was admirably endowed, both in face and in fortune. And what better way to avenge Alanna's betrayal than by causing her daughter to fall in love with the jilted suitor's son, who would marry the girl for her fortune! So caught up was Briavel in this aspect of the matter that he entirely failed to realize that he had associated the idea of marriage with a living, breathing, readily accessible young lady, which he had never before done in his life.

In quite another carriage, Rora and her relatives were being driven home by Lady Liscarrol's coachman, and there was a great deal of conversation. Joan teased her cousin mercilessly upon being the first girl in the neighborhood to waltz at a party, and with so illustrious a gentleman as Lord Briavel. In return, Rora twitted Joan on her obvious preference for Sir Nicholas Tobin's company.

"He is known to me slightly—I recognized him at once as one of the gentlemen who came to buy horses from Papa last autumn. And new faces in old surroundings are always most welcome: witness your own warm reception this evening, dear cousin!"

"Sir Nicholas seems an agreeable gentleman. I like him very well."

"He is amusing, but what do you think of Lord Briavel, Rora?"

"I dare not say, since one occupant of this carriage is so very well disposed toward him."

Lady Liscarrol, who had appeared to be dozing, opened her eyes and asked her granddaughter what she found objectionable in young Gavin.

"He appears to me to be cold and aloof, both condescending and yet overly familiar by turns, and unnecessarily high in the instep. He's probably selfish as well."

Her ladyship laughed at this condemnation and said that perhaps in time Rora would come to like the fellow. "It's to be hoped you will, because you'll come in one another's way the rest of your lives, unless he sells Hargrave House someday, which I don't think at all likely—it's too prosperous an estate."

Joan shook her head at Rora, a secretive smile playing about her lips. "For my part, I find Lord Briavel every bit the gentleman: elegant, handsome, and very kind." She looked down at her lap thoughtfully, completely missing Rora's expression of surprise at these words. "And I don't think him at all selfish."

"Well," Rora said sharply, "his lordship can pride himself on having made *one* conquest this evening!" Would Joan fall in with her father's wishes if they included setting her cap at Briavel? The gentleman had not singled her out this evening as he had Rora— not that his attentions were anything to pride oneself on, Rora told herself severely. She was concerned about Joan's evident admiration for his lordship, for she had no wish to see her cousin hurt in any way, and she was utterly convinced that the man was dangerous. This fear, however, she elected to keep to herself, hoping that Joan's comments stemmed more from her innate liking for people than from any partiality for Briavel. Or maybe he thought more highly of Miss Newburgh than he did Miss Donellan, and did not provoke her into unseemly behavior. And he had asked Joan to dance first that night, Rora recalled, and she mulled over this disconcerting memory throughout the rest of the journey home.

CHAPTER V

Lady Liscarrol and Joan had driven out for an airing when Peyton Newburgh next visited the castle, but as he had come in search of Rora, this in no way discommoded him. He took her by surprise outside the stables, and found her on the point of departing for her morning ride, with her groom. Ever since her encounter with Lord Briavel at the folly, she had given Slaney permission to go with her as escort. He had just helped his young mistress into the saddle when Mr. Newburgh appeared. As Admiral's hooves scattered gravel in the yard, Peyton shouted that he was very glad to see his cousin mounted and in riding dress, because he had something magnificent to show her if she was willing to return with him to Newburgh Hall.

"The hall? Good God, Peyton, it had best be something magnificent indeed! I had planned to ride all the way to Kilkenny-town today," Rora informed him, a crease between her brows.

"Go tomorrow," he suggested. "If what I have is to your liking, you'll be thanking me within the span of an hour!"

Something about his enthusiasm awoke in Rora a welcome suspicion. "Oh, Peyton, is it a horse?"

"Well, aye, if you must have it so—it is, not one but several. I had wanted it to be a surprise, but now you've destroyed it, so I may as well spill my news: Papa returned yesterday, and with the finest string of hunters you'll ever—"

"Slaney," Rora called to her henchman, interrupting her cousin's raptures, "we're going to Newburgh Hall at once—to have a look at the new hunters!"

The groom grinned with one side of his mouth and hastened to follow the cousins, who had already turned their horses toward the main road.

"You said Uncle Brendan has returned—will he require Joan to go back to the hall?" Rora asked.

Mr. Newburgh gave his cousin a cautious glance before he replied. "Hard to say. If no one makes mention of—of the gentlemen at Hargrave House, he may find no harm in letting Jo remain at Ardara."

"But I thought Uncle Brendan fancied Briavel as a match for her." Rora reminded him. "I should think he'd want her to stay."

Swallowing convulsively, Peyton directed another sidelong glance at her. "Faith, you *are* a sharp one, Rora!" he said with admiration. "Fact is, there's no knowing what Papa will take into his head. He could be against the match by now, for all we know, and what's more, he never tells us what he's thinking. For my sister's sake, the less said about Briavel—and his guest—the better!"

Rora's sensibilities were slightly ruffled by this cautionary tone. "I'm not one to go spilling tales! Although I don't see how it can remain a secret, since Uncle Brendan will see Joan and Briavel in company often enough, if he attends any of the local assemblies and balls."

"No fear of that. Papa don't much care for such foolery—he hardly ever stirs beyond the gates of the hall, unless there's a horse fair about. And with the new horses arrived, and the Kilkenny race meeting coming up, he won't give a rush for the entertainments going on."

They rode the rest of the way in eager conversation about the horses, and Rora was flattered that one fine specimen had caught Peyton's eye as a possibility for her. In less than an hour they arrived at Newburgh Hall, a square house of faded red brick, whose lawn and gardens were not elaborately planted; Sir Brendan expended his energies and moneys not on gardeners, but upon grooms and stable hands. Still, the estate had a neat and comfortable appearance that told as clearly as any words that this was Joan's home as well as her father's. Peyton led the way around to the stables, proudly detailing the many improvements he and his father had instituted in that all-important region. He scarcely allowed Rora time to take them in, however, before he was conducting her to the area where the new hunters were still penned.

Rora leaned against the fence, oblivious to the danger of splinters in the rough wood, completely absorbed in admiration of the string of animals frisking in their enclosure. Most of the horses were young, three to four years of age, although several more mature ones stood calmly lipping at the hay strewn along the lower end of the paddock. There were chestnuts, bays, one gray, a cream-colored horse, and a black. Peyton lifted his crop and pointed toward a handsome bay. "That's the one I picked out for you, Rora—he's called Troilus. Our head groom tells me he's the most promising four-year-old he's seen this age!"

Miss Donellan was no fool when it came to purchasing horses, and although she trusted the Newburghs implicitly in all matters of horseflesh, she could not forbear to ask, "Then why are you so eager to be palming him off on me, Cousin?"

Peyton sighed down to his toes, reflecting his unfeigned and quite considerable displeasure at his inability to keep so fine an animal. "I'd give anything to keep the beast for myself, but Papa says he can't have another hunter eating its head off in the stables. The price we can get for Troilus is too great to pass up."

Rora knew this was her cue to begin bidding. "What might you be wanting for the creature?" she asked, turning away from the paddock and fixing her cousin with an intent look.

"Faith, you'll have to make me an offer, Rora. *Garsún!*" Peyton called to a young stable hand, employing the Irish term for boy. "Bring the horse Troilus out—the one the color of *madra rua.*"

"Ah, how true—the color of the fox!" Rora said with a smile.

"What a lovely figure altogether you'll make upon him, Cousin —your fine hair is like *madra rua* as well," her cousin said handsomely.

When the horse was brought out and after Rora had run her hands over the animal, carefully judging his points, she returned her attention to her cousin. "You think he will carry a lady?"

"Aye, to be sure—to admiration!"

"Hmmm." Rora considered for a long moment before making her offer. "Fifty."

"Guineas?"

"Naturally."

Peyton looked the animal over, going so far as to walk around behind it, patting the glossy rump as he did so. "I'm not sure but what I could get more—much more—from another buyer."

"Wretch!" Rora laughed. "Have you no family feeling whatever? Oh, very well, seventy-five."

"One hundred."

She stared at him in mute disbelief. "Oh, you're coming it much too strong! Do you take me for a flat?"

"Nay, you're no flat—you're an *oínseach*—a fool, Rora, if you'll let such a bargain fly away. Why, he's cheap at two hundred, and well you know it! In England he'd fetch—"

" 'Tisn't England we're in, and besides, you know just as well as I that Uncle Brendan paid only a fraction of my original offer for Troilus at the fair in Galway—if not a good deal less! I stand by my offer of seventy-five, Peyton."

"But, Rora," he protested, scratching his fiery head, "how could I sleep nights knowing I let the creature go for less than one hundred?"

"Console yourself with the fact that you'll have made a considerable profit from the transaction," Rora replied tartly, gathering up her skirts and making as though to leave.

"Wait!" Peyton called after her retreating figure, giving a brief nod in the direction of the stable boy, who was standing wide-eyed at the sight of so hard-bargaining a lady.

Rora paused and turned back, her face wreathed with a smile. "Well?"

"Congratulations, Cousin, you've got yourself a rare beast there." Peyton crossed the grass to shake her hand, sealing their bargain, and Rora gave orders to Slaney to see Troilus tied to his horse for the trip back to the castle. The groom nodded and told his mistress under his breath that she had bought one of the grandest animals it had been his privilege to view.

The cousins, each pleased with the transaction, strolled up the hill toward the house; Rora wished to greet her uncle, for she had not yet seen him since coming to the country. As they neared the rear of the house, Sir Brendan himself came down the steps, followed by a tall, dark-haired gentleman whose figure looked disastrously familiar to Rora.

"Faith, if 'tis not my little niece!" Sir Brendan Newburgh cried in greeting, quickening his step. "Peyton, my lad, I've been searching high and low for you this hour past, but now that I know you were with your cousin Rora, I'll forgive your absence." He turned to his visitor. "So, Lord Briavel, do they not make a fine pair, this son of mine and Donellan's lass?"

The gentleman flicked his eyes lightly over the cousins. "Yes, indeed," he murmured thoughtfully as Rora and Peyton exchanged looks of mingled shock and amusement.

Sir Brendan continued, "Rora, lass, have you had the pleasure of meeting Lord Briavel—his lands march with my mother's, but you'll be knowing that."

Before Rora could reply, his lordship said, "Miss Donellan and I have come across one another on more than one occasion, Sir

Brendan. In fact, I count your niece among my many new friends in the district."

Rora longed to give him an icy set-down, but felt Peyton's restraining hand on her arm.

"Rora's just bought one of the young hunters, sir," the youth told his father with a certain measure of pride. Any sale of a horse must reflect well upon him, and he yearned to be treated more as a valued partner by Sir Brendan than as merely one of the many underlings involved in the family business.

The cousins joined the gentlemen as they walked toward the enclosure. "Did she indeed?" Sir Brendan responded pleasantly. "So, too, has Lord Briavel. Which of the fair beasts did our Rora find to her liking?"

"The young bay—Troilus, the four-year-old," Peyton answered proudly. "And we made a rare deal, Papa, I can assure you!"

His father appeared thunderstruck by this news, and Briavel showed signs of being highly amused as he regarded Rora. "Troilus?" Sir Brendan bellowed. "How can that be, you young jackanapes? For I've just sold the creature to his lordship for two hundred and not a penny less! We had a glass of Madeira up at the house to seal the bargain!"

"Two hundred!" Rora cried, turning a look of scorn upon Briavel. "Why, I purchased Troilus for seventy-five guineas—and think that a high price, to be sure!"

"Seventy-five?" Sir Brendan thundered, turning upon his son. "You call that a rare deal? What are you about, sapskull, to let that bay go for such a price as that? *Bodach!*" he spat.

"Less than two hundred," Briavel mused, looking toward the handsome bay. "And you would hardly agree to part with the animal for less than three, Sir Brendan? In all fairness, sir, you must now let me have him at the lower figure!"

"But Troilus is mine!" the young lady reminded the gentlemen hastily. "Peyton and I shook hands on the deal."

"You're out there, lass," her uncle informed her with a quelling frown. "His lordship and I shook hands before you ever arrived at the hall, which nullifies your purchase, and what's more, he'll be paying cash, which I doubt is in your power to do. Lord Briavel, the bay is yours for seventy-five guineas, but it costs me such a pang to part with him at the price, you'll never know." Another frown was directed at Peyton, whose carelessness had thoroughly botched the deal, as had the presence of Sir Brendan's troublesome niece. He knew that the odd hundred and twenty-five guineas was as no more than a shilling to a man as rich as Briavel was reputed to be, but now it was impossible to insist upon the original price, thanks to the lad's clumsiness. Now the girl was angry—and a fine creature she looked in a temper—and she would probably hold it against her cousin Peyton that she lost the horse to his lordship. That was even a greater pity than the lost guineas, for a match between Rora and his youngest son was Sir Brendan's fondest dream.

"Perhaps another of the pretty horses takes your fancy, Rora, my dear," he essayed hopefully.

Peyton's downcast expression lifted. "Why, yes, Rora—what of the cream-colored one over there? He'd be a fine lady's mount."

"Yes, a most superior animal," Briavel suggested easily. "What a figure you would look on him, too, Miss Donellan."

"You!" she uttered with loathing, momentarily forgetting the presence of the Newburghs. Her bitter disappointment at losing Troilus was all but lost in her intense dislike of the person at her side. She took a deep breath in order to gain a measure of control over her temper, then addressed her uncle coolly. "Yes, the cream-colored horse is fine indeed. I'll take him for fifty pounds, and instruct Papa to send you a draft upon his bank as soon as possible. Good day, Uncle, Peyton." She ignored his lordship's bow and whirled away, the stables her destination. At least she had turned her moment of defeat into one of triumph, for her uncle would be forced to let her have the cream hunter for the exact sum she had offered, which would infuriate him no end; the animal was worth nearly thrice that amount by Irish standards, and a good deal more by English, as was Troilus. But he would not risk offending her a second time that day, so she was assured of having nearly as fine a horse as the bay for a great deal less money. She informed Slaney of the substitution, and waited impatiently as he brought the horse from the paddock and tethered the animal to his own mount for the ride back to Ardara.

Rora nevertheless rode home under a cloud of utter frustration, for again Lord Briavel had bested her. Her only consolation was that Slaney approved her second choice of horse, saying that if she could not have the bay, then this one was as fine as she could ever hope to have. He then proceeded to tell a long-winded and probably aprocryphal tale of a horse-dealing cousin of his who had, during his long career, frequently managed to sell one animal to two people at the same time, amassing a fortune but engendering excessive ill feeling among those whose earnest money he was able to keep. The story did not cheer Rora at all, and she soon ceased holding Falstaff back to a pace matching Slaney's. Urging her mount forward, she found herself fervently hoping that Briavel would ship the young bay to England immediately and never hunt or ride the animal in her presence; to see his excellent figure upon that particular horse would be galling in the extreme.

When she heard the sound of hooves behind her in the road, she supposed that it was her cousin, hurrying to apologize to her for the incident of the bay. Great was her surprise, therefore, when instead of Peyton's long-tailed gray, a large black horse materialized at her side. She twisted about in her saddle to look for Slaney, but the groom was some distance behind, encumbered by the new hunter and riding so slowly as to be barely visible on the horizon. She straightened her spine and stared straight ahead, wishing that Briavel would realize that she had no intention of speaking to him, and praying that he would ride on.

"Tongue-tied again, Miss Donellan? We seem to find ourselves in this situation all too frequently! You turned a similarly stony countenance upon me during our waltz some evenings back."

She said nothing, but maintained her haughty silence.

"It is your own fault, you know," he went on conversationally. "If you did not look so magnificent in a rage, I doubt that I would take so much delight in tormenting you. Are you *very* angry about the horse?"

Not daring to speak for fear she would give him a tongue-lashing that would show her in a most unbecoming light, Rora gave a curt shake of her head. Naturally, it did not deceive him as to her state of mind.

"I see. Well, I suppose I could set things to rights by making you a present of the bay—"

"How could you do so?" she interrupted him, forgetting her resolve not to speak. "A gentleman does not make such a gift to a lady!"

"—but I am a gentleman," he continued glibly, unperturbed and seemingly unaware that she had spoken. "Besides, then you would have two of the finest hunters in all Ireland, if your uncle is to be believed, and that would be insupportable. I must always have the best, Miss Donellan."

"The best horses, perhaps—the best manners, never!"

He ignored this aspersion and said coolly, "Tell me, ma'am, if you will be so good, is your cousin Miss Newburgh at home to visitors today?"

"When I left Ardara, she was not at home at all."

"A pity. I had a pressing matter to discuss with her. Be so good as to convey my respects, and tell her that I shall call at Ardara upon my return to these parts."

Rora looked up and met his eyes, nearly flinching at the intensity of his gray gaze. Undeterred by it, she said eagerly, "You are leaving, sir?"

"So I am, Miss Donellan. I see that the news pleases you, so I must count myself happy—for to please you is of all things what I most desire."

"You needn't exert yourself to flirt with me, Lord Briavel. I am impervious to such flattery."

"Are you?" he murmured wonderingly. "You almost tempt me to put your claim to the test. But back to my journey: Nicky and I are leaving for Dublin tomorrow and will not return for at least a fortnight. Shall we call upon your father to assure him that you are well—and in good spirits?" His eyes glittered with mockery.

"I don't care what you do!"

"Yes, that is one of the few things I do like about you, Miss Donellan. Good day, ma'am—try not to miss me too much!" He touched the black horse with his silver spur and cantered off.

"One of the *few!*" Rora echoed in outraged accents, but he was long gone and her only auditors were the birds perched in the furze bushes along the road.

Briavel had left her with much to ponder. She could not imagine why he had asked after Joan so particularly, nor what he could possibly have to say to her cousin. To the best of Rora's knowledge, he had not met Joan above twice. Unless—and her heartbeat quickened strangely at the thought—his lordship had visited Newburgh Hall for more than the purchase of a hunter. Perhaps Lord Briavel had been asking Sir Brendan for permission to pay his addresses to Joan. Rora would be very sorry if her cousin agreed to marry him; she didn't believe that the viscount would be a comfortable sort of husband, and she was not at all sure that he cared for Joan—or any woman—as a gentleman should for a lady he wished to marry. She knew, however, that many men, particularly noblemen, were inclined to marry for purposes of material gain rather than love, but what could Briavel hope to gain from wedding a lowly Miss Newburgh, with no marked degree of beauty, nor any portion to recommend her? And why did he persist in treating Rora herself to his odious attentions if he planned to make Joan his wife? That seemed monstrously wrong of him. She wondered whether she should warn Joan of Briavel's shockingly familiar manners, but decided that she hardly knew her cousin well enough to speak of it. Joan had never confided in her, demonstrating a noticeable reluctance to discuss her abortive affair with that Englishman; it mystified Rora. And whatever Joan's lingering feelings, if any, for the unknown and possibly unlamented suitor, Briavel expected that she would receive him with complaisance upon his return to Kilkenny. It was all quite puzzling, and disturbing.

As Rora turned Falstaff into the drive, she realized with odd pleasure that no word of Lady Alanna had passed Lord Briavel's lips that day. And for that, she told herself with a half-smile, she was almost willing to forgive him his purchase of the bay horse. But she followed this with a stern reminder that she was nonetheless relieved that the neighborhood would be devoid of his odious presence for a fortnight. She set about planning all manner of delightful, solitary rambles about the estate, in an attempt to convince herself that she would enjoy her tormentor's absence.

CHAPTER VI

Rora's peace was interrupted a week after Briavel's departure when Lady Liscarrol announced over dinner that she planned to invite his lordship and Sir Nicholas to dine at Ardara immediately upon their return from Dublin. At this news both young ladies colored faintly. The auburn-haired one fidgeted with her napkin, and the dark-haired one stared straight before her and breathed somewhat more heavily than she had been a moment before. Her ladyship noted this, but said nothing more except that next month there would be a race meeting at Kilkenny and she had a fancy to hold a race party again. The young ladies' reactions to this pronouncement were less marked, but the news of the races was particularly meaningful to them both, if in different ways.

Joan knew that her father and brother would be too greatly occupied with their racehorses to pay her much mind, and was glad of it. Rora reflected that if there was to be a race meeting in the district, Lord Briavel would likely remain at Hargrave House until it was finished, however much she wished it otherwise. According to everything she had ever heard about his set, gentlemen of that sort were addicted to all manner of sporting pursuits, and the impending Kilkenny Races ensured that both he and Sir Nicholas would linger. That was her first thought. Her second was that if his lordship did become engaged to Joan, any hope of his leaving the neighborhood must be abandoned. As yet, her cousin had given no hint of her feelings on the matter, and Rora almost longed for Briavel's return, in order that her own burning questions might be answered at last.

When she had told Joan of the gentleman's message, her cousin had done no more than nod and smile. "Yes, I supposed that he would be wishing to speak to me. You saw Lord Briavel at the hall, you say? How did Papa appear to be?"

"Vexed, but more so at Peyton and me than anything else. In fact, he was cross as a bag of weasels!" Rora then explained the circumstances of her visit to Newburgh Hall, carefully omitting the fact that Briavel had angered her almost to the point of insanity.

"Poor Peyton—he will have borne the brunt of Papa's anger, then. A pity, because he's the most sensitive of all us Newburghs, and hopes so much to do well with the horses and be a credit to Papa."

"I'm beginning to think 'twas a mistake, my going to the hall, not but what I came away with a fine hunter, when all's said and done. Slaney and I have taken him out twice, and he fairly flies over the hedges. You must come and try him, Joan!"

"I will indeed, if only to make sure that he is everything you say. I wonder, do you care for aught but horses and fashions, Rora?"

"Add Papa and Ardara to the list, and you'll have nearly the whole of it. And Grandmother and you, and Peyton, and—"

"Lord Briavel?"

Rora could scarcely believe her ears. "Good God, Joan, you must be mad! How many times have you heard me say how I loathe him?" Recalling Joan's possible *tendre* for the gentleman in question, she amended this scathing condemnation. "That is, I think I could like him perfectly well if he were less—well, I don't know what! The sad fact is that we are always at dagger-drawing."

"It is a great deal too bad," Joan said easily, "for I fear you misjudge him. Yet I know you well enough, dear Cousin, to realize that it would be impossible to convince you that he is other than the veriest ogre!"

The result of that interview was that Rora now more than ever believed that her cousin was on the verge of making a disastrous marriage to Briavel, and she felt helpless in the face of Joan's calm imperturbability. Never had she met so firm and decisive a girl as her Newburgh cousin, and for the first time in her twenty years felt positively bubble-headed by comparison and less than certain about most things, Lord Briavel in particular. If that man was about to become a connection of hers, she supposed that she would learn in time to meet him with complaisance. But had their several *contretemps* been her fault alone? It seemed to her that he delighted in setting her on edge, and she herewith resolved not to allow him to do so in future, for Joan's sake. And mayhap, once Joan perceived that she had relented toward the gentleman, Rora would be honored with those confidences Joan kept to herself. There was a secret, and Rora was not altogether sure that it had solely to do with Lord Briavel, although he was clearly a part of it.

On more than one occasion she had ridden to Kilkenny, and sometimes drove herself and Joan there in the gig that Lady Liscarrol kept in addition to the chaise and the barouche. In town Rora had enjoyed the shops and the sights, and she thought Kilkenny a miniature Dublin, with all of the larger city's strata of society represented but with less of the squalor than the former capital possessed. She was therefore not displeased when one day at luncheon Lady Liscarrol informed her granddaughters that they had been invited to take tea at the Bishop's Palace in the town.

"But that is perfect!" Rora exclaimed. "The dressmaker promised my new habit today, so I shall be very glad to go to Kilkenny."

"You may take Joan with you to Miss Rose's, then, while I change my book at the library and look in on Sally Jervis in Parliament Street. And Rora, I do wish you will prevail upon your cousin to purchase some new ribbons for that primrose gown. It becomes you well enough, Joan, but those green ribbons you wore with it the other evening looked so deedy!"

"I know, Gran, but they were the best I had," that young lady replied, not at all distressed by this censure.

"Well, my granddaughter can do better than that! Listen to Rora's advice; she may be a madcap, but she dresses in excellent taste." Her ladyship cast an approving glance at the other of the two girls.

"Blue ribbons might be a good notion," Rora suggested. "Or white. We must see what we can find in town."

"I wish you will find something, because Joan should wear the primrose next week for the assembly at Kilkenny. And while the two of you are shopping, I would be grateful if you'd take it upon yourselves to purchase a pair of white kid gloves for me, on account. Miss Rose has my measurement. Now, be off and be dressed, girls, for I have ordered the barouche for half an hour from now, and old Jack hates to let his horses stand too long, as well he should!"

Within the specified time the young ladies tripped downstairs. Rora demonstrated a more lively form of excitement than did Joan, who teased her cousin for flying into alt over a mere visit to town. Rora replied that while she delighted in country life, at times she was starved for gaiety and would therefore be glad when the subscription balls and assemblies began, to say nothing of the race meeting. She declared that although she had sometimes been bored by the constant flow of entertainment in Dublin, in the country these things took on more significance, for they had to be regarded in the light of a treat.

Tea was taken at the Bishop's Palace, in the shadow of the imposing St. Canice Cathedral. The younger ladies spent the period of the visit sitting quietly in polite boredom, listening to the discourse of the two dowagers. It mostly concerned events that had occurred long before Joan and Rora had been born, but both girls reacted immediately when their hostess mentioned the gentlemen at Hargrave House: Rora's eyes flew to her cousin, who nearly succeeded in looking unconscious. Miss Donellan noted that attempt, however, and as she returned her green gaze to the bishop's good lady, she wished that Joan had less control over herself and her emotions. Rora knew that if she had been upon the point of receiving a flattering offer from a wealthy and titled gentleman (however disagreeable a person he might be), her ready blushes would have betrayed her whenever his name was introduced into conversation. Why, even she had felt aflutter when Briavel was being discussed, and she didn't even like the man! Another surprise was in store: Lady Liscarrol was apparently well versed in the particulars of Sir Nicholas Tobin's history; she rattled off his holdings in England and claimed a long-ago acquaintance with that gentleman's grandmother. A pity that he was not at all the sort of man that she fancied, Rora thought to herself; there was little doubt that her ladyship would not look askance upon him as a match for her.

After they left the palace, the young ladies dropped off her ladyship on Parliament Street before continuing on to the dressmaker's establishment. Ribbons of an azure blue were purchased for Joan's ballgown, along with the gloves for Lady Liscarrol. After these commissions had been completed, Miss Rose carried out the handsome new habit that Miss Donellan had bespoken. This creation was of a fine rust-colored cloth and fashioned in the Glengarry style, ornamented with black silken frogs and corded trim. There was a fetching hat as well, high-crowned and finished with a tuft of nodding black plumes.

"What a stylish riding dress!" Joan exclaimed when the habit was lifted from its box to be proudly displayed by its creator. "The color will be vastly becoming to you, for it matches your hair. I'll look a dowdy beside you now, in my old gray, but that is an experience I'm rapidly becoming accustomed to," she jested.

"Well, I own myself pleased, and cannot wait to wear it. Now, let me see, what else do we require? I could do with another pair of riding gloves," Rora remembered as the shop assistant began taking their purchases out of the shop to be bestowed in the barouche. "And I believe that you must have that wreath of yellow silk flowers, Joan, as it will match your ballgown." By the time the ladies followed their packages into the carriage, they joked that there would hardly be room for their grandmother, whom they were to meet outside the lending library.

As the barouche moved into the thin stream of traffic, Rora spied a familiar pedestrian strolling along the opposite side of the street. "Look," she said, nudging her cousin, "there is Lord Briavel!"

"So it is—and he is alone. I wonder how long he has been back from Dublin?"

It was not very long before they learned the answer to this. His lordship skillfully skirted the horses and carts that separated him from the barouche and came up beside it at the bottom of the street. "I am fortunate indeed, coming upon my near neighbors in this way," he greeted the young ladies pleasantly. "I might have missed you, for I am on my way home."

"On foot?" Rora asked irrepressibly.

He shook his black head, but his eyes were on Joan as he said, "No, I go to the hostlery that is stabling my horse. Perhaps I may ride alongside you, at least as far as Hargrave House?"

Before Joan could speak up, Rora informed him that they were on their way to meet Lady Liscarrol. " 'Tis unlikely we'll be leaving Kilkenny just yet—Grandmother may have other errands," she pointed out innocently.

Briavel's look of amusement showed how transparent Rora's excuse was to him. "Then I mustn't detain you. I, too, should be on my way; I was performing a trifling service for Sir Nicholas and he awaits my return. But you may be sure that I'll put in an appearance at Ardara ere long—perhaps tomorrow. I look forward to seeing you both then, and you may tell Cousin Hester that I wish to speak with her." He bowed and walked on, swinging his malacca cane jauntily and looking every inch the London-bred gentleman that he was.

"That was quite rude of you, Rora," Joan did not hesitate to point out to her cousin. "I hope you're satisfied in driving him away, as was clearly your intention."

"I did nothing of the kind—I merely spoke the truth! Anyway, we shall have the burden, I mean, the pleasure of his company tomorrow, and I'll be at pains to be conciliating, if that will make you happy."

"Don't waste a thought on me; 'tis his lordship I'm thinking of. You should be friendly toward him for his sake, for I promise you he deserves your regard."

"Deserves it? Why, because he has undertaken to perform a trifling service for his friend? Certainly that is the only thing I have heard to his credit since I first met the man!"

"You wrong him, Rora," Joan said simply.

"It would appear that you know him mighty well, for one who never laid eyes on him till three weeks ago, if as long!" Rora retorted, already angry with herself for failing to keep to her resolution to behave well in Briavel's company.

"I know him well enough to like him, at all events. Perhaps you should try to know him better."

Rora agreed to do so, and gave her promise that she would begin on the following day when his lordship called at the castle.

She was occupied in letter writing in the smallish back parlor at the hour of his visit and was quite unaware that Briavel had arrived until she saw him through one of the windows; he was strolling leisurely across the lawn, obviously in search of someone. Rora didn't believe that person could be Lady Liscarrol, who was even now going over accounts with the estate agent in the library. She was not greatly surprised when Joan emerged from the rose garden, where she had been employed all afternoon in taking some cuttings for her garden at Newburgh Hall. The face that she turned up to Briavel when they met was as calm and serene as ever, but the interesting pair wandered into the rosebushes and out of Rora's line of vision, and it was impossible to know more. She could only be glad, for she felt worse than an eavesdropper, sitting there spying on her cousin from the window. Returning to her letter to her father, she tried to continue her glowing description of the new hunter, but found that her concentration had been utterly destroyed by the little scene she had just witnessed on the lawn.

She set aside her letter to be finished later and began pacing the floor agitatedly while she waited for her cousin and the gentleman to emerge from the garden. Was he even now making her an offer, she wondered, and felt a queer pang. Would he take Joan into his arms and kiss her, or would he be businesslike and aloof as he asked her to be his wife? Finally, she was unable to stand the anticipation any longer and went running to her bedchamber to change her dress. She expected to be called down to the saloon to hear her grandmother announce the engagement; probably she would be required to drink a glass of wine in toast to the happy couple, and therefore wanted to look her best for the occasion. Despite an inexplicable feeling of lowness, she rang for Mary and selected a sea-green cambric gown with Mameluke sleeves and white silk ruchings on the bodice.

By the time Rora was dressed, no summons had yet come from downstairs, so she decided to go down at once. Hitting upon the perfect excuse for her change of raiment, she carried with her a white silk sunshade, as though she had no other purpose than to enjoy a pleasant stroll in the rare sunshine. She went gracefully down the carved staircase, the very picture of maidenly beauty; in the front hall a footman sprang to attention and informed her, when she asked about her grandmother's whereabouts, that her ladyship was entertaining a visitor in the library. Rora supposed this to mean that Mr. Crosbie was still closeted with Lady Liscarrol, but nonetheless she wandered toward the rear of the house and the library; or if anyone asked, to the terrace.

The door of the library was ajar, and her ladyship's strong voice could be heard from within.

"You're a fool, Gavin! I wish you'd consider a betrothal now, but it's early days yet, and I don't despair. At least you don't turn your nose up at this match I've held out to you—on a silver platter, I might add! The girl could be brought to agree at once, you know, and would fall in with the plan at the slightest word from me on the subject, or do you doubt my power over my granddaughters? Moreover, her father would welcome the marriage." There was a pause; then her ladyship asked reflectively, "Will yours, I wonder?"

"That is not at issue just now. I have not completely made up my mind, Cousin Hester. I admit, there are advantages that cannot be overlooked, but I beg you will not set your heart upon it." Lord Briavel's tone, for it was he, was apologetic.

Rora stiffened; she had understood at once that the occupants of the library were discussing a marriage between Joan and his lordship. So Briavel's mind was not made up—that was a new wrinkle! But courtesy demanded that she make her presence known, so summoning up her courage and fastening a look of splendid unconcern on her face, she sailed into the room.

"Rora, my girl! You look the picture of spring, doesn't she, Gavin?" Lady Liscarrol prompted Briavel, who nodded curtly.

Rora smiled brilliantly at him. "How do you do, my lord?"

"Perfectly well, Miss Donellan."

"Are you going for one of your walks, Rora?" her grandmother asked. "Gavin, you ought to walk with Rora through the shrubbery. You've had a tête-à-tête with one of my granddaughters already this day—you must show the other one the same civility!"

Briavel's gray eyes glinted as he replied that he would be happy to take a turn through the shrubbery with Miss Donellan.

"Excellent. Mind, Rora, put your sunshade up—Joan came in from the rose garden a few moments ago looking quite flushed; I do hope she hasn't taken a sunburn."

"Yes, Grandmother," Rora answered, feeling propelled by forces beyond her power to resist. A stroll through the shrubbery was not exactly what she'd had in mind as a start to inaugurating friendship with her escort, but for Joan's sake, she must comply, and with apparent willingness. As they crossed the lawn, Lord Briavel quizzed her on her new hunter, but Rora withstood her inclination to fly out at him over his perfidy in snatching Troilus from her; she said evenly that Prince Hal suited her very well. In turn, she asked about his recent trip to Dublin, whereupon he told her that he had enjoyed himself there.

Walking between the tall hedges, she was uncomfortably aware of the gentleman's sidelong scrutiny. She was about to ask him tartly if she had a smudge or a speck on her face, when he calmly suggested that they avail themselves of an elaborate marble bench conveniently nestled in a niche cut into the hedge, flanked by urns and topiary. He guided her toward the seat inexorably.

After reposing herself gracefully on the bench, Rora plucked up her courage and abruptly voiced the question that had long been on her mind. "I observed you and Joan among the roses a little while ago. Are you perchance attempting to fix your interest with my cousin, sir?"

At her words he interrupted his inspection of the opposite hedge and turned his head, giving her a long, inscrutable look. Then he answered her question with one of his own: "Whatever makes you think it?"

She frowned at this masterfully noncommittal response, but said airily, "The rumor is on many tongues that Lord Briavel has come to Ireland to seek a bride. Your attentions to Joan have not gone unremarked, particularly by members of her family." She wondered if her interrogation was too personal, but decided that he looked more thoughtful than angry at her boldness.

"Meaning remarked by you, Miss Donellan. Forgive me if I disappoint you, but that was not my intention in coming to Ireland. Had I wished to become a tenant-for-life at any time these past ten years, I assure you it could have been accomplished with great ease in London." His voice had taken on a hard edge, but he seemed to have noted it himself and his next remark was uttered with less constraint, although somewhat coolly. "No, my visit to your country was rooted in my excessive boredom with my mode of life, and a desire for, ah, rustication. Because I chose Hargrave House rather than another locale is my concern alone."

Rora flushed at this set-down, however well deserved. It was on the tip of her tongue to reply in kind, but she was unable to think of a scathing enough retort. She had the lowering feeling that she was treading thin ice and was of half a mind to introduce another topic of discussion, when Lord Briavel forestalled her.

"My attentions, as you phrase them, to Miss Newburgh arise out of my sincerest admiration for her."

"That is understandable," Rora agreed warmly. She clasped her hands together in her lap, and looking up at his profile, said confidingly, "I am quite fond of Joan, but somehow being near her always makes me feel as though I have no—no direction. Do you have any idea what I mean by that? It is most disconcerting!"

Briavel's mouth twitched, but he answered with perfect seriousness, "Of course it is! Your cousin is the enviable sort of person who knows precisely what she wants from life, and has the resolution to achieve it. She has great determination, Miss Donellan."

" 'Tis true, but you make her sound odiously scheming, which she is not. But I only wish I knew as well as she does what I want out of life!"

"A natural desire, ma'am, and one we share."

"You?" she cried, startled out of her reflective mein. "It seems to me that you of all people must know what you want, and unlike so many, have the wealth and influence to obtain whatever it might be."

He frowned, but not at her. "You are mistaken, for no man has so little knowledge of his—wants, for lack of a better term—than I. I am tolerably certain of what I *don't* want, and that is in part my reason for coming to Ireland. I became bored, a disagreeable condition which invariably leads to impatience and a sense of ill usage. So I left London."

"I thank you for the warning, sir, and I will be at pains not to bore you again, for fear of those disastrous consequences already familiar to me! The next time you become impatient and disagreeable in my company, I shall know the cause."

An appreciative laugh greeted this playful remark. "You need have no fears on that head, Miss Donellan, and whatever your faults, you don't bore me! Tell me, for you must have some notion: what do you want from life?"

Rora looked up at him uncertainly, but he appeared to be interested in her reply, and his smile was encouraging, not mocking. He was not simply making idle conversation, and therefore she gave an honest answer. "I no longer want to live in Dublin keeping house for my father, because I cannot now conceive of leaving Ardara. So I suppose my only aspiration is to continue as I am, here with Grandmother. Not an unpleasant prospect: all my life I have longed to call the castle my home!"

"You love this place so much?"

"More than anything! When I was young, my mother would tell me all about Ardara and the amusements she and her Newburgh brothers enjoyed here. It sounded like paradise on earth to a child brought up in a city, within the confined spaces of Dublin." This sounded disloyal, so she enlarged upon her previous remark. "Not that I haven't always been glad to live in Dublin. It is a very stimulating city, and of course, the shops are perfectly delightful!" She cast an impish glance upon him, a characteristic twinkle in her green eyes.

"So at last you have your wish. Ardara Castle will belong to you one day."

"It would have in any case, but I shan't hurry Grandmother into a premature grave for all that!" She laughed. "My happiness stems from living at Ardara, not in owning it!"

"What of marriage, Miss Donellan? Surely you don't intend to make the supervision of the estate your sole occupation in life."

She shrugged one shoulder in dismissal. "It seems to me that marriage is not something one either decides upon or does not, like a bonnet or a horse. It results from love and understanding and common interests between a man and a woman, things that I've not yet experienced with a member of your sex, sir."

Her optimistic notions disappointed Briavel and he said in a clipped voice, his eyes on the ferrule of her white parasol, "You are a romantic, ma'am, and a misguided one at that. Come now, you are an heiress and must know that you can't expect to be sure of the true state of a gentleman's heart. Any clever fortune hunter might persuade you of his regard—have you thought of that?"

"You must think me uncommonly stupid, Lord Briavel! Recollect that I have seen enough of the world to judge when a gentleman is in earnest and when his is being conciliating for the purpose of—of pulling the wool over one's eyes. I am more than seven, you know."

Looking down at her, his forbidding expression softened. "Indeed you are, but not by much. There is nothing for it, ma'am, but for you to marry a man of greater substance than yourself, for only then could you be certain of his affections. A gentleman like me, for example."

She gave this suggestion considerable thought before admitting that he had a good point. "But I cannot *will* myself to love another simply because that person is vastly wealthy. And if I fell in love with one less well endowed than myself, what difference would our unequal fortunes make? Disparity of wealth should be no impediment to a marriage of true minds." She chuckled softly and shook her head. "This is the most preposterous conversation, sir! Do you realize that I could have taken your previous remark for a proposal? Suppose I had taken you at your word: then you *would* be in the basket!"

"No, no, I don't fear it on two counts: you dislike me, and you have clearly informed me that you desire a love match above all things. Not but what a marriage between us would be eminently suitable, Miss Donellan, more so than one between me and Miss Newburgh. The lands of Ardara and Hargrave House would be joined, and not only are you an heiress, but I am creditably informed by your cousin Peyton that you are the prettiest lady in the district."

Now it was Rora's turn to frown. "You needn't say such things to me, or *I* shall become bored. And how could you forget—you didn't come to Ireland to seek a wife, or so you claimed only a moment ago!"

He humbly begged pardon. "I was rather forgetting that," he

said, looking chagrined. "I hope I wasn't leading you on. Anyway, I expect we shouldn't suit."

"Not in the least," she agreed pleasantly, rising and smoothing out her skirts. "Besides, I'd probably bore you to tears, and you would be impatient and out of sorts all the time, which I would dislike excessively. If you will excuse me, sir, I ought to go assist my grandmother. It is very nearly teatime and she will want me to preside over the table. Will you stay? We should be most happy."

Briavel was regarding her closely, an odd little half-smile lurking about the corners of his mouth. He declined the invitation, saying that Sir Nicholas had been left to his own devices for quite long enough.

Rora expressed her regret, although privately she was glad to see him go. Their dialogue had left her feeling strangely dissatisfied, despite the fact that it had been the most amiable one they had exchanged since their thorny meeting. He might try to give the impression that he had no intention of offering for Joan, but clearly he admired her a great deal, more so than he did Joan's frivolous cousin. Rora tried not to mind, but why this suspicion should make her feel an unwonted tug of jealousy, she had no idea. His ridiculous talk of the advantages of a marriage between them rankled; she saw in it an attempt at flirtation on his part, which further dissatisfied her. Seemingly he viewed her only as a suitable flirt, while Joan was worthy of his respect and admiration. For some reason, Rora felt she would be happier to receive Briavel's friendship than his gallantries.

Lord Briavel was also less than content with the conversation he had held with Miss Donellan, and as he rode back to Hargrave House, he went over its shortcomings in his mind. When he had pointed out to her how excellent a candidate he was for her hand, she had seemed not at all discomfited, leading him to believe that she was a more sensible female than he had guessed. She had taken it as a joke, laughing it off, and had not been the least bit self-conscious. Some of her remarks, however, were cause for considerable alarm. For example, her innocent prating of love as it related to marriage had irked him no end, not only because it brought Lady Alanna's love match to mind, but also because it made him wonder with what sort of man Miss Donellan would be liable to tumble into love. Having lately visited the city of her birth, he conjured up visions of the suitors she must have had in Dublin—probably good, worthy men, students and scholars with whom she came in contact as her father's hostess. Likely they had been a set of dull dogs, since none of them had awakened in her that—what was it?—love and understanding—that she deemed so necessary to marriage.

Did she have no notion of what could exist between male and female, he wondered with a grim smile. Foolish little innocent! His earlier resolve to make her fall in love with him had strengthened immeasurably, and not merely as a result of their half hour in the shrubbery together. The desire for revenge against Alanna, once his primary motive, had receded so far as to be barely perceptible as he considered how best to go about the intriguing pastime of engaging Miss Donellan's affections.

CHAPTER VII

Not until the night of the assembly did Rora again set eyes upon Lord Briavel; he did not visit Ardara once during the days following their stroll through the shrubbery. She frequently found herself recalling their discourse, and the more she thought of it the more disturbed she became. Joan was going about wreathed in smiles and with a glow that betokened a girl in love, although her demeanor remained one of unimpaired calm. Whatever Briavel had said to her in the rose garden must have led to her bloom, Rora mused, yet she'd heard with her own ears his lordship's denial of any interest in matrimony; he had told her the same, and she had overheard him say it to Lady Liscarrol. She wondered if Joan, borne aloft by her high hopes, was in for a heartbreak, and wished that the disaster she couldn't help but envision might be averted.

These were her thoughts as Lady Liscarrol's closed carriage conveyed the three ladies and Peyton, who had dined at Ardara Castle and would be staying the night there, to Kilkenny and the assembly rooms. Joan was looking quite her best in the primrose sarcenet, now freshened by pale blue ribbons, and she wore the floral wreath in her black hair. Peyton was suffering a restricting shirt collar and an elaborate neckcloth; his usual attire was comfortable buckskins and riding coat, with a simple stock or Belcher handkerchief tied negligently around his neck. But despite his present discomfort, he announced himself perfectly happy to attend the assembly, as he was fond of dancing; besides, selling the cream hunter to Rora had made him plump enough in the pocket to anticipate a pleasant evening at the gaming tables, provided the stakes were moderate. His grandmother sat beside Rora, on the opposite side of the carriage from the Newburghs, regal in her evening dress of gray satin, a fortune in rubies draped about her person.

The arrival of the Ardara party occasioned something of a commotion outside the assembly rooms; lackeys rushed forward to see the ladies out of the carriage, and the family were admitted without having to show their tickets, for Lady Liscarrol was a person of considerable consequence in Kilkenny. She was greeted warmly by the master of ceremonies, who professed himself honored to make the acquaintance of Miss Donellan; he ventured to hope that the young lady would often grace the gatherings now that she was come to live at the castle.

Most of the gentlemen between the ages of seventeen and seventy flocked around Miss Donellan, but Joan had her own set of friends and did not lack for attention. Rora's ball gown was variously admired and envied by the other damsels present, since it was one of the most elegant in the room and had obviously come from the hands of one of the many French émigrées who had set up as modistes in Dublin. The dress was fashioned of parchment-colored silk with a thin vertical stripe of maroon; the neck and sleeves were edged with black velvet piping. Rora's auburn curls were bound by a bandeau that matched the silk of the gown, and she carried a white fan with ebony sticks; her only jewelry was a simple gold and garnet necklet. It was a dashing toilette for a young lady still unwed, but ever since attaining her twentieth year, she'd no longer held it necessary to array herself in the whites and pastels of the debutante.

She had no dances left for Lord Briavel when he attempted to engage her, but she was willing to go down to supper with him. They made up a foursome with Joan and Sir Nicholas Tobin and were eventually joined by Peyton and a Miss Fanshawe, the lively daughter of a Kilkenny merchant. Rora was amused to see that the young lady was more interested in the gentleman than he was in her; Peyton was engrossed in his conversation with Sir Nicholas, and treated his supper partner with only common civility.

Rora enjoyed a light flirtation with Briavel; it had been instigated by his lordship and she was practiced enough in the art to willingly pass the time in such a manner. She was not altogether displeased when he informed her that he had secured a dance with her after all, and she had a pretty good notion of how it had come about.

"Have you and Sir Nicholas traded off partners again?" she asked him as he escorted her back to the ballroom.

"No, it was your cousin Peyton who was so obliging as to relinquish his reel to me," Briavel explained. "I am most grateful, for otherwise I should have left the assembly quite unsatisfied."

"You should make it a point to arrive earlier, sir, for the purpose of securing dances with the ladies of your choice," Rora advised him demurely, a telltale dimple showing at the corner of her broad mouth.

"True—or perhaps I ought to make it a habit to bespeak my dances several days in advance, as must be done with the London belles. You should be pleased, Miss Donellan. In my recollection, I have never before considered going to such lengths over any female!"

She laughed at this, for he had uttered it lightly and in his usual mocking fashion. "You would only ask for waltzes, and thus be disappointed, for they are never danced at assemblies in Ireland, I can assure you!"

"In that case my only recourse is to induce some lady of the neighborhood to give a waltzing party. Let me see, who would be most likely to do so? It would have to be someone with young daughters, I daresay. I must give the matter some thought."

"I wish you luck in your endeavor, sir, but fear you will be disappointed. Waltzing parties may be all the rage in London, but even in Dublin they are infrequent, for not many of the dancing masters are familiar with the steps." Her bantering with Briavel came to an end when her next partner moved forward to claim her for a jig.

Rora was glad when Sir Nicholas Tobin requested that they sit out their dance, for her only respite had been at supper, and she was thankful of another opportunity to catch her breath as much as for the chance to become better acquainted with him. They spent a pleasant half hour talking of Dublin, a city he admired, describing it as one of the finest he had ever seen. She was gratified by this remark, as much as she was delighted with the gentleman himself. He was sensible, thoughtful, and attractive; she could only be sorry that a man of such obvious worth elicited no spark in her breast, but then, neither did he appear to hold her in any higher regard than did, for instance, his noble friend. Strange that it was a relief to be admired in so detached a fashion by Sir Nicholas, but oddly frustrating where Briavel was concerned. She was perfectly happy to flirt with the viscount, if that was what he wished, but she was also piqued by his reluctance to honor her with more serious conversation.

She half hoped that Briavel would also be willing to sit out their dance together, but he preferred to join in the eight-handed reel. It was an intricate dance that had evolved from a simple country reel to its present form as a result of the embellishments of the itinerant dancing masters of the previous century, and Rora was surprised to see how well Briavel danced it. At first she'd regretted that Peyton was not her partner, for her cousin was one of the most skilled dancers in the room, but she had no cause for complaint. After the music drew to an end, she quizzed Lord Briavel on his knowledge of the reel, and he reminded her that as a child he had spent part of every year in Ireland, where he had learned all the local dances.

"Of course, I had quite forgotten!" Rora said. "Most of the English botch our dances most thoroughly, or perform them as insipidly as though they were at their stuffy Almack's—without proper feeling or spirit. As dancers, Englishmen are not normally up to my weight at the pace," she concluded, lapsing into the vernacular of the hunt.

"Englishmen?" he echoed. "And do you not consider yourself English, Miss Donellan?"

She shook her head gently. "But I have no intention of embarking upon a discussion of politics, and that it would surely be if I were to reply to that question."

"Oh, no, we need not strive against becoming political," he assured her, "and I am truly interested in knowing your sentiments." He drew her a little way apart from the crowd; the ball had ended with the reel but people had not yet begun to call for their carriages. The ladies stood milling about, still engaged in conversation, waiting for their gentlemen to emerge from the card room.

Rora tapped his arm lightly with her fan. "Nay, any such discussion must wait, sir, for 'tis late, and Grandmother will be wishing to depart momentarily. Besides, I couldn't express myself very briefly, I fear."

There was an arrested expression in his gray eyes as Briavel informed her that he would call upon her soon to continue their conversation; Rora inclined her head gracefully. She did not set much store by his remembering it, although she hoped that he might begin to take her more seriously. If he ever did engage her in a political discussion, she suspected that her loyalties would give him a disgust of her; he was a true-born Englishman, after all, however Irish his title. But most likely he would forget the matter, and by the time Lady Liscarrol's party arrived back at Ardara, Rora had practically forgotten it herself.

Great was her surprise, therefore, when Briavel came calling a few days later. She had been visiting the gatekeeper's wife and had intended to stop there for a short time only, but she stayed to tea and listened with amusement to Mrs. Drennan's tales of the days when the Lady Alanna had lived at the Big House. After bidding the kindly woman goodbye, she was assisted into the saddle by young Tomsy Drennan, who was unfortunately still quite childlike despite his sixteen summers. As she adjusted her skirts before setting out, she was greatly pleased by the delightful contrast of the rust-colored sweep of her habit against the creamy whiteness of Prince Hall. She scarcely remembered that Lord Briavel had ruthlessly absconded with the bay.

She had hardly got beyond the lodge gates when that gentleman's handsome black horse came cantering along in her wake, unexpectedly casting her into transports. As Briavel slowed his pace to match hers, she hoped her triumph didn't show.

"Have you come to call upon Grandmother—or Joan?" she asked coquettishly, fairly certain of the purpose of his visit.

"Neither, as you should know, Miss Donellan! I have come to continue our discussion of the other evening."

She toyed with the idea of feigning complete ignorance of any such discussion, but chose instead to smile upon him. "I must admit that I'm surprised at your remembering mere ballroom discourse, sir. I'd have thought that as experienced as you are in such flirtations, they must escape your mind within moments of their having been concluded."

His black brows drew together for a moment, then relaxed. "Oh, I was not *flirting* with you, ma'am, when I said I was interested in your opinions. Granted, I did flirt at supper—and enjoyed it immensely, I might add. You are no novice in the art, and I suppose I have the young bucks of Dublin to thank for it."

"Perhaps," she answered briefly, unwilling to discuss her past flirts with this gentleman. She wondered if he meant to mock her by his last remark, but the blandness of his tone and the absence of the frequently malicious gleam in his eye argued that it could not be so.

"Where can we talk—privately?" he murmured provocatively, and was amused by her sudden look of confusion, which was followed by an attempt at archness.

Said she airily, "Practically anywhere. We have already tried out the shrubbery—perhaps the gardens should be next." This was a cautious suggestion on her part; most of the gardens could be seen from the rear terrace and thus she could be private with his lordship without being completely unobserved. "You may visit with Grandmother—or Joan—while I change my dress."

He turned about in the saddle to look at her. "Must you do so? I must applaud your taste, Miss Donellan, for you never fail to appear anything other than charmingly."

"How am I to take that, sir? Most of our meetings have occurred when I have been in riding dress!"

"Nothing shows you to greater advantage, and I was right in thinking that you would look magnificent on that horse. But you forget that I have seen you in the ballroom on two occasions: at the Whitneys' and at the assembly." He paused, then went on, "Am I wrong in guessing that those were paltry gatherings compared to those you have been used to appearing at in Dublin?"

"I am not one to belittle my present circumstances in order to puff myself off," Rora said in answer to his question, the purpose of which she could not fathom. "Both of those parties were most enjoyable." She forbore to mention their waltz at the Whitneys', not so pleasant a memory, but turned the subject. "Do you care to race me to the house? I assure you that if you let me win, as some of my Dublin acquaintances commonly do, you will sink in my esteem past all reclaim! You and I have been going on so well lately, it would be a shame indeed to be at outs again!"

Laughing, he readily agreed to the race, and as Rora expected, he won it easily. The couple entered the house in good spirits, only to meet Lady Liscarrol coming down the great staircase.

"Gavin! You here again? I hope you aren't encouraging Rora to behave in an even more hoydenish fashion than she already does, though I must say that whatever mischief you've been up to, it's left you in high bloom, my girl!"

"I have just bested your granddaughter in a race, Cousin Hester, and am about to take a turn with her in the gardens—subject to your permission, of course," Briavel added with a wicked grin.

"I don't care what you do with her!" the lady said rather snappishly, "as long as she comes to no harm in your company, which I'm sure she won't."

Rora was not so certain of that as her grandparent, but nonetheless she tripped upstairs to change out of her habit and to wash her face. From the upper landing she could hear the faint murmur of voices in the hall below and wondered what Lady Liscarrol was saying to Briavel to cause him to break into loud laughter. Probably she was teasing him on his attempts to turn both of her granddaughters up sweet. Rora was beginning to like him, and even to look upon the probability that they would one day be related with complaisance, but she was not at all sure that his attentions to both her and her cousin Joan were a matter for laughter. She was assailed by a sudden feeling of guilt, for if Joan cared for Briavel, it was the height of disloyalty to have invited him to walk with her in the gardens, and in such a brassy way. She probably deserved any familiarities the gentleman might choose to take, for she had all but encouraged him to do so by signifying her willingness to be alone in his company.

She changed into a cotton print gown and tied a gypsy straw hat hastily over her curls, and peering into her glass, she noted that her cheeks were becomingly pink and her green eyes large and lustrous. Although she was not a vain girl, she took great pride in her appearance, and as she forced herself to walk slowly downstairs, she wondered if Briavel thought her beautiful. He was surely used to seeing the dozens of beauties that graced London: great ladies, actresses, and the girls of rank and wealth who frequented Almack's and the ton parties. She tried to imagine how well she would figure among them; in Dublin she had been a belle, but who could say what was admired in London?

Lord Briavel and Rora walked leisurely through the formal gardens, and no topic other than local ones was vouchsafed. Not until they came to the rose garden did he broach the subject that had ostensibly brought him to Ardara that day.

"I admit, Miss Donellan, I'm all agog to hear the answer to my question of several days back. Do you not consider yourself an Englishwoman?"

"The Act of Union between England and Ireland argues that I ought to do so," she said seriously. "But as I have never visited England in my life and have limited knowledge of the parent country, it is very difficult for me to describe myself as English."

"Don't you count yourself wholly assimilated, then?"

"My heritage is Ireland," Rora replied simply. "I was born here. My own mother never visited England during her lifetime, and my grandmother hasn't been there for many years. My family, though their origins may be English, have always preferred to live here, ever since the day they first came to these shores to found their plantations. After generations of Morres marriages into the

Irish aristocracy, to say nothing of my Donellan blood, I'd be hard put to claim any Englishness at all, as Grandmother so often says."

Shaking his head in apparent disappointment, he said, "I suppose that like most Irish, you heartily disapprove of absentee landlords."

"Yes, in general I do, for I believe they foster the great gap existing between the Irish tenant and the English landholder. I know very little of specifics, however, for nearly everyone in this neighborhood has resided here since the time of the Boyne—well over a hundred years."

"The Hargraves have certainly been absent from this area of late."

Rora permitted herself a slight smile. "Yes, but there were—well, certain circumstances that apparently rendered that absence prudent."

Briavel looked down on the russet head which barely reached his shoulder, and a smile teased at the corners of his firm mouth. "In my father's case, perhaps. But you must agree that I have been remiss. Oh, my Hampton cousins were happy to take the part of my family and saved Hargrave House from falling into a ruin, but it is no longer the place I remember from my boyhood. I should like it to be so again."

"From all I hear, sir, you have put your lands in fine order and are liked by your tenants—all you lack is a wife to set your house to rights!" As soon as the words were out, Rora regretted them, but it was too late. In sudden embarrassment, she left the path and walked toward one of the bushes, bending to sniff at a few fragrant roses. When she straightened, her blush had receded and she noted that Briavel was regarding her somewhat cryptically from the gravel pathway.

"My housekeeper keeps the house running well enough, Miss Donellan," he remarked, before returning to the original topic. "In sum, then, you consider yourself wholly Irish."

"A simple act of legislation cannot affect my loyalties, sir."

"Your father's sentiments, perhaps?"

Rora disliked his assumption that she merely followed her father's politics, for she prided herself on holding her own views. "Oh, no! I mean, he feels so too, but I am supportive of the Irish cause in my own right, and am against the penal laws, and—and—" She cudgeled her brain for examples of other iniquities of the conqueror against the conquered, but in the face of his cocked eyebrow she broke off.

"Your father was involved in the '98 Rebellion, I believe."

"Well, he was aligned with the United Irishmen, for university professors are frequently open to radical thought, but he had a falling out with the leaders. He disapproved the use of violence and was not enamored of the prospect of soliciting French aid in the cause." She laughed and added, "He was enough of an English-man at heart to know the French for an enemy, and he considered their revolution unnecessarily bloody, besides."

They continued along the path. "But he was opposed to the Union of 1801?"

"Indeed, yes."

Briavel nodded. "So was I, and my father as well. He hated the extensive bribery and bullying of influential persons, and disliked the result. But in the end, it was his own class, the ruling class, that adopted the Act, and most of them more English than anything, as you well know."

Rora was pleased that his sympathies fell in with her own, for until now she had supposed him to be one who cared only for squeezing the profit out of his Irish estates with no thought for the people of the country. "Papa did hope at first, after the Union, that he might be elected to Parliament as one of the two members from Trinity College. But he is at heart a scholar, and although he is a man of great political acumen and enlightenment, he's not really a politician, so it was better that he didn't stand. Although I will admit that the thought of being in London during a session of Parliament almost makes me wish he had done so!"

"You have a fancy to visit the metropolis?"

Rora's eyes were on the path and she failed to catch the watchful expression in the gray eyes. "Oh, yes! As much as I delight in leading this country life now, I must own that I am a town creature by habit. Poor Dublin has now been relegated to a second-best capital since the Union was effected, and I think it sad, for it was used to be even gayer and more glittering than it is presently. But I don't despise the thought of London simply because it is now the seat of government. In theory it always was, I suppose."

They were about to turn down the path into another of the narrow alleys that crisscrossed the rose bed, but the sound of footsteps on the gravel halted their progress. It was Joan who appeared on the walkway; evidently she had followed them.

She hurried up to Rora and Briavel, becomingly flushed and with an apologetic smile. "Pray forgive me for interrupting your walk," she said, a look of concern in her guileless blue eyes, "but I have something of—of an urgent nature to discuss with Lord Briavel, and I knew that you would permit me to borrow him for a moment, Rora."

It was all Rora could do to keep from staring. Joan was closer to being flustered than she'd ever been, and never before had she uttered such disjointed and breathless sentences, or twisted her hands about in agitation. Concerned by this, Rora replied, "Of course you may speak with Lord Briavel, Joan, and you mustn't apologize for interrupting. The discussion between his lordship and myself is concluded, and you may carry him off with my goodwill." She looked up at Briavel to gauge his reaction to her generous speech, and was a little hurt to see that he seemed relieved. All that was left to her was as graceful an exit as possible, so she turned away from them, walking toward the succession houses with apparent indifference.

She had hardly gone half a dozen steps when she heard Joan say in an undervoice: "Come with me back to the house, if you please! Oh, Gavin, the most disturbing news—you must help me!" He murmured something soothing—Rora could not hear his exact words—and the pair disappeared around a corner.

She stood perfectly still, as immobile as though turned to stone. Her cousin's use of Briavel's Christian name shocked her, for it argued an intimacy that she had not guessed existed between the two. She followed the couple's progress with curious eyes, watching as they approached the huge white house. They walked up to the terrace, moving purposefully across the thick green lawn: Briavel's taller frame close to Joan, his black head bent to hers as though he was listening carefully to her every word. He reached out to pat her shoulder comfortingly, and as he did so, Rora felt more alone and left out than she could ever remember being.

The pang was strangely familiar, yet unidentifiable, and she put it down to jealousy. Not jealousy of Joan; she could only wish her dearest cousin to be happy, and if Briavel was the man of her choice, well, Rora had little interest in him except as a friend. In that respect she was envious of her cousin, envious of her friendship with the viscount. For she couldn't care less, she told herself fiercely, where he bestowed his name and title, but she would like very much to be his friend and was sorry that they had been interrupted when on the verge of coming to a closer understanding.

After a half hour of wandering alone through the succession houses, Rora had to admit to herself that she was more than a little jealous of Lord Briavel for being the one in whom Joan chose to confide. In all other respects, she and her Newburgh cousin were on terms of greatest intimacy, but Joan still skillfully skirted any conversation during which she might be likely to open up about her present relationship to Briavel, or her past relationship with an Englishman. Rora knew everything about life at Newburgh Hall, since Joan had been quite open in discussing her trials as mistress of her father's establishment and her worries about Peyton's future; neither had she been reticent about her unsisterly dislike of her two older siblings, who had been cut right out of her father's cloth. Likewise, Rora had told Joan about her life in Dublin, the interesting people she had met there, and her suitors. She had even confided to her cousin her desire for a love match, and Joan had nodded as though in agreement but had offered no similar insights into her own hopes.

It was all very puzzling; Rora wondered if she would ever understand Joan's motives and secrecy, or Briavel's for that matter. He had exerted himself to be conciliating lately, but she had a suspicion that his unbending of late was more a result of wishing to please either Miss Newburgh or Lady Liscarrol, or both. Well, Rora's similar change in attitude toward him had its roots in consideration for her cousin, but had somehow, unfortunately and against all inclination, been replaced by a genuine regard for the gentleman.

CHAPTER VIII

Rora was not long in discovering what Joan's distressing news had been, although how Lord Briavel could provide help remained a mystery to her. Lady Liscarrol had received a message from Sir Brendan Newburgh, in which he asked if he could stay at Ardara during the upcoming races at Kilkenny; this request had been enough to greatly discomfort Joan and displeased her grandmother just as much.

"I'll not have it!" her ladyship said on more than one occasion after the arrival of Sir Brendan's note. "I'm of half a mind to fill the castle with company during Race Week, just so I won't be obliged to give him houseroom! Brendan has no business coming here and cutting up my peace, which you may be sure he'll do, for we can't meet without engaging in argument. And I won't have him hounding you to return to the hall, Joan—not yet!"

"You'd need to invite a vast number of people in order to fill Ardara," Rora pointed out to her grandmother with a merry laugh. "We can sleep upwards of forty here, I expect, and I don't think you'd fancy that one bit!"

"Nor do I know of forty people who would come, so I'll have to think of something else." Noting Joan's downcast look, Lady Liscarrol added, in an attempt to cheer her, "Never you mind about your papa, my girl. I've always been able to handle him and will contrive something, I assure you!"

In the end, it proved unnecessary. Sir Brendan wrote the following week that because he was running several promising horses this year, he believed that he and Peyton would do better to take lodgings in Kilkenny; that way they might be closer to the racecourse.

"I might have known!" was his parent's triumphant response to this brief epistle. "Brendan must be sure of his horses—no doubt he's counting on the purse money to pay his shot at the inn! There, Joan, now you may be easy again! By the way, I wrote to Liscarrol's nephew that he may come to Ardara to visit me during Race Week. Remind me to inform the housekeeper, Rora."

"Who is this nephew?" that young lady wanted to know. "Papa once mentioned having met him."

"I expect Jasper came across Hubert Manville in London last year," her ladyship replied. "My correspondents in England tell me he's to be seen everywhere: one of those fellows of good birth and little fortune who fancies himself a dandy. Hubert is the son of Liscarrol's younger sister, who ran off with a half-pay officer in the teeth of her parents' opposition—back in the days when I was still wed to Sir Hugh Newburgh and living at the hall. I never set eyes on her again after she left Ardara, though she wrote most kindly when Liscarrol and I were wed."

"The Morres women certainly have a penchant for runaway marriages," Joan observed with a twinkle. "Will you carry on the tradition of your great-aunt and your mother, Rora?"

"She most definitely will not!" Lady Liscarrol said heavily. "Rora, when she marries—if ever she does, which I begin to doubt, so finicky as she appears to be—will be wed out of Ardara, as Alanna should have been, with all the proper pomp and cere- mony."

Rora observed that a bridegroom was a prerequisite before she could set about ordering her bride clothes. "Dearest Grand- mother, I have been here only a month, and already you are planning how you may be rid of me!"

"I'm doing no such thing, miss! Not but what I'd be glad to see you wed, and soon. Brendan is going to do his best to throw you and Peyton together come Race Week, and that is one reason I've invited Hubert Manville, although he's been angling for an invita- tion to Ardara this twelve-month. Liscarrol's nephew is in his thirties and still unwed, and from all accounts he's a gentleman, at least. 'Tis to be hoped that his presence in the house will put my lickpenny son Brendan's nose out of joint and deter him from setting his hopes upon your marrying Peyton, Rora, because that match would not do at all!"

"Grandmother, 'tis a *slibihn* you are!" Rora cried teasingly, but not without admiration.

"Yes, she's a schemer, but a very dear one," Joan added. When she left the room a short time later, she looked as thoughtful as she had upon entering it.

Rora had noticed her cousin's pleasure in learning that the

threat of Sir Brendan's visit to Ardara was gone, but Joan was the least of her own worries. She had concerns about the forthcoming visit of Hubert Manville and sensed that her grandmother had a hidden purpose in inviting him to the castle. Privately she feared that the invitation had been tendered in order to promote a match between the late earl's heiress granddaughter and his nephew, and that suspicion was enough to set her against the gentleman from the start. She cautioned herself to keep her objections quiet until she had made his acquaintance; perchance he would be amiable company. Yet when she remembered that Jasper Donellan had once described Mr. Manville as repellent, she blindly accepted the fact that her father must be right and rejected all thought of her unknown relation as a marriage prospect.

Rora wasn't sure why Lord Briavel had not put in an appearance at Ardara for so long. Her grandmother still spoke of inviting the gentlemen at Hargrave House to take their potluck at the castle, but as far as Rora was aware, no invitation had been penned as yet. The most frequent caller these days was Peyton, full of enthusiasm for his father's string of racehorses and, in particular, the great hope of the Newburgh stables, Comet. Rora was soon heartily sick of this horse's very name, and was thankful whenever Peyton allowed her to introduce some other topic of conversation, which was not often enough to suit her. The young gentlemen in the neighborhood were assiduous enough in their attentions to her to make up for her cousin's preoccupation with horses, however, and before the first of May she had gently but firmly declined an offer of marriage from the eldest Whitney scion, but also one from an uncomfortably flushed Peyton.

This offer surprised her a great deal more than the one from Mr. Whitney, since she and Peyton had agreed at the outset that neither of them had any intention of marrying at the present.

"Dearest Peyton, you *know* I can't marry you," Rora told her cousin apologetically, trying to preserve her countenance at the sudden relief breaking across his freckled face.

"Well, 'tis no less than what I expected, but I had to ask," he explained.

"Had to ask? Oh." She giggled, comprehending from these words the real reason behind his proposal. "Uncle Brendan!"

"Just so!" Peyton replied with a grin. "Papa asked me how we were getting along, and I told him the truth, that we got on famously and that you're a great gun, and then he wanted to know if I'd offered for you yet. When I said no, he told me that I must do so at once. I tried to stave him off by asking if I oughtn't first ask Uncle Jasper's permission to pay my addresses, but he said not to waste time with such stuff and advised me to sweep you off your feet! Can you imagine?" Mr. Newburgh burst into helpless laughter at the thought, in which he was instantly joined by his cousin, who had a great appreciation for the joke.

Wiping her streaming eyes, Rora finally said, "Uncle Brendan may urge you to appeal to my romantic sensibilities, but I fear I have none! What will you tell him now, Peyton? 'Tis certain he'll ask you what was my reply—I hope he isn't even now hauling up champagne with which to toast our betrothal!" The cousins succumbed to another fit of laughter and were found in an advanced state of mirth by their grandmother, who had come to the book-room in search of Rora.

"Peyton! Why did no one inform me of your presence?" she asked, looking down her fine nose at the red-faced, breathless young man.

"Because he has been making me an offer, Grandmother, which I have refused—although I'm very sorry to have to do so!"

"Well, I'm glad to hear it!" Lady Liscarrol said approvingly, relaxing her tone. "Drat that son of mine! He put you up to this, didn't he, lad?"

Peyton nodded. "He ordered me to—to sweep Cousin Rora off her feet!"

Her ladyship was as much struck by the hilarity of this suggestion as the cousins had been, for she laughed softly. Taking a seat, she declared, "Pretty fine talking for an old sobersides like Brendan! What will you tell him, pray? He'll cut up pretty stiff, you know."

"Tell him that my feet are firmly rooted to the ground," Rora suggested helpfully.

"He'll do no such thing, girl. Would you wish for Peyton to have his father haranguing him from now till Doomsday to coax you 'round? No, my boy, you must leave this to me; you may carry a letter back with you to the hall. I'll put a flea in Brendan's ear, you may be sure, and only wish I could give him the scold in person! If he asks you a single question about this business of you and Rora, you may tell him that I burst in upon the pair of you and gave you a piece of my mind. Which I certainly shall not do, for you are both of you bright, sensible people, even if some of your elders are not!

Now, Rora, please to fetch me writing paper and a pen, for I want to write my son while I'm still at the height of my anger at his foolishness."

Rora did so, then sat down beside Peyton, where they conversed in low voices. Several wicked chuckles from the direction of the writing desk indicated that Lady Liscarrol was taking great delight in penning her displeasure to Sir Brendan. When she had finished the letter and sealed it with a wafer, she handed it to Peyton and adjured him to be off with it at once.

"There goes a very well-behaved young man," she observed to her granddaughter when he had taken his leave of the two ladies. "But he wouldn't do for the heiress of Ardara—I was married to a Newburgh and I should know. Now, miss, what do you think about my plan to give a party here?"

"It has been so long since you broached the subject that I'd begun to think it by no means a settled thing," was Rora's candid response. "Have you gone so far as to select a day?"

"We'll invite everyone for Thursday next, and since you young people will think it a very sorry affair if there's no dancing, I intend to hire the musicians who play for the assemblies. Hubert Manville is supposed to arrive Monday or Tuesday; I've just had a letter from him telling me so. In the drawer of my writing table you'll find a list of the guests I wish invited; you and Joan may begin directing the cards of invitation as soon as you please." Having said this, Lady Liscarrol swept out of the library with a rustle of mauve silk.

Rora was not startled by any of the names on the list, which she subsequently retrieved from the desk, but she was surprised by one glaring omission: the two gentlemen from Hargrave House. Neither the names of Briavel nor Sir Nicholas appeared, although every other house in the neighborhood was represented.

At dinner when she brought up the fact that those gentlemen had not been included, Joan's blue eyes flew to her grandmother's face in wonder. "Why aren't they invited, Gran?"

"Gavin and Sir Nicholas may not be in the neighborhood during the races," her ladyship replied tartly. "Not that it's any business of yours."

"Not here for the races?" Rora echoed, unable to imagine why two gentlemen who were reputed to be sportsmen would forgo the opportunity to attend a race meeting. She could not have explained to herself or anyone else why she felt so disappointed. It suddenly seemed that all her own anticipated pleasure in the treat had evaporated into thin air with her grandmother's statement. She looked over at Joan to judge her reaction, but her cousin had her face in order and exhibited not a sign that she was in any way disturbed.

"Don't worry your head about why, miss, but send out the cards at once," Lady Liscarrol concluded.

On the following day the two young ladies set about writing and directing the gilt-edged cards of invitation to some thirty persons. Miss Newburgh was in her usual good spirits, but Rora was on edge. Her pen sputtered and dragged across the snow-white cards, ruining at least three of them before she flung the quill down in frustration and stalked out of the room. She wandered toward the door giving onto the terrace, hoping that the fresh air would enable her to clear her thoughts.

She left the house and park behind and walked in the direction of the folly, heedless alike of the drizzle and the strong wind that betokened an oncoming storm. It was three quarters of a mile from the house to the ruins, a brief jog on horseback, but a ramble of some length by foot. By the time she reached the domed temple, she was glad of the shelter its columned porch provided; the rains were becoming heavy and her kerseymere gown was quite damp. She sat down upon the cool floor and wished, as she had done weeks before, that the interior were not locked. Now she would have to wait out the storm before daring to venture back to the castle, and she hoped that Joan and Lady Liscarrol wouldn't be overly concerned about her absence.

Rora had nothing to do but sit and think, and for some reason that was now an unwelcome pastime, where thirty minutes before she had longed to escape the back parlor for that purpose alone. To divert her mind from such an unpleasant subject as the possibility of Briavel's departure, she began to compose a letter to her father in her head, but that was little help; all she could think to tell him was of Briavel's surprising sympathy with the Irish cause and his laudable intention of bringing his house and lands into good order. Then she turned her mind to the hitherto exciting prospect of the Kilkenny Races, but again Briavel intruded upon her thoughts. Well, if she was going to sit there thinking about Briavel, Rora decided, she might as well do so in his context of Joan's suitor. But this was worst of all, because the memory of his black head bent to

Joan's as it had been the other day was insupportable. In fact, it was almost painful.

She could not imagine how she had come to regard as interesting a man who plainly considered her little better than a hard-riding Dublin miss, frivolous and foolish, and just as likely as her mother had been to run off with the first gentleman who offered. No, that couldn't still be true, because Alanna's name had not cropped up between them for some time. Nor had he teased her or treated her in an odious fashion lately. She could only wish he had visited Ardara more often, instead of staying away for so many days.

Rora's reverie was interrupted by the sound of hoofbeats on soggy earth, and she looked up, to see who was coming her way. As though in answer to her unspoken wish, Briavel appeared on the worn path that ran through the park to the folly, mounted on his fine black and wearing an extremely angry expression. She rose and as he rode toward her one of her damp arms encircled the nearest column as though for support.

Relief washed across his lordship's face, but by the time he dismounted, the thundercloud look was back. He came swiftly up the steps to stand before her, and asked curtly, "Are you all right?"

"Only wet!" She laughed softly, nervously. "What on earth are you doing here, sir?"

He wiped his rain-dampened face with his handkerchief before answering. "I called at the house an hour ago, only to learn from Joan—Miss Newburgh—that you had disappeared, she knew not where. When the storm broke and you had not returned, I offered to look for you. I combed the gardens and the park before thinking of this place."

"Surely Grandmother and Joan didn't fear an accident had befallen me?" Rora asked, still amused.

"No, they were not much concerned—too little, I thought, but—" He broke off as though he realized what he'd just said, and thundered at her, "What the devil were you thinking of, you foolhardy young vixen, to go running out into the rain?" He struggled out of his riding coat and placed it roughly about her shoulders.

Bemused, Rora looked up at him, and as their eyes met, a liquid warmth flooded her veins. His actions were oddly at variance with his words, yet familiar to her for some reason, and also comforting; she struggled to come up with the memory. It came to her: the one and only time she could remember her father ever being truly, furiously angry with her. The incident that had incited Jasper's wrath had been her taking his newest and untried young horse out of the stables and riding alone and unaccompanied all the way to St. Stephen's Green. Slaney had discovered her absence almost at once and had gone after her, and when he brought her back to Merrion Square, Jasper Donellan, after a half second of relieved silence, had vented an uncharacteristic rage upon his twelve-year-old daughter. Even now, eight years later, Rora remembered his fury and her own fear that her father would never love her again. And just as clearly, she recalled her mother's soft whisper: "Hush, my love, of course Papa doesn't hate you! 'Tis only that he was frightened for your safety—he loves you so much and it is often easier for a man to express anger than love."

All of this, and most especially Alanna's comforting words, came back to Rora in the space of a heartbeat, and it was a wondering face that she turned up to Briavel's scowling one.

"I promised to bring you back," he growled, angered beyond all reason by the softness in her eyes, "although it would serve you right if I left you here to walk back through the rain!"

"You needn't concern yourself," Rora said with a shrug, no longer unsure of why she felt such elation at his every sharp word. He cared for her! She had no time to ponder it, but the knowledge made her tingle all over with happiness.

"I oughtn't to concern myself at all, you're right, but I promised. Come along, Miss Donellan, you'll have to ride before me, for I've no intention of leading my horse all the way back to the house."

She said nothing and allowed him to toss her onto his saddle, then he mounted and gathered up the reins, his arms reaching around her. It was an embarrassing and overly familiar position in which to be, and she felt almost faint with confusion.

"Pray do not let my coat fall to the ground, Miss Donellan," Briavel said acidly, and as they started off, she obediently clutched at the garment he had wrapped about her shoulders. She tried to assume an air of unconcern, and it took all her powers of concentration. His very nearness was both disconcerting and also exciting, and she tried to ignore its effect on her, although she fancied she could feel the hammering of his heart through the thickness of his coat and her own clothes.

When they reached the house, he jumped to the ground to help her down, and just as quickly he was in the saddle again. Rora thanked him for his kindness in a subdued fashion, and began what she hoped was a dignified and unruffled approach up the front steps. Just before Purdon admitted her into the house, she turned and called out, "We shall miss you next week at the races, Lord Briavel."

"I have no intention of leaving Kilkenny," he informed her grimly, and she was sorry that he was too far away for her to read the expression in his eyes.

Her heart leapt at the substance of his words, but she dared not even smile. "I had heard otherwise."

"You were misinformed. It is Sir Nicholas who has been called away for a time." So saying, he put his heels to the black horse and cantered down the drive, sending gravel and mud flying.

Rora entered the house, casting so glorious and happy a look upon Purdon that the long-faced butler fairly goggled and failed to utter a single syllable about her bedraggled appearance.

Once in her room she listened to Mary's scolds and cluckings with half an ear, hardly hearing them as her thoughts raced. Briavel cared for her, and he was not going away! She hugged this knowledge to herself exultantly while her maid brushed out the damply curling tresses. Rora dared not delve into the reasons for the considerable elation she felt, fearing to examine why all at once Lord Briavel alone had the power to rule her happiness. If anyone had suggested to her that she might be passing through the early stages of love with alarming rapidity, she would have denied it with the last breath in her body. Besides, he was popularly believed to be courting her cousin Joan, and this recollection caused her to fear that it would be she, not her cousin who would ultimately suffer a heartache at Briavel's hands.

CHAPTER IX

When it transpired that Miss Newburgh was already aware of Briavel's intention to remain fixed at Hargrave House for Race Week, Rora supposed that his lordship had told her of it himself. It was Joan who said, sensibly, that Lady Liscarrol must now send him an invitation to her dinner party and ball.

Her ladyship took this suggestion in good part and sent her granddaughter away to carry it out at once. Fixing Rora with an eagle-like stare, she asked, "Cat got your tongue, miss?"

"No. Only—Grandmother, do you believe Joan has a *tendre* for Lord Briavel?"

"I don't know and it's none of my business, no more than it's any of yours. I won't deny I'd welcome an alliance between one of my blood and Gavin Hargrave, but I'll likely live to see both of you girls dwindle into spinsters, for you've no more notion how to handle your affairs than a pair of babies!" With this scathing remark, Lady Liscarrol took herself off majestically, leaving Rora seated alone on the terrace, her attention completely removed from the ladies' fashion journal she had lately purchased in Kilkenny. The issue was woefully out of date, but until Joan had exhibited her prior knowledge of Lord Briavel's activities, Rora had been perfectly well absorbed in its modes.

Her elation of the previous day, at what she had believed to be a significant revelation of Briavel's true feelings for her, was now shattered. For weeks she had been living in hourly expectation of receiving the news of his engagement to Joan, and a single softening of his expression coupled with several curt remarks could go only a little way toward proving that his intentions had changed. On the face of it, it seemed that he held her in as great a contempt as ever. And because by now she understood that she was in danger of conceiving a *tendre* for the gentleman herself she resolved firmly, then and there, to steel herself against him. In future she would not be so easily beguiled into flirtations or other sorts of encounters that had proved so agreeable in the past.

Miss Donellan's resolution was all the easier to effect for the simple reason that at subsequent meetings Briavel demonstrated little inclination to engage her in conversation, much less in a flirtation. They came across one another frequently enough in the days before the Kilkenny Races, at parties or excursions, and on one memorable occasion at Lady Liscarrol's dinner table. After Sir Nicholas left Hargrave House, her ladyship invited Briavel to join her and her granddaughters and to take his potluck at Ardara. The meal itself went off without a hitch, but afterward the evening went downhill, for at the whist table Rora found herself partnered with her grandmother, while Joan and Briavel were engaged against them. The familiarity and camaraderie between her cousin and the gentleman could not but rankle; by the end of the evening Rora was exhausted from her attempts to maintain her composure in the face of Briavel's evident preference for Joan. He may once have claimed to do no more than admire Miss New-burgh, but unless Rora was greatly mistaken, that admiration had ripened into something else, something that tore at her heart and kept her awake at night, her mind endlessly going over his cool civility toward herself and fashioning excuses for it.

He was more aloof from her now than he had been early in their acquaintance, if less critical. Long into the night she pondered this change, coming as it did on the heels of their damp meeting at the folly. The memory of the way she had felt as they had ridden back to the house that day, his arms around her, his warm breath on her neck, caused her to blush in the darkness, and when she recalled how he had squeezed her waist the one time they had waltzed together—well, that did not bear thinking of. Nowadays he seemed always to be found in some corner with Joan, their black heads so close together that they nearly touched. At times Rora would feel herself being raked by Briavel's gray eyes; at her grand-mother's table she had once looked up to see him regarding her watchfully, almost speculatively, and even in company when he was speaking to Joan in warm, low tones, he would occasionally give Rora a glinting, scorching look. His behavior distressed her, but she could only ignore his glances and accept his waning atten-tions with apparent unconcern. She prayed that the races and the social whirl that would surround them would necessarily offer her a diversion.

She was granted one in the person of Mr. Hubert Manville,

whose hired carriage drew up in front of Ardara only two days before the races began.

The gentleman who alighted from the vehicle was of no more than moderate height, but of such a leanness that he appeared taller than he was in actuality. As soon as Rora was introduced to him, she recognized him as a man of fashion, from the toes of his highly polished and gold-tasseled Hessian boots to the top of his perfectly coiffed head, from which he removed a high-crowned beaver. His locks were the color of burnished gold and arranged in an artfully careless manner. Mr. Manville wore a coat of blue superfine; its cut proclaimed the hand of a master tailor, but Rora, not unused to the Dublin dandies, detected the telltale buckram padding in his shoulders. His pale pantaloons were of the first stare, his waistcoat in excellent taste, and only a few fobs and seals hung from his watch chain. Rora, although she had never seen Bond Street in her life, nevertheless fancied that her grandfather's nephew would appear more at home there than at an Irish country estate. Like everything she had ever heard of the famous Beau Brummel, Mr. Manville was not handsome, although his face was attractive, and his manners were such as must please.

He greeted Lady Liscarrol with profuse thanks for her kind invitation to visit Ardara before turning to the two young ladies. He mistakenly supposed Joan to be Miss Donellan, and when his error was made known to him, he could be said to have looked at Rora with surprise and a little relief. She took this as a compliment, but was angry at what she deemed a slight to her cousin, until Joan caught her eye, an appreciative laugh in her bright blue orbs, evidence that she was not in the least offended. Both girls' suspicions were confirmed at once: the certain but unstated intention behind Mr. Manville's visit was to have a touch at the heiress. With his ready smile he begged their leave to address them as cousins, although he was in no way related to Joan, and when he complimented his Aunt Hester on possessing two such lovely granddaughters, the girls exchanged glances once more.

When he came down to dinner he was resplendent in his evening attire, which to Rora seemed a bit overdone for a country house visit, but she could not in truth fault him for his adherence to proper modes. Lady Liscarrol, surveying the younger members of the party with a tolerant and amused eye, observed to Mr. Manville that he was just what they needed at Ardara to keep them looking respectable. As she was herself dressed in satin with a necklet of pearls at her throat, the intent of this remark could only be judged as kindness, but Mr. Manville was much gratified by it. Over dinner he and his aunt discussed the intricacies of Morres blood relationships, which apparently included nearly every peer in all England as well as Ireland; then they turned to London gossip, about which Mr. Manville found the old lady surprisingly knowledgeable. Through most of this discourse the young ladies sat quietly, their minds occupied with more personal concerns. Although they knew most of the names by repute, they cared not a jot that Lady Caroline Lamb, to whom Mr. Manville referred familiarly as Caro, had embarked upon an affair with a poet, Lord Something or Other, who was all the rage. And the fact that Brummel was increasingly at outs with the Prince Regent was of even less interest to them.

Before settling down to whist with the ladies, Mr. Manville presented Rora with a slim volume. As he pressed into her hand, he said smilingly, "I wished to offer you a gift, Cousin, yet could come up with nothing to sufficiently convey my great joy at meeting you at last. I hope you will accept this small token."

Rora looked down at the book. *"Childe Harold's Pilgrimage,"* she read from the title page. "Why, this is by that nobleman you mentioned at dinner—the one who has taken all London by storm." She looked up to meet Mr. Manville's brown eyes. "Do you think Lord Byron as interesting a poet as he is a topic of conversation?"

"As to his poetry, I am not much of a judge, but I fancy you will enjoy this work. I brought it with me to beguile the tedium of my crossing, and as such it pleased me. Since you are the daughter of a respected scholar, Cousin, I know I shall benefit from your opinion of his lordship's verse."

Rora disclaimed any qualifications as a critic of poetry, saying that the only poets for whom she had any particular affinity were Dean Swift, and perhaps Mr. Wordsworth and that odd Mr. Blake, both of whom dealt with the subject of nature. But she thanked Mr. Manville for his thoughtfulness and then hurried away to order a footman to set up the chairs at the card table.

Peyton visited Ardara the next morning, staying only briefly; he was on his way to Kilkenny with a string of Sir Brendan's racehorses and the innumerable underlings who looked after them. Rora wished that she could have gone with him instead of remaining at home and riding sedately around the estate in Joan's and Mr.

Manville's company. She approved of the way their visitor sat Falstaff, who had been lent to him for the ride, and he knew enough about horseflesh, although he was not as impassioned as would have pleased her. She and Joan exchanged amused glances at the many pertinent questions Manville put to them about the acreage of Ardara, the extent of its flocks, the numbers of tenants and freeholders. These were asked in the most disinterested of tones, but neither girl was unaware of his thinly veiled pleasure at the magnificence of Rora's future inheritance. It was a relief to Rora that here was something she and her cousin could share, this joke of a suitor.

The three riders returned to the house and were comfortably seated on the terrace with the tea tray when Lord Briavel came strolling toward them, evidently having left his horse at the stables, since he came from that direction. Each person was surprised by his arrival, but in a different way. Rora, while inexplicably happy to see him, was inwardly seething at the way in which he chose to make good her grandmother's invitation to make himself at home at Ardara. Joan started and spilled her tea, her wide, catlike face betraying a pleasure that she did not scruple to hide. Mr. Manville was startled out of his customary composure long enough to mutter, "Good God, it's Briavel!" under his breath.

Briavel greeted everyone easily, asking Manville in an affable manner how had been his crossing, addressing him with the ease of familiarity. He seated himself beside Joan at her invitation and entered into the conversation, occasionally regarding Rora and Manville through hooded gray eyes. In a little while Mr. Manville excused himself, saying that he ought to devote himself to his Aunt Hester, since they had had little opportunity for a private cose. Joan, too, rose and begged leave to change her dress before the tea stain became too set for even Mary to remedy. This left Rora and Briavel with no other company save that of the teapot, the plates of cold meat, and each other.

"Are you well acquainted with my grandfather's nephew, sir?" Rora asked after a moment of awkward silence.

"Manville? No, not well, but he has come in my way often enough in town. I fancy he was not pleased to see me here at Ardara, for I believe at our last meeting he heartily wished me at the devil." He paused, then elucidated, "The occasion was at White's Club in St. James's, and he left the table four thousand pounds the poorer."

"Four thousand!" cried Rora, astonished by the sum. "And you were the winner?" she ventured. At his answering grin, she could not keep the smile from breaking across her face. "That must have been where Papa met him."

"Your father is a member of White's? Odd that I have never seen him there."

" 'Tisn't the least bit odd, since Papa resides in Dublin and only visits London once a year, if that, for the purpose of lecturing," she retorted. "Grandfather sponsored him, and Papa has been a member this age, but unlike you, Lord Briavel, he has neither the time nor the fortune to while away his life at the gaming tables!"

"You're taking the wrong man to task, my girl," he informed her lazily, stretching out his booted legs before him and crossing them at the ankles. He had all the appearance of a gentleman who had no intention of removing himself from that position for some length of time. At any moment Rora expected to see him close his eyes.

"Are you perchance implying that Mr. Manville is a gamester?"

"Come now, Miss Donellan, it is against my code to belittle a single gentleman to a single female! I would no more tell you the worst I know of Manville than I would dare to, ah—" He broke off and his eyes went to her mouth. "Well, it probably wouldn't be worth the effort."

Rora noted his glance and bristled at his unspoken imputation that she wasn't worth kissing. She asked frostily, "What is the best you can say of him?"

He shrugged. "That he dressed well." His hand went to the pocket of his riding coat and he drew forth a slim volume, placing it on the table. "Perhaps you will be interested in this, ma'am. From what I hear it's all the rage in London and my aunt kindly sent me a copy."

She knew before picking it up, and gave out her rich laugh. "I'm thinking 'tis *Childe Harold* again! How he does get about! But you are behindhand, sir; Mr. Manville gave me a copy of Lord Byron's work last evening."

"Did he now?" Briavel's tone was neutral, but his mouth twitched as though he was struggling to suppress a smile.

"Oh, you may laugh if you choose," she informed him, correctly interpreting his desire. "Joan and I already consider it quite a joke amongst ourselves. Mr. Manville has come to look me over as though I were a prime horse or a promising foaleen, and to see if

Ardara will suit him." She sighed to her toes and added in a confiding tone, "But I doubt that he would care had I a squint or—or even some agonizing deformity! I believe he has an eye to my fortune, and if you are hinting that he's a gamester, then I am sure of it."

"Your fortune? Oh, yes, I was rather forgetting that," Briavel murmured inscrutably.

" 'Tis perfectly true! But it doesn't matter, for I am quite used to it by now."

"Indeed, I recall your telling me that you were experienced enough to judge when a man is in earnest, and when he is merely trying to—how exactly did you put it? To pull the wool over your eyes?"

"Possibly I said so. 'Tis no more than the truth."

"You have quite steeled yourself against Manville's charms? I assure you, he's quite the thing in London, up to every rig and row in town. Drives all the ladies mad with his air of fashion, dapper dog that he is. Doesn't that appeal to you?"

"Lord, sir, it's the man I must admire, not his clothes or the fashions he apes! Besides, Papa doesn't like him—I know it from something he said before I left Dublin. And if Papa feels that way, I wouldn't be caught dead at a pig fair with Hubert Manville!"

His eyes gleamed, but as he was regarding the tops of his boots, she didn't see it; he was enjoying some private joke as much as he was her rich and descriptive phrase. "To win you, then, a gentleman must secure the liking of your father?"

She shook her head. "You mistook my meaning. That is not the only thing that would induce me to marry. There must be esteem and love on my part—I told you that, too, weeks ago."

"So you did. Tell me, for I ask it only as an idle question: Suppose that you fell in love—my, how vulgar a phrase to bandy about in such genteel surroundings!—fell in love with a man of whom your father disapproved? What would you do? For you, unlike some ladies of my acquaintance, are upon excellent terms with your parent, and he with you."

She wondered how he could know so much of her relationship with her father, for what he said was true: as father and daughter, the Donellans were remarkably close, and she guessed that Lady Liscarrol had spoken of her son-in-law in such a way as to leave that impression. "I imagine I should do what my mother did—choose the man over my family and work toward achieving better understanding with Papa afterward, after the marriage. Grandfather relented within a year of Papa and Mama's elopement, but I can't imagine anyone remaining angry with my parents, for they were so happy!"

"Miss Donellan, I used to think you take after Alanna, but now that I have, ah, come to know you better, I fancy there is much of Jasper Donellan in you."

Rora looked over at him in wonder, half expecting that he would be frowning, but quite the opposite—he was smiling back at her in a mild fashion. It seemed that her grandmother had indeed been describing Jasper to the viscount.

Briavel noted her surprise, but went on speaking. "And in some ways, though you mightn't realize it, you are like your cousin Joan. She, too, would agree 'all for love, and the world well lost.' "

Rora was unsure what he meant by this, for she knew perfectly well that there would be nothing lost to Joan if she wed Briavel; Sir Brendan would fall over himself in his eagerness to catch so eligible a husband for her. True, he was at present more concerned about his horses than his daughter, not an unusual situation, but Rora and her grandmother had agreed that the only possible reason for his permitting Joan to remain at Ardara was Briavel's continued presence at Hargrave House.

Miss Newburgh rejoined Rora and the viscount, having changed into another gown, and Rora was bemused when, for the first time in quite a while, Briavel treated both cousins with an equal degree of interest and attention. But she could not allow herself to refine upon this overmuch. Any budding hopes had to be dashed when, before taking his leave of the young ladies, he dropped a sealed letter onto Joan's lap. She looked down at it and blushed fierily, and before Rora's startled eyes she jumped out of her chair and ran into the house without a word, clutching the note to her breast.

"What on earth—" Rora began, more to herself than the gentleman standing behind her on the terrace steps. Then she whirled around to find him regarding her quizzically.

"Did you believe me incapable of composing *billets-doux*, Miss Donellan?" he asked, cocking his head slightly. "Alas, I fear you would be correct in that assumption! Let me give you a single bit of advice before I go, although I doubt very much you'll heed it: do not accept at face value everything your pretty eyes take in! There, you will do so, I expect, despite my warning, and I will leave you alone to abuse me to your heart's content."

So saying, he strolled off with a flourish of his whip and a grin at her shocked face. She could hardly accept his audacity in carrying on what must be a clandestine correspondence with Joan, much less his boldly giving her a letter while both were observed! She very much feared that she ought to inform Lady Liscarrol, but checked herself; Rora despised tale-bearing. Besides, Briavel had warned her not to accept things at face value: a patent appeal to her to keep silent about the letter. Well, her grandmother approved of the match between him and Joan, so perhaps his passing letters to her was not so bad. Still, Joan's reaction had been odd; in the same situation, Rora decided, she would remain in her beloved's presence as long as possible, and wait until he had departed to carry his note to her room, to read it in privacy.

She looked down at the volume of Lord Byron's poetry, resting on the table where Briavel had left it. Why had he given it to her instead of to Joan? Rora picked up the book and pressed it to her breast, much in the same manner Joan had done her letter, and went into the house, feeling quite foolish and unaccountably touched by his gift.

CHAPTER X

On the first day of the Kilkenny Races the Ardara ladies were judged by the onlookers at the racecourse to be quite the best dressed and most distinguished in the crowd. Rora's spirits, so flagging of late, were elevated by her fetching amber promenade outfit and straw bonnet; she was mobbed by her admirers. Joan, in less dashing attire, was in high bloom, flanked by Peyton and Sir Brendan. These gentlemen were in a nervous but affable state; their excitement was due to the fact that Newburgh horses would be running each day, but they were also exhausted by the ceaseless activity required to bring a string of racehorses, grooms, and trainers from the hall to town. Furthermore, Sir Brendan's relations with his mother were strained at present. He resented the fact that she had intervened in the matter of Peyton and Rora, and he was infuriated to find that his late stepfather's nephew was among the Liscarrol party, paying extravagant compliments to the heiress.

He knew Manville for a fortune hunter in a single glance, and made no attempt to conceal his hostility toward the outsider. Had anyone accused Sir Brendan of coveting Miss Donellan's fortune for his son, he would have denied it and immediately pointed out in justification that the cases were quite different: Peyton was Rora's half-cousin and deuced fond of her, besides. Sir Brendan expected that his formidable mother would catch cold at trying to arrange a match between Jasper's girl and that man-milliner Manville, and Peyton could then step in and renew his offer.

Sir Brendan found cause for delight in Lord Briavel's kind attentions to Joan, however; the fellow was obviously on terms with her, and she just as clearly liked him. Satisfied, he nodded to himself when the nobleman drew Miss Newburgh aside for a bit of private conversation, and he imagined that within a few days—if not hours —he would be granting the viscount permission to pay his addresses. The family had been trying to achieve an alliance with the Hargraves for generations, and once had nearly done the thing, but Alanna shabbed off with young Donellan in the midst of her betrothal party. Sir Brendan had had a vague fondness for his lovely half-sister, but he'd also considered her a spoiled, flighty bit of femininity and a fool for whistling the Hargrave fortune down the wind, and all for a scholar, a man of parts but only moderate fortune. Well, now the long-lost alliance would be made, albeit twenty years later. True, Joan was a Newburgh, not a Morres, nor was she of the late earl's blood, but she was granddaughter to Lady Liscarrol; Sir Brendan was certain that his stepfather would have been pleased to know that the two houses would be united at last.

The afternoon grew warmer; between races Mr. Manville hurried away to procure some refreshment for Rora. The Newburgh gentlemen and several of the young bucks who had been hanging around the heiress departed for the stables. Briavel did not do so, but availed himself of the opportunity to engage Miss Donellan in conversation.

He didn't regard Manville as much of a threat and was able to observe quite dispassionately as the dandy paid transparent and effusive compliments to the girl. These were evidently growing wearisome to her, for by the time her fashionable swain took himself off, a small crease had formed to mar the usual serenity of her marble brow, and an expression of acute relief crossed her face as Manville exited the box.

"You've had a tedious sort of day, ma'am," his lordship sympathized as he took Manville's empty seat.

Rora suppressed a sigh and merely said, "How can you think it when I won ten pounds on the last race?"

"I was referring to your cavalier."

"I know you were, and I was trying to avoid your quizzing me by turning the subject." She shook her head, glancing down at her lap.

"Now why should I do so? I could see that you were becoming uncomfortable and have no desire to make you more so," was his surprisingly warm reply.

She raised her green gaze to his face and what she found there caused her heart to give a little jump. Then she remembered the letter he had given Joan and quickly dropped her eyes again. It was useless to build hopes upon so shaky a foundation as his kind sympathy and the negligent gift of a book of verses. "You are very good," she said coolly.

The sudden chill in her manner did not go unnoticed by Briavel, and he was quick to guess its cause. "Come, come, Miss Donellan, let us cry a truce! Did I not warn you yesterday that you shouldn't trust everything you see? How many times should I tell you that Miss Newburgh's letter did not come from my pen before you will believe me?"

Rora desperately wanted to believe him, but everything she had observed since Joan's arrival at Ardara belied his words. She replied, "It will take many denials to offset what I would term an understanding between you and my cousin. And while I can scarcely believe Joan capable of a clandestine correspondence, you, my lord—oh, yes, I can readily believe it of you!"

"You are a damnably stubborn female, but I suppose you have been told that many times before. I pity your poor father, and do not wonder that he packed you off to the country as soon as Cousin Hester offered an invitation." As Rora gasped, he lifted one hand, the one on which his heavy signet ring gleamed. "Now, not another word will I say on the subject of that letter to Miss Newburgh by way of explanation or excuse, except to repeat once more that I did not write it. Spare me your questions! I have already betrayed your cousin's trust by speaking of the matter, so we will consider the topic outworn."

Rora might have taken exception to his peremptory tone, but, she was too overcome by surprise at his words to do anything but stare at him. Questions were forming rapidly in her mind, but he was already talking of the weather and the crowds, so she could do nothing but swallow the inquisition she would have liked to subject him to. If Briavel hadn't written the letter, who had? That was the primary question, but she dared not voice it for fear he would leave her side, and all afternoon she had been longing for him to approach her. She replied to his commonplace remarks in monosyllables; he didn't seem to care, or even to notice. Without realizing what she had done, she agreed to let him partner her for two dances at the Fanshawes' ball that night, wondering why he had asked when a few moments before he had seemed angry with her. Now his eyes gave off teasing lights, although his manner was one of detachment. Before she knew it, he had coaxed her into the sort of flirtation that not so long ago she had vowed to deny him.

When Mr. Manville returned to his seat, he was not best pleased to find Lord Briavel ensconced with Rora Donellan and chatting with her on terms of apparent friendliness. He considered the viscount's presence in Kilkenny a most unwelcome one and could have wished that any other gentleman in all England was in that fellow's place. Briavel probably guessed not only the extent of his debts, but also his purpose in visiting Ardara; one word of these, either to Lady Liscarrol or her granddaughter, would do him no good—would wreck his chances, in fact. He hadn't considered Briavel as competition for the heiress, for that gentleman had seemed to be too taken up with the Newburgh girl, who, although a pretty enough female in her way, had an uncomfortably direct way of looking at one, as though she could see into his mind. Moreover, she didn't have the degree of fashion that Miss Donellan had, which would be preferable in the future Mrs. Manville. He didn't really want to marry, but circumstances required that he do so; just as well that the Donellan chit was a beauty—there was no denying it. Manville had a strong appreciation for beautiful objects and within the space of a day had found the match even more advantageous than he had dreamed. Of course, Ardara Castle was the primary one. Manville could easily envision himself as lord of the manor, spending the hunting months on the estate, the season in London, and the summer in Brighton, just as his more well-heeled cronies did. Still, there was a drawback to this profitable marriage: the lady herself. He had quickly discovered that Miss Donellan was allowed a great deal more license than were English girls of high birth; she was outspoken, and her manners were certainly more direct than he was accustomed to. But these faults in no way disgusted him, and he counted himself well able to amend these deficiencies of character in a short period of time.

His finances pressed him toward an early marriage, but he knew that he must go more slowly than he had originally intended— otherwise Lady Liscarrol might thrust a spoke in his wheel. She looked to be the sharp, all-seeing sort, like Miss Newburgh, and to a lesser extent, Rora Donellan; Manville knew that pleasing the old lady was the key to achieving his goal. Gaining her goodwill would go farther toward helping his cause than making himself agreeable to the granddaughter, who would probably have little say in the matter of her marriage. So after he handed Rora the lemonade that he had brought for her, he devoted himself to her grandmother, exerting himself to amuse her with those bits of London gossip that she might find interesting.

Lord Briavel remained at the heiress's side, and during the next heat, he derived more enjoyment from observing Miss Donellan than he did from watching the race itself. He was not certain, at this stage, whether or not the lady liked him; he believed that his attentions to Miss Newburgh had piqued her, and for that alone he would have continued them. But there were several considerations, apart from Joan, that prevented him from even thinking about pursuing his original plan, and the impossibility of doing so made it difficult to know how he ought to proceed. It seemed to him a long time since he had considered marriage out of motives of personal gain, or as a sort of revenge against Lady Alanna. Aurora Donellan was stubborn, and there were unmistakable signs that she had the devil's own share of temper, but he had never met so lively nor so engaging a young woman, not even after years of attending the fashionable London squeezes at which well-born, marriageable females were presented. This young lady was unaffected, possessed of high spirits, and was an intrepid, if occasionally foolhardy, horsewoman. Inwardly he strained at the fetters that kept him bound and unable to do more than flirt with her, a pleasant enough pastime, but ultimately unsatisfying. He wanted more, yet at this time there could be no more between them. Or could there? He had the suspicion that, if carefully sowed and even more carefully tended, something akin to friendship might sprout and grow between the lady and himself. That expectation, as much as any desire to woo her, resulted in his turning his mind away from thoughts of her and toward concocting a scheme whereby they could contrive to be alone together, so that he might talk with her freely and without the constraints imposed by onlookers.

Rora's thoughts were tumultuous for the rest of the afternoon and throughout the drive to the inn, where the ladies and Mr. Manville changed and dined before leaving for the ball at the Fanshawe house. Joan was at ease that night; her father would not be present, since he considered Mr. Fanshawe and his family vulgar mushrooms of the merchant class. It was just as well that he had declined the invitation: had Sir Brendan seen the way Miss Fanshawe's rather protuberant eyes followed Peyton around the room, he would have been incensed. When that young gentleman engaged his cousin for a dance, Rora teased him about his conquest.

"Shall I hint Miss Fanshawe away by informing her of my prior claim upon you, Peyton? She may not be aware that you have laid your heart at my feet!"

"Come off it, Rora," he replied, flushing uncomfortably. "I must do the pretty to Susan because old Fanshawe buys his horses from us. Papa don't like the family above half, but if I was remiss in my attentions, it would go hard with me, I can tell you! Besides, Gregory Fanshawe's a great gun—we've known each other all our lives and went to the Kilkenny school together."

"I'm sorry for roasting you," she said penitently, "and I should've remembered you're not in the petticoat line. Poor Susan must needs have a mane and a tail for you to accord her the interest that she deems her due."

He laughed at that and readily agreed to the truth of it. "And I'm wondering myself what it would take to secure your interest in a gentleman, Cousin," he returned with a grin.

Now it was her turn to color up, ever so slightly. "I suppose he would have to be worthy of my respect, a man of character. Kind and good and brave—all the usual nonsense," she said, shrugging.

"Does that Manville fellow qualify?"

"Oh, Peyton, how can you ask it? Of course he doesn't!" She gave a rueful laugh. "I fancy I am too nice in my requirements and will end as an ape leader, though I suppose there's hope for me in the fact that Grandmother married my grandfather at twenty-five!"

"True, but he was her second, and anyway, she'd known Grandfather Liscarrol since she was a girl. If I was you, Rora, which I'm not, I'd look to Briavel. If you're thinking *I'll* marry you to keep you from leading apes in hell, you're far off the mark! Seems to me Briavel's not as interested in my sister as you thought a whileen ago, and I'm all but sure Jo's not caring for him any more than she is anyone else. You could do worse, and—"

"Thank you very much for your advice, Peyton Newburgh, but I don't recall having asked for it," Rora interrupted him loftily. "I am not the sort of female to throw myself at a gentleman only to save from ending an old maid, and I'm all but certain Lord Briavel has plenty enough ladies on the catch for him in London."

"Well, none of 'em could be half as pretty as you, nor have so fine a seat on a horse," Peyton said handsomely, making an adjustment to his overly tight collar. "Faith, but I'm hungry—my stomach will be thinking my throat is cut! Care to go down to supper with me, Cousin?"

She declined, since she had been engaged for supper by another gentleman. Whether or not Peyton was right about Briavel and Joan, the gentleman in question didn't seem disposed to dangle after any particular female that evening, preferring to remain in the card room. Nevertheless, he bestirred himself long enough to favor Rora with the requested two dances, and Joan with one reel. Mr. Manville, on the other hand, was quite attentive to all the ladies of his party; he escorted Lady Liscarrol to supper, causing Rora and Joan to fall upon each other in helpless giggles when they met in the ladies' cloakroom at the end of the party.

"Oh, Rora," Joan cried, " 'tis a great deal too bad that Gran is his aunt—or Mr. Manville could dangle after her instead of you! By the way, do you think he is unaware that she has a life estate in Ardara—that she holds it in trust for you? Someone really ought to warn him—Gran could live to be a hundred, you know."

"I hope she does! I have said nothing to Mr. Manville about the trust, nor do I intend to—it's not my place to do so. I'll leave it to Grandmother to tell him."

Joan chuckled. "She will when she's ready to be rid of him, for I cannot believe she wishes you to marry that man! She'll have to tell him the truth sooner or later—I should think she'd be tired of him buzzing 'round her like a fly on a horse. And if she doesn't let him know about the trust, you'll have to endure his making you an offer—an odious prospect!"

But Lady Liscarrol seemed highly pleased with her guest: his appearance, manners, and attentions to herself could not but satisfy; the girls supposed them to appeal to her vanity. Whatever she thought of him she kept to herself, and whether or not she was aware of her granddaughters' amusement at Mr. Manville's expense couldn't be ascertained from her impassive countenance as the foursome made their way back to Ardara Castle in the cool spring night.

CHAPTER XI

There was great rejoicing among the Ardara party the next day when Comet won his race, especially as nearly everyone in her ladyship's enclosure had bet upon him to win. Champagne and high spirits flowed, and groups of other spectators came over to congratulate the Newburghs on their win and to make numerous offers for the horse. In the excitement the ladies were all but forgotten by the gentlemen, so Lady Liscarrol and Joan wandered across the way to visit with friends; Rora stayed behind to enjoy the horsey conversations going on about her.

Not long after her grandmother's exit Briavel approached her and asked if she would like to stroll beneath the trees behind the stands, where it would be a great deal cooler. Rora agreed, unfurling her pretty sunshade before she placed her gloved hand upon his lordship's arm. She didn't suppose that her absence would be remarked, owing to the fact that her swains were, to a man, engaged in discussions of sporting matters; she was therefore rather grateful to her escort for remembering her existence.

But within a few moments of departing the stands in his company, Rora was staring at the gentleman in abject amazement, for as soon as they were alone, he asked her, without preamble, if she would consent to meeting him at the temple folly at Ardara—at midnight!

"Are—are you mad, sir?" was her startled reply. "A touch of the sun, perhaps? Faith, I'd be lost to all propriety if I agreed to so shocking a thing! You must have windmills in your head, Lord Briavel!"

"Oh, as to that, I will admit that my mind is somewhat disordered, Miss Donellan. But let me relieve you of one objection: not a soul will know of this tryst but ourselves. And I assure you I have no harmful intent in suggesting this, ah, slightly irregular sort of meeting."

"Then—why?" Rora was all at sea; moreover, she was finding her breathing processes strangely impaired.

"Doesn't it sound a pleasant interlude, the ruins at midnight, uninterrupted conversation—we are so often interrupted—and the opportunity to become better acquainted?" he answered smoothly, guiding her around a puddle in their path.

"But—"

"Of course, if you find it outside your powers to effect your escape from the house . . ." He trailed off disappointedly.

Rora released his arm and turned to face him, the corners of her broad mouth quivering. "Oh, you wretch! Are you going to tease me into meeting you? 'Tis most unfair!"

"Craven!"

"I'm *not* a craven! Only, I can't conceive of why you should want to meet me in so—so clandestine a way. You don't even like me!"

"Now what can have given you that impression, Miss Donellan? I like you very well, and given the chance, could like you even better. You seem to forget that we have been alone at the folly twice in the past: on the occasion of our first meeting, and again after your ill-judged excursion in the rain. And if the latter has escaped your mind, then you are not the woman I think you."

There was a gleam in his eye that brought the color surging into Rora's face, for she was far from forgetting the day of the storm and his arms around her as they rode his black horse back to the house. "If you are going to make such—such *odiously* insinuating remarks as that, then I must naturally refuse to meet you!" she declared hotly, knowing full well she had no intention of agreeing to his outrageous proposal.

Briavel drew up short and peered into her face. "What if I give you my word, as a gentleman, not to do anything that might make you uncomfortable or put you to the blush? Word or action—I swear it!"

"I'm not sure," she wavered. It wasn't that she didn't trust him to keep the line, but why she should feel vaguely disappointed by his assurances that he would do so, she had no idea. "Oh, very well! I daresay you think me lost past all reclaim, and 'tis no more than I deserve. If Grandmother ever learns of this—"

"Never! At midnight, then?"

"Yes, but I mustn't stay long." Why had she agreed to meet him at all? It had seemed to be a challenge on his part, and therefore she had little choice in the matter; to appear afraid of him she would not. Whatever his purpose, she had his word that he meant her no harm, and any fears on that head must be laid to rest.

Despite danger to her reputation, it was a highly intriguing prospect, and one that appealed to her, this midnight meeting. Half of the fun would be in escaping from the house without alerting anyone. By the time she and her escort had returned to their places for the next race her plan was half formed. She was a little alarmed by the distance between the house and the ruined castle, but if it was a clear night, there would be sufficient moonlight, and in any event, her eyes would eventually become accustomed to the dark.

That night Rora had to force herself to keep her eyes averted, so brimful of mischief were they; even Mary had noticed it and asked what queer start she was on.

"You've got that look in your eye I've been knowing since ye was a tiny lass, and I don't doubt I ought to warn her ladyship of it!" the abigail declared with a wary glance at her mistress. "Poor, decent lady that she is! If I could fall down dead this minute 'twould be more than a relief to me, knowing the trouble you're apt to find. Like as not I'm an *oínseach* for not letting on to the mistress you're brewing mischief!"

"Dear Mary, you're no more a fool than I am this night," Rora said merrily, twirling around before the glass to admire her gown. It was a plain but becoming coral pink, and as she draped her Indian shawl over her arms, she wished that Briavel could see her now.

Hubert Manville greeted her happily when she went down to the Great Parlor. "Cousin Rora, you're a picture of beauty!"

Because neither Lady Liscarrol nor Joan was downstairs yet, Rora found herself wishing that she could back out of the room. "You are too kind, Mr. Manville," she murmured, eyes demurely downcast. Please God he wouldn't make her an offer tonight!

"I address you as cousin—can you not bring yourself to do so as well?" he asked plaintively, pulling out a chair for her.

"Very well—Cousin." She sat upon the satin upholstery as though on eggs and arranged her skirts with great deliberation.

"Have you been enjoying the races?" Manville asked as he took a seat beside hers.

"Yes, indeed! Today I won a hundred pounds on Comet—would to God I had put more on him, but I fear I'm not much of a gambler."

At the mention of gambling, the gentleman looked acutely uncomfortable. "Yes—I mean—no. Tell me, Cousin Rora, do you have a fancy to visit London someday?"

He was working up to a declaration, Rora feared, and she prayed that someone would enter the room to interrupt him. "How strange that you should ask that, Cousin. Why, Lord Briavel and I were talking about London just the other day!"

Manville's brown eyes glinted on hearing his lordship's name. "Were you indeed? I oughtn't to be surprised—Lord Briavel is certainly fond of town life. I cannot understand why he has immured himself in the Irish countryside, for such a thing is not in his line at all, I assure you."

Her eyes narrowed and she might have questioned him further about Briavel's likes and dislikes, but in answer to her prayers, Lady Liscarrol came sailing into the room.

"Rora! And Hubert—goodness, I'd no notion I was so tardy! And where's our Joan?"

Rising from his seat, Manville informed her seriously, as though it were a matter of some concern, "I saw Cousin Joan walking toward the gardens carrying a basket. I noted it from my bedchamber window as I was dressing."

"How odd, to be sure," her ladyship murmured thoughtfully. "Well, we must wait for her return. I wonder if I should warn Cook to hold back dinner?"

This drastic measure proved unnecessary. Joan joined them a few minutes later looking pink and quite pretty, and she apologized for being late.

"Did you cut any blooms?" whispered Rora after Purdon announced dinner.

"That's none of your business!" Smiling beatifically, Joan pinched Rora's cheek and put an arm around her waist, adding, "Someday, dearest Rora, I shall tell you everything I'm so wicked to keep to myself nowadays!"

" 'All these woes shall serve for sweet discourse in our time to come,' " Rora quoted.

Joan stopped short in the hallway, an arrested expression on her face. She asked Rora whence came the quotation.

"*Romeo and Juliet,* I'm thinking."

"How wonderfully clever you are! 'Tis perfectly apt, little though you know it."

Lady Liscarrol, on Mr. Manville's arm, turned and called back to them, "Hurry along, girls, or our dinner will be as cold and hard as a brick!"

Had Rora not been so caught up in her plans to meet Briavel later, she would have been much struck by Joan's words and strange manner. As it was, all her attention was on the image of the mantel clock in the gilt-framed mirror across from her place at the table, but it was difficult to read the time; the hands and numerals of the clock face were reflected backward. The meal seemed endless, and while course after course was served by Purdon and his underlings, Rora tried to keep her eyes downcast, stifling the impulse to look back at the clock every few minutes. Joan noticed and threw Rora a questioning glance that nearly caused her to choke on a mouthful of lamb. She winked back as their grandmother passed a dish of potatoes to Mr. Manville, all the time feeling like a naughty schoolgirl on a prank.

After dinner it was the usual game of whist till sometime past ten o'clock, when Lady Liscarrol finally declared that she could keep her eyes open no longer. Each person took his or her candle from a table at the bottom of the staircase and went to his or her room just as they had done every other evening. Mary sleepily helped Rora to undress and brushed out the gleaming auburn tresses before being dismissed, too tired to remark on the young lady's alertness.

As soon as the servant was gone, Rora bounded out of bed and slipped into a long-sleeved cotton dress. She searched her wardrobe for a shawl, selecting one too large and dark for fashionable wear, but warm and shielding. The bracket clock told her that she lacked but a few minutes to eleven o'clock: it was far too early to make her exit. She sat in the darkness for three quarters of an hour more, her heart pounding harder with every passing minute. Finally she judged it time to leave and went silently and stealthily down a back staircase.

Once she was safely beyond the house, she drew the shawl over her head and ran toward the path leading to the folly and the Old Castle. As she had guessed, it took only a little while for her eyes to become accustomed to the night, but she forced herself to walk slowly down the worn track, wondering if Briavel would be at the folly at the appointed time. She was impatient with herself for not remembering to bring the tiny gold watch her father had given her on her last birthday, for now she had no way to judge how long she ought to wait for Briavel if he should be late.

But her concern was unnecessary. From the point where the path gave into the clearing, she saw a cloaked figure walking in front of the domed temple. The folly looked starkly white in the glow of the moon, thrown into pale relief against the dark, looming ruins and the trees.

On seeing her, Briavel said softly, "Miss Donellan, allow me to congratulate you on your fortitude." He sketched a bow, then removed his cloak and spread it upon the steps of the folly. "You will be quite safe from the damp here, I should think. But you strike me as the sort who almost never takes a chill—am I right?"

She nodded, dropping down to sit on the step. She didn't know what to say now that she was here, so she turned her head to look at the ruins, barely distinguishable in the blackness of night, now that she was so close to them. The sight was neither frightening nor eerie, as she had sometimes imagined it might be; the tower and walls of the Old Castle were strangely comforting, as was the gentle rustle of leaves stirred by the breeze. She let the shawl fall from her head to her shoulders and faced Briavel, a slight smile lending a softness to her face.

"What are you thinking?" he asked her before she could speak.

"That this scene is like something out of a novel, only to me it isn't the least bit mysterious or frightening, as it would be if described by Mrs. Radcliffe or Mr. Lewis!"

"Too true!" he agreed with a laugh. "Tell me, why was this charming example of classical architecture placed in so unlikely a spot?"

"It is dreadfully out of place, isn't it?" Rora drew her knees up and encircled them with her arms in a most unladylike fashion, but one that her father would have recognized as her confiding pose. "Great-grandfather built the folly, I suppose because his architect told him 'twas the thing to do—all the crack, as you would say! Many nobles have constructed false ruins on their estates; at least ours at Ardara are genuine enough! This is where the Newburghs and I played as children. The temple folly was the castle where the captive princesses were held, and the crumbling walls were the fortress of the soldiers who freed them." She chuckled low in her throat and pushed back a loose strand of hair that had strayed onto her cheek.

"You must have made a delightful captive princess."

There was a warm note in his voice that she could not mistake, and she went first hot, then cold all over. "Oh, no, sir, I was one of the band of rescuers! I always considered being a princess a paltry role to that of soldier." Her voice quavered slightly on the last word and she bit her lip.

"Are you nervous, Miss Donellan?"

"No, not in the least," she lied. "Only, 'tis odd to be here, and at this hour."

"And alone with me," Briavel supplied.

"Well, yes, there's that too," she admitted, meeting his eyes squarely. "You don't think worse of me for coming? The sad fact is, you fairly flung a challenge at me, making it all the harder to refuse. I was more afraid not to come than to do so!"

"There could be no danger in meeting me; I promise you no one will know of it."

She sighed. "Of course there is danger, and all of it for me. You are a man and I a woman, we are alone, and I am probably already ruined."

"Can this be the intrepid Miss Donellan? I gave you my word not to, ah, to molest you, did I not? Don't you trust me?" He smiled wryly down at her worried face. "You are not ruined, my dear. And you must agree that it is pleasant here, as I foretold." He lounged against the stone steps and stretched out his legs in a way already familiar to her.

"Yes, 'tis pleasant." She could not deny the truth of it.

They were silent for a moment, each listening to the wind in the trees overhead. Rora's anxiety soon subsided and she began to feel more comfortable in his presence. When he spoke again, she looked into his face wonderingly, unable to determine what it was about this man that often made her behave like a romping school-girl, this time going so far as to creep out of the house at midnight, and for nothing more than a little moonlight conversation. He was handsome, but she had known other handsome men; he could be amusing and witty, but there were many such in Dublin. She supposed that it was the way his gray eyes met hers, looking at her as though he knew so much about her and wished to know all. Impossible, of course, but an intriguing notion. Certainly no other gentleman had ever made her feel so breathless and fluttery, as though nothing she did in his presence was quite right, and at the same time making her want to tell him all about the time she had run away from home because her music master had patted her on the knee. Such a silly memory, yet significant, and she had never

told anyone in her life, not even her father, but something about
Briavel made it possible to speak of it, and so much more.

But as much as talking did she enjoy listening to him. And when
they hit upon the subject of books, and she learned that from the
time he had been a lonely little boy, literature had been his greatest friend. And for him, too, *Gulliver's Travels* had been a favorite.

"Dean Swift visited Ardara in my great-grandfather's day," Rora
told him proudly, "during the time he was at St. Patrick's in Dublin. I enjoy *Tale of a Tub* greatly, just as much as I do Gulliver. I
don't know why it is, but satire inevitably appeals to me whatever
the form, whether verse, novel, or drama. Mr. Sheridan's plays are
among my favorites for that very reason—and also because he's a
distant connection of Papa's!"

They talked of their very different childhoods, a strangely unso-
phisticated topic for two people who had been used to banter
cleverly with one another. Their experiences had been widely
divergent: Rora had been raised in a comfortable home with loving parents; Briavel was on good terms with his father nowadays,
he told her, but freely admitted that as a boy he had been sulky
and rebellious, raised mostly by tutors and relations whom he had
disliked.

"My hopes for a mother were dashed when Alanna went away,"
he explained to Rora with a twisted smile. "I was no more than
eight years old and that seems a lifetime ago, but still I cannot
forget the disappointment I felt when I learned she had gone.
Now, of course, I have cause to be grateful for her choice: the
result is admirable!" Another of his warm glances wafted over
Rora and she ducked her head, so that she missed the bleak expression in his gray eyes as he continued, "That experience has no
doubt been the reason for many of my misdeeds toward your sex."

She lifted her face to look at his. "Now, at least, I understand
better why you disliked me at first," she mused aloud. "I knew you
resented Mama's behavior, but I thought 'twas on your father's
account, not your own. How long ago that day seems now."

"You were certainly a shock to me, sitting on the ground over
there, looking much as Alanna did twenty or so years ago." Her
resemblance to her mother seemed to trouble him and he did not
speak again for some minutes, but frowned abstractedly into
space. Then he murmured reminiscently, "And how angry I made
you in those early days, on purpose and out of revenge. It has been

many weeks since I have tried to do so; I hope within that span of time you have come to forgive me."

"Oh, I don't know that I have!" she told him spiritedly. "Only remember, *I* was the first one to cry friends, yet you remained aloof. Then when you bought Troilus out from under me, I wished you at the devil!"

He was amused by that expression, coming as it did from a lady. "Someday," he drawled in his lazy, caressing voice, "you will have to teach me those Irish curses I heard coming from your lips on the occasion of our first meeting."

She only laughed and said that he had best go to Slaney for instruction, since that was where she had come by them. She asked the time, and upon being told, bounded to her feet, cried in consternation, "Two o'clock! Good heavens, sir, I'd no notion 'twas so late! And you've had your watch by you all the time—you are a villain for not telling me. I only meant to stay but a whileen!"

"Must you go? You'd have been up later than this and still dancing, at a Dublin ball," he pointed out.

"I know, but—oh, yes, I must go!"

"Tomorrow, then, at the same time?"

"Very well, tomorrow," she agreed hastily, wishing to be off and yet hating to leave him. She held out her hand impulsively and was surprised when he lifted it to his lips, for until now he had not seemed in the least disposed toward making love to her, except, perhaps, with his eyes. As his mouth touched her flesh, lingeringly, her spine tingled, and she withdrew her hand reluctantly. Replacing the shawl over her head, she ran off in the direction of the path. She could see it almost as well as if it had been daylight, her eyes were now so used to the darkness.

By the time she closed her eyes that night, or rather, early that morning, Rora felt deliciously tired, as she hadn't felt for ages, and wonderfully alive, as though she had been hunting and had spent a long satisfying day in the saddle. Snuggling deeper among her pillows, her mind was filled with thoughts of Briavel's face in the moonlight, its hard edges softened as she had never thought they could be. Had they really talked for two hours? A month ago she would have thought him likely to be bored by the sort of reminiscences she had shared with him. If she hadn't asked the time, they would still be talking, she thought to herself, very pleased. And tomorrow evening she would meet him again, and the night after that—no, that night was the one of her grandmother's ball, and it would last till well past the hour of midnight. But he would be present, and there would be dancing. Upon this blissful thought Rora buried her cheek in her pillow and soon was dreaming of Lord Briavel and his warm gray eyes.

CHAPTER XII

Lady Liscarrol and her granddaughters elected not to attend the races the next morning; there was a steady drizzle of rain and the skies were ominously overcast. Her ladyship, admirably assisted by Joan, busied herself with the preparations for the Ardara Castle ball, but Rora, who was in a flow of spirits that day, couldn't bear to be kept indoors. When the rains stopped shortly after noon, she was happy to drive out with Mr. Manville, who had spent the morning writing letters to England. She half expected him to turn up his fashionable nose at the only form of conveyance available to them, but he accepted the news in good part, so Rora sent a message to the stables ordering Slaney to harness the gig. Then she went to change into a dress that would not suffer from the inevitable mud and dirt that they would encounter during the course of their drive.

She felt so happy that it required little exertion to be pleasant to her companion; she was in a mood to like everyone and everything, including Hubert Manville. Under her beatific gaze he expanded and was able to keep her tolerably entertained by his stories of the London world, peopled by such luminaries of fashion as Beau Brummel, Lords Petersham and Alvanley, and the Prince Regent. That Manville admired these men and wished to emulate them as far as was in his power was clear, although Rora was amused that the cut of a coat or the shine on a pair of boots could engender so much enthusiasm when there were so many more interesting things in the world: horses, people, books, music, and estate business. Had he exhibited more than a cursory interest in anything else but the fact that he someday hoped to dine with Prinny at Carlton House, she might have liked him better for it; she thought him a shallow man, though an undeniably well-dressed one. Moreover, she found herself comparing him unfavorably to Briavel, who might on occasion have been exasperating, but who at least was a man of sense as well as fashion.

"Have you become well acquainted with Lord Briavel during his stay in the neighborhood?"

Rora started at Manville's question, most particularly at the mention of the man who figured uppermost in her thoughts. Reminded of the leaps her friendship with Briavel had taken the night before, she blushed faintly and turned away her head to observe the damp, leafy trees they passed along the lane. "Yes, we are becoming friends," she admitted.

Manville laughed, an unpleasant, snorting sound. "On your side, perhaps, Cousin Rora, but I very much doubt what Briavel feels for you could be honored with the name 'friendship.' To my certain knowledge he has never been particularly friendly toward those of your sex. Although how a man can be both a notorious misogynist and a womanizer at the same time, I cannot fathom!"

Rora stiffened. "What do you mean, sir?"

The gentleman looked at her, mingled amusement and shock in his face. "Dear me, Cousin, not you, too? You will not take it amiss if I offer you some advice?" She embarked upon a protest, but he held up one elegant gloved hand, skillfully controlling his horse with the other. "Oh, I know it is unsought, but you would do well to hear me."

"I can see you are bent on speaking and I cannot stop you," she said in a tight, clipped voice. She had an inkling of what was to follow and had little wish to hear.

"It is no secret in London circles that Briavel has libertine tendencies," Manville went on silkily. "As long as he confines his—attentions—to the West End comets and demireps, his behavior cannot be considered injurious. But on occasion he has devoted himself to young ladies of impeccable birth and breeding, and with disastrous results for his fair victims!"

She must not be hurt or disappointed to learn that Briavel had mistresses, she cautioned herself. It was not unexpected and was no more than she had believed from the moment of her meeting him. Maintaining her composure, she asked calmly, "Are you perchance trying to tell me that his lordship has made it a practice to seduce young ladies of quality? For I won't believe you."

"You speak plainly, Cousin! I see that I need not scruple to do the same. As to how far he goes, no one can say: such things are quickly hushed up by the parents, of course. Money and influence can go a long way toward covering up the proofs of his reprehensible deeds."

"Good God, sir, are you suggesting that—" She broke off. That Briavel had sired bastards was possible, she supposed, but that their mothers had been well-born young women of the *ton*, she could not accept. "This is preposterous, Cousin Hubert! I am not so ignorant as to be unaware that young girls are chaperoned and guarded from the notice of rakes, whether in London or in Dublin! Your allegations are absurd."

"Are they? I have known Briavel much longer than you, my dear, not that I am proud to admit it. When I learned he was here, I—well, never mind my feelings. But as to his shocking conduct in the past—they say he has a grudge against all females, stemming from some kind of disappointment in his youth—"

"His youth," she repeated, taking hold of the side of the gig. That much was perfectly true, for only last night Briavel had told her of his reaction to Alanna's elopement. What had he said? Something about the early disappointment being responsible for his misdeeds toward females—oh, but he couldn't have meant what Mr. Manville was so cruel to imply!

"He has sought out young women for the purpose of ruining them," her companion continued, seeing that Rora was suddenly looking thoughtful. He had not hoped for such success and congratulated himself on his cleverness. "Briavel's campaigns are so well known that he has lately caught cold at them; the mamas and papas are prepared for his stratagems nowadays. First he gets up a flirtation with some pretty young bud, then he makes a declaration —false, of course. It is a fact that he is one of the most charming gentlemen in England, Cousin, and you cannot wonder at a girl's fancying herself in love with him."

"But he can hardly ruin someone by flirting with her. If that could destroy a reputation, Cousin, then mine is in shreds by now, I'll have you know!"

"I imagine his next recourse is to induce a young lady to meet him in clandestine fashion, enabling him to—ah, I dare not say more! Aunt Hester would be appalled if she knew I had spoken of this to you."

Rora sat silent and perfectly still, staring unseeingly before her; then she turned to look hard at her escort. What she saw in his face allayed her fears that he knew anything specific of her midnight meeting with Briavel, but she had to be certain he didn't suspect it. "Just why did you tell me these things—this gossip?"

"Because, dear Cousin, I have noticed that Briavel is becoming

most particular in his attentions to you and knew that you could
have no idea of what is said about him in England. And when I saw
you leave the stands in his company at yesterday's race, it was all I
could do to keep from running to stop you!"

"Have you told Joan of this, too, or even my grandmother, who
acts *in loco parentis* to us both? Briavel has lately been attentive to
my cousin as well; there have been rumors circulating about the
neighborhood that he will offer for her," Rora informed him.

"Marry? Briavel? Dear God, if any of his London acquaintance
heard that, how they would laugh! Cousin Rora, he has no thought
of marriage, and has become the most complete hand at evading
all the traps set for him by conniving parents—"

"How can he be considered such a prize, then, if he is known for
a debaucher of innocent girls?" she asked sharply, frowning at the
gentleman. "That is certainly inconsistent, don't you agree?"

"Oh, he—well, he is very wealthy, of course, and will be an earl
one day. For some people those attributes must outweigh his—his
reputation," Manville finished lamely. He didn't like clever
women, especially those more clever than himself, and it was with
an effort that he managed a creditable assumption of unconcern.
"I know that such considerations would not weigh with you,
Cousin. Not that there's any chance of his giving up being a bache-
lor, if you'll forgive me saying this, not even for a lady of birth and
beauty like yourself."

Their drive did not last much longer; the clouds were building
up once more, threatening to spill their rains on the already
drenched and muddy countryside. When Rora returned to the
house, she went directly to her room, but it was some time before
she rang for Mary to come and help her undress.

She knew that those things Hubert Manville had told her of
Briavel could not be entirely true, but there was a grain of truth in
some of his assertions, for Briavel had admitted that Alanna's
elopement had affected him, even to the point of leading him to
torment Rora out of motives of revenge. It wasn't hard to believe
that he had behaved ill toward other females, demireps and opera
dancers, using them for his pleasure and then discarding them
when he became bored; that would be very much in character.
Manville had suggested that there had been numerous mistresses,
from which she surmised that his lordship was incapable of fidelity;
that was more disappointing to her than the existence of other
women. The tales about his seducing young ladies of quality must

be discounted, however, for now that she knew him better, it was absurd to think of Briavel as a ravisher of innocent youth, and besides, Manville had slipped by mentioning that he was also considered a matrimonial prize.

But Manville had succeeded in planting a seed of doubt in Rora's fertile brain. She thought no less of Briavel, for the dandy had hinted at little more than what she herself had already suspected: that Briavel was something of a rake, and that he had mistresses. So did many gentlemen, she knew. Still, unfortunate as it might be, considering her growing pleasure in his company, the wisdom of meeting him at the folly had to be examined. Suppose Briavel thought she had acquiesced only because she was another of the many girls on the catch for him? That would be fatal, for it would surely give him a disgust of her, and more than anything did she want his respect and admiration. Her belief that he was interested in Joan had flown out the window since the moonlight meeting, and Rora was all but certain that if Briavel took it into his head to offer for one of the cousins, it would be to herself that he would pay his addresses. The thought was exhilarating but was soon pushed aside by another nagging doubt: whether or not Viscount Briavel, already immune to the lures of marriageable society females, would take to wife a romp of an Irish girl who was so heedless of her reputation that she would readily meet him in a wood at midnight. Perhaps he thought her little better than one of his lightskirts. He had kept his promise not to annoy her with making advances, but why would he have given his word not to do so unless he had thought of making them in the first place? He might think that in time she would grow amenable to them. Engaging to meet her by night might be a first step toward his inducing her to join the ranks of his mistresses; possibly her open manners and disregard for chaperonage had encouraged him to think she would be willing to accept a *carte blanche.*

Rora was more subdued that evening than she had been all day, but Joan's vivacity compensated for her cousin's lowness of spirits. Lady Liscarrol cast several sharp glances at the thoughtful face of her younger granddaughter and wondered to herself what had come over the girl who was more typically the livelier of the pair. Very interested in the state of Rora's heart, her ladyship would have liked to be privy to whatever thoughts and feelings were being concealed there. She hoped that Hubert Manville had not pressed his suit during their drive earlier; Lady Liscarrol knew that it would bring matters to a head all too soon. But had he done so, he would have come running to his dearest aunt with the news of Rora's answer and it was more than likely that Hubert would ask the grandmother's permission to pay his addresses before making them. At which point her ladyship would inform him about the trust that allowed her to remain mistress of Ardara for her lifetime. She was not one to regret a decision, and she had had more than one purpose in inviting her late husband's nephew for a visit, but she would not be sorry to see him go. A selfish woman, but quite well aware of this flaw, she recognized in Manville a man even more selfish, and one who was an opportunist, a thing she despised. She thanked God that Liscarrol had died before ever making the fellow's acquaintance; the earl must be turning in his grave to see what a dandified coxcomb was making up to his cherished Rora.

Manville, unlike her ladyship, could not have been better pleased by Rora's quietude, for it betokened her acceptance of his warnings about Briavel. If the girl had been developing a *tendre* for the viscount, he hoped that he had now nipped it in the bud; even if she had not, she would be certain to avoid that gentleman from now on, making it easier for Manville to occupy her time and thoughts. He couldn't wait too much longer before he became engaged to the heiress, but he knew that he ought to let a few more days pass before offering for her. He had effectively undercut his only rival, which he had known Briavel to be, whatever gossip said of his attentions to the Newburgh girl, and could now direct his energies toward turning Rora up sweet. Then they would announce the betrothal and he could hurry back to London, where his creditors would cease to pester him as soon as the word of his alliance to a great heiress became known.

By the end of the evening Rora had come to the painful conclusion that she must not go again to the folly to meet Briavel. It was unfortunate that she had no means of letting him know her intention ahead of time, but she trusted that he wouldn't wait there long before realizing that she was unable to come. Wishing that the weather had cooperated to give her an acceptable excuse, she looked out of the window just past the hour of midnight and noted that the clouds had blown away and the stars and moon were visible in the clear night sky.

Regretful, she was about to turn away from the window, when she caught sight of someone down below, in the region of the gardens. Surely Briavel had not dared to come up to the house! Straining her eyes to see through the darkness, she spied a figure hurrying along the path that led into the garden. It was a female; she knew it from the long skirt, and in the space of a heartbeat saw that it was none other than Joan. Her cousin was meeting someone, and Rora forgot all about her own ill-fated assignation as she tried to imagine who was hiding among the rosebushes in wait for her cousin.

She recalled Joan's disappearance into the gardens yesterday: perhaps that had been another meeting with the mysterious gentleman. That it was a gentleman Rora was positive, and she cast about in her mind for who he might be, deciding that it could easily be Peyton, on a lark. She had convinced herself that this must be so, when a sudden fear gripped her that Joan was meeting Briavel. The walkway through the garden gave out onto the path to the Old Castle, and even now Joan could be making her way to the ruins. But that was a ridiculous notion, for how could Briavel be meeting Joan at the same hour he was expecting Joan's cousin to arrive at the folly? By the time Rora finally climbed into bed, she had no more answers than she'd had on first seeing her cousin scurrying toward the garden. Her brain was too worn out from thought and worry already; she would not wait at the window for Joan's emergence from the rosebushes. She couldn't spy upon one of whom she was so fond, whatever threat that person might be to her own happiness. Before closing her eyes, she consoled herself that it had to be Peyton whom her cousin was meeting, and she further reflected on how odd the past two days and nights had been. She wondered sleepily if Briavel had been at all disappointed by her failure to appear at the folly, as disappointed as she had been to remain in the sanctuary of the house, safely hidden away from the attentions that were becoming increasingly necessary to her well-being.

CHAPTER XIII

Rora failed to attend the races on the day of the ball, pleading a headache that was real enough, and a reluctance to spend the heat of the day in an uncomfortable crowd. Since she didn't go down to breakfast either, but sent a message by Mary, she had no knowledge of how her relations received the news. No sooner did the carriage drive away in the direction of Kilkenny than Rora bounded up from the daybed where she had been reclining in case Joan or her grandmother came to inquire about her indisposition. She donned her riding habit without Mary's assistance and crept down the back stairs and toward the stables.

Slaney greeted her with his characteristic gruffness, stumping forward on his bowed legs to ask why she hadn't gone to Kilkenny with the others. "For 'tis sure the races have begun already. Even if ye ride like the divil, ye'll be missing the first heat, Miss Rora."

"I'm not riding to town, Slaney, but you may saddle Falstaff for me. I intend to ride the estate, so you needn't accompany me."

"Now, miss, ye'll not be going out alone again? I thought we'd done with that, sure and I did! And whatever would the master say?"

"He'll never know of it, so you may stop your moaning and groaning this instant and ready my horse," Rora commanded firmly before wandering out into the sunshine, where she waited impatiently. The best way to deal with her aching head, she had decided, was to ignore it, and she was sure that once she was cantering across the fields, the rush of air would blow the pain—and her heartache—away.

As soon as Slaney threw her into the saddle, she adjusted her skirts and gathered up her reins, urging Falstaff forward. She felt a delicous freedom, one she had missed for some days now. Her emotions had been wearing down her spirits, but if she was fortunate, soon all her troubles would be done with. Manville would probably make his offer soon and she could refuse him and send him on his way, after which Briavel would come to realize, having nearly lost her to another, that Rora was the ideal wife for him and then he would propose. Joan could remain at Ardara to keep Lady Liscarrol company while Briavel carried Rora to London, where she would be a dazzling success, and eventually her grandmother, or Rora herself, would arrange an advantageous match for Joan. Whatever affair Joan might be carrying on must be with an inferior person; if Briavel was in Miss Newburgh's confidence, then perhaps he could induce her to give up the man, whoever he might be. Letters, clandestine meetings at midnight: these bore all the trappings of a secret love. Rora felt she should tax her cousin with that telling observation from her window last night. That Joan had been meeting Peyton seemed very unlikely in the clarity of daylight.

The only obstacle to her glorious vision of the future (and it was a significant one) was the fact that Briavel, if Hubert Manville was to be believed, had no intention of marrying. Briavel had even admitted as much during their stroll through the shrubbery together. Well, other men had been known to act contrary to what they believed their true inclinations, and certainly his lordship would require an heir someday, and thus a wife as well. Searching her heart, Rora knew that while she would prefer for a true love match, if Briavel ever offered for her, she would have him whether he returned her love or not. That she was perilously close to loving him she knew; that he desired anything more than a pleasant flirtation she could not believe, for she was not a fool. Well, retaining his friendship would probably be of more value to her in the end, so her aim must be to maintain the excellent relations that had lately cropped up between them rather than to attempt to provoke his short-lived and transitory passions. If he ever did marry her, she would have to learn to accustom herself to his inevitable desires for other women—most wives did, except those extremely fortunate ones like Alanna and Lady Liscarrol, both of whom had prided themselves on the fact that their husbands had never looked at another female. Rora resolved that Briavel should never know she loved him; he was so unpredictable, and she could just imagine his amusement at her expense if the true state of her heart were revealed to him. Doubtless he had laughed at all the silly fools he had attached in London, and how much harder would he laugh at his own wife if she were so misguided as to admit her feelings. But that was many weeks, perhaps many months, in the future, and it was entirely possible that his affection might one day animate toward her, Rora reminded herself optimistically.

She guided Falstaff in the direction of a small river she knew, seeking the cool comfort of rushing waters that flowed into the great River Nore and southward to Kilkenny. There, beneath the branches of tall alders, she allowed the horse to drink. Along the banks several varieties of wildflowers bloomed, among them the delicate cuckoo flower and the white stitchwort. Rora had long been enchanted by the beauty of the Kilkenny spring; she loved growing things, and the plants she had been used to seeing in the Dublin parks were cultivated and therefore not the least unusual or interesting.

In her absorption of the scene around her she did not quite forget her headache. During the ride back to the house she counted the different types of blooming flora, hoping that by concentrating on something else, she could divert her mind from discomfort. Despite the beauteous flowers in meadowland, thicket, and hedgerow, she discovered that the most spectacular display was waiting for her at the end of her ramble. As Falstaff rounded the drive and began the long approach to Ardara, the glorious sight took Rora's breath away: the park was lavish with bluebells, their purple-blue heads bobbing in the breeze. The prospect was so delightful that she reined in and sat for some moments in rapt contemplation of the graceful white house, carpet and sky of blue, and ornamental pond that reflected these glories—all of these filled her with pride.

Within the walls of the great house she found that all was in an uproar; the servants were rushing about performing the final cleaning and arrangement of the rooms, while Purdon was struggling manfully to maintain his composure and his control. The carpets had already been taken up in the saloon for the dancing and the card tables were arranged in the back parlor, but the housemaids were still dusting surfaces and polishing candelabra, and affixing new wax tapers into the holders. As Rora climbed the staircase, she heard a crash and a shriek emanating from the Great Parlor and could only hope that the loss had been minimal. There were so many treasures at Ardara that one would not be missed, except for the fact that at some point her grandmother's sharp eyes would detect any attempt to hide the evidence of a disaster.

After changing her dress, Rora stretched out upon her daybed once more, her chosen companion *Childe Harold* (the copy given her by Briavel; she had loaned Manville's gift to Joan), her intent to recruit her energies for the night's revelries. She lay back lazily and sighed in gleeful anticipation of the ball. She had never been to a big party at Ardara, not even during her grandfather's tenure, and none had been held in the four years since his death. The staff was noticeably rusty, but nevertheless it promised to be a wonderful evening.

Rora must have dozed off, for her eyes flew open at the sound of a knock upon her chamber door. Joan peeped in and shook her dark head on finding her lively cousin in a reclining position. "Does your poor head still ache?" she asked, coming into the room and sitting at the foot of the chaise.

Rora moved her legs aside to make room. "Only a little. Please don't tell Grandmother, but I went for a long ride, and I think it actually helped! How were the races?"

"Nothing could have been better! We had three winners today— or rather, I should say Papa and Peyton did. You never saw anyone so happy, and I think they'll make their fortunes if they wish to sell some of the racehorses. Gran is as proud as a peacock, for all she says if Papa means to conduct his horse trading at her party tonight, 'twill be much the worse for him! Briavel asked most particularly after you today, and Peyton was sorry to hear you were unwell, but I told them you preferred to be invalidish all day in order to dance yourself into bits tonight, as I'm sure you will. Oh, I nearly forgot: Cousin Hubert told Gran just now that he would do anything in the world to please you, and do you know what she said?"

"I can't imagine—do tell!"

"She told him that he ought to buy himself a decent hunter while he's in Ireland!" Joan crowed. "I nearly died from holding in my laughter, for she pretends to loathe Papa's business, but she's as much of a horse coper as he, I think! Gran is such a downy one—a *slíbhín*, as you said the other day. She can't wait to be rid of her nephew; she looked over at me once while he was extolling your virtues, and she rolled her eyes!"

"Did she indeed?" Rora laughed, sitting up.

"And just now in the hall she whispered to me, 'Hubert's the kind that if he went to a wedding, no doubt he'd remain for the christening!' Which makes it clear that in her mind he's outstayed his welcome. Oh, how I shall miss her, the dear old dragon!" Joan colored suddenly and added, "When Papa drags me away from Ardara, that is, which he'll surely do soon."

"Why should he? Grandmother won't give you up to him," Rora declared staunchly, taking hold of her cousin's plump hand. "And I won't either!"

Joan surprised her by enfolding her in a warm embrace. "Rora, you are the dearest dear, and how glad I am that we have come to know one another better! You think me a strange creature, I know, but one day I'll tell you all. You'll guess most of it soon enough." She jumped up from the chaise and smoothed out her wrinkled skirts. "Now I must hasten to my room and desire your good Mary to whip the flounce on my blue ball gown, while I write some pressing letters. 'Tis spoiled I've become by having a maid's services—I shall require one henceforth, I think!" So saying, she left Rora.

Joan's reassurances that someday she would tell all were comforting, if puzzling; Rora fell to speculating once more on the identity of Joan's rose-garden gentleman. It was a futile pastime; had she not been so certain of her cousin's excellent sense and taste, Rora would have supposed him to be a servant or a groom, or someone from the village. The doctor was wed, but there was the curate—only he was fifty if he was a day, and a widower, and quite unlikely to meet Sir Brendan Newburgh's daughter by moonlight. Perhaps Joan had a Kilkenny swain no one suspected. Rora intended to take the bit between her teeth and put a few questions to her cousin after the excitement of the ball was past.

Before she knew it, the time had come to dress for dinner. Her ballgown was a new one, never before worn, and fashioned from pomona-green silk finished with a gauze overdress. For jewelry she wore a pair of gold-fringed eardrops and a simple gold chain, but her finest ornaments were the delicate butterflies she wore in her hair; they were made of fine gold wire and had belonged to Alanna. The butterflies caught up the russet curls, arranged to perfection by Mary, who had allowed a few tendrils to frame her mistress's oval face. When at last Rora went downstairs to receive the dinner guests, she was confident that she looked well and hoped that Briavel would think it, too.

That he was looking fine in his own evening attire could not be denied, and her heart nearly skipped a beat when he drew her aside for private conversation after dinner, just as the ball guests were beginning to arrive.

"Where the devil were you last night?"

She had not forseen this question, nor the dark, penetrating look that accompanied it, and consequently had prepared no excuse for her absence. "I—I'm sorry that I failed to meet you," she faltered, dropping her eyes in her inability to meet his angry gaze.

"I was afraid you were ill, or had injured yourself in the dark. Then today Joan told me that you had the headache, but I cannot believe you would have failed me for such a reason as that. Why didn't you come, Miss Donellan?"

"It wasn't possible for me to leave the house," Rora explained reluctantly, disliking to tell him an untruth, however small. "Joan was with me—I was unable to slip away."

He glared at her in patent disbelief, then shook his head and stalked away, leaving her standing there, alone and puzzled.

She could not know, but Briavel was angrier at himself than at her, which was very angry indeed; his greater fury was over his admission of his concern for her. Last night he had harbored the fear that she was unwell, or hurt, for only one of those two things, he felt, could account for her failure to join him at the folly. He lent no credence to her excuse about Joan, for he had a pretty good idea where Miss Newburgh had been at the hour of midnight, and it had not been in her cousin's company. Rora's lie angered him because he had thought better of her, but he did not dwell on it; he wondered if she had been avoiding him, last night and today. She had seemed glad enough to see him upon his arrival before dinner, however; nothing could have pleased him more than the friendly smiles they had exchanged in greeting. But something had caused her to shy away from him, and he fancied he hadn't far to look for the cause. Even now that fellow Manville was leading her into the saloon, where the musicians could be heard tuning their instruments. Briavel glared at the man whom he suspected was his detractor, and strode into the room set aside for the card players, determined that he would proceed cautiously that evening. Somehow he had lost Rora's trust, and he was determined to win it back. And just as important was his great need to speak with her privately, even if it was only once more.

Rora was relieved, a little while later, when Peyton rescued her from Hubert Manville. "I say, Rora, do come and hear about the racing! I was sorrier than anything when you didn't come to Kilkenny today, but if you care to sit out this dance, I'll tell you everything." She allowed him to take her out of the saloon and in the direction of a refreshment table, where Peyton helped himself to a number of lobster patties and procured a glass of champagne for his cousin. They retired to the library, in which most of the sportsmen had congregated to discuss the week's racing. Sir Brendan, flushed with champagne and success, nodded approvingly when his son sat down with Rora on a sofa and engaged her in animated conversation.

"You wouldn't have believed Fire Rocket, Cousin," Peyton declared. "He broke ahead at the start, and none could touch him the rest of the way! And on a wet track, too! 'Twas a piece of fine riding by Bevins, but a rider don't make a smidgen of difference if he's not supported by flesh and bone and spirit."

Rora nodded sagely. "And Fire Rocket has all three. But now the racing is over, what comes next for the Newburgh stables?"

"Why, the Dublin Races, of course! Papa and I have hit upon an excellent arrangement: he will see to the racing side of the business, and I'm to take charge of the hunters—what do you think of that? This autumn I'll be visited horse fairs all over Ireland!"

"Oh, Peyton, 'tis beyond anything great! How happy you must be!"

"Well, I admit I'm pleased about it. 'Tisn't as noteworthy as being a famous scholar like Uncle Jasper, or a soldier like Uncle Matthew Newburgh, but at least in sporting circles the name 'Peyton Newburgh' will become known. I was feared that after the Troilus episode, Papa would never trust me with another sale. 'Twas a pretty near run thing, I can tell you, but he soon got over it. And I was able to hire a trainer away from Lord Ashford today, so my credit is mighty high just now. He's a capital fellow—the trainer, I mean—and exactly what we need to head up our racing stables."

"That requires a great deal of money, doesn't it, to build up a racing stable?" Rora asked with a troubled frown. "I hope Uncle Brendan isn't counting upon—well, you know what I mean."

Peyton grinned back at her. "Faith, don't I just! But you're out there, Rora—I don't have to marry you for us to expand the business. The Newburghs ain't paupers, you know, despite Papa's squeeze-purse ways. Symon's going to be riveted to an heiress in a few weeks, and Louisa is her husband's concern now, so they aren't a drain upon the estate, and the hall can be kept up without a lot of fuss—it's prosperous enough. Poor Jo may have her dowry paid out in racehorses if Papa has his way, but I'll not let him. Nay, you may be easy on that score, Cousin—we aren't counting on your fortune to support our stables. 'Twould be nonsense, anyway, for you don't come into it till Gran is gone, and to tell the truth, I'd liefer have her around!"

"So, too, would I," Rora agreed warmly.

"You've still no intention of wedding this Manville fellow, have you? Greg Fanshawe says the man dropped five hundred pounds at their party—he's a gamester, you know. I'd hate to see Ardara gambled away someday!"

"There's no chance of it," she reassured him. And she flashed her brightest smile, for she had noted Briavel's figure in the doorway.

"Well, I'm glad to hear it!" her cousin declared fervently. "Look, here's Briavel come to claim his dance, I'll be bound. I think I'm engaged to m'sister for this one. Oh, now that the racing is done, I'll be over for one of our rides, Cousin—what say you?"

Briavel was approaching them now, and she was a bit afraid of looking up. "Do come tomorrow," she begged, fixing her eyes on her cousin's face. " 'Tis my plan to call on Mrs. Drennan, so I'll be at the lodge in the morning, but tomorrow afternoon—"

"What of it, Briavel?" Peyton asked, rising from his place and greeting the viscount. "My cousin and I intend to ride out tomorrow. Do you wish to join us? We might make a party of it, with Jo, and Manville, of course."

"I'm afraid I'll be otherwise engaged," Briavel said, looking down at Rora with a half smile of regret.

"Estate business, I'm thinking—devil of a bore!" sympathized Peyton, before rushing off to the saloon.

"Might I engage you for this set, Miss Donellan?" Lord Briavel asked, hand outstretched. "I am creditably informed that it is to be the eight-handed reel and am emboldened to ask you, since you admired my execution of it some weeks past."

She accepted with pleasure, thankful that he was no longer angry with her. After their dance, Briavel left her side, returning to the card room, and Rora was surrounded by her cavaliers.

Mr. Manville, who figured among them, was looked upon with disfavor by the local lads, he possessed an enviable degree of fashion and address, and they feared his London touch might appeal to Miss Donellan. In this assumption they were quite wrong, as Peyton was thoughtful enough to inform his cronies while Manville partnered Rora in a Scotch reel. Hope sprang anew

in many a male breast, especially that of Mr. Whitney, the most
determined of Rora's local suitors.

Lord Briavel departed rather earlier than many of the guests,
but before he left, he managed to cause Rora no little distress. He
undertook to stroll with her across the well-lit terrace, where
several ladies had retreated for a breath of cool, fresh air, then he
guided her to its edge, a little bit apart from the rest, and fixed her
with a stern eye. "I expect to see you later, Miss Donellan—shall
we say, two hours from now, at our usual meeting place? I realize
that it will be an unconscionable hour for running around in the
night, but I have something of a particular nature to say to you."

She sucked in her breath and raised large eyes to his face. "I
ought to tell you, sir, that I have vowed not to meet you again."
She tried to imagine what he might wish to say and came up with
only one thing, although she knew that any raised expectations
would inevitably be dashed to the ground. Her head ached horridly as she shook it. "Say whatever you will, my lord, I cannot do
what you ask."

"Oh, yes, you can—and will!" he said through gritted teeth.
Lowering his voice somewhat, he continued, "You'll meet me
tonight, my girl, or I'll come up to this house in two hours' time
and break the door down! I don't think you'd enjoy that very
much, or the stir that it would cause, so I shall expect to see you at
the folly."

Rora stared after his retreating figure in offended silence. There
had been an implacable note in his voice, and knowing him as she
did she could not doubt that he would have the audacity to come
up to the house—he was capable of anything! The suspicion that
he was foxed had crossed her mind; his face had been slightly
flushed and his eyes had glittered almost dangerously. But no, that
fear had to be discarded; in the words of Rora's estimable parent,
Briavel was not drunk, but merely had drink taken. That, and the
fact that she had failed him last night, must be the reasons for his
anger.

She was too tired to be very angry herself, and could therefore
be more easily beguiled. She decided that she would go to the
folly, albeit unwillingly, swayed not by his threats but by her wish
to tell him that she would never do so again. Rora returned to the
saloon, where she saw Joan in deep conversation with Peyton.
Watching her cousins wistfully, she found herself wishing desper-

ately that she had a brother of her own, or even better, a sister, to whom she might confide her troubles. But with a half-hearted smile, she reflected that if Briavel proposed to her, those troubles were in a way to being over.

CHAPTER XIV

By the time the two hours had passed, Rora was in a state of exhausted wrath, most of it directed toward Briavel. How dare he order her to meet him, after a long, fatiguing party, and when she had the headache and was thinking only of her bed? She had another reason to be anxious to put a speedy end to her trysting with Briavel; it had resulted from a bedtime conversation with Lady Liscarrol.

Mary had undressed her and was lovingly brushing out the thick hair when her ladyship came to Rora's bedchamber and begged a private word.

"Grandmother, you must be dead on your feet—I know I am," said Rora with a weary smile. "That will be all, Mary, you may go." The servant left the room, and Rora smiled up at the old lady. "Shouldn't you be in bed, ma'am, if you'll forgive me for being so impertinent?"

Lady Liscarrol sank down onto the chaise. "I should be, not that it's any of your business, miss!" She replaced the curtness in her tone with warmth as she said, "There's something I must tell you, Rora, and I'll be brief. But 'tis something you ought to know straightaway."

Twisting about on the dressing stool, Rora turned her green gaze upon her grandparent and waited.

The old lady wrinkled up her brow and began to speak. "In a matter of months you'll attain your majority, and I have formed the intention of altering the trust. In fact, I'm going to set it aside altogether, and in November, Ardara will become yours, part and parcel." A smile broke across her tired, fine-boned face. "With the provision, of course, that you don't rivet yourself to that walking tailor's sign, Hubert Manville!"

Her granddaughter chuckled in amusement. "I must tell you that there's no chance of that, ma'am, but are you quite sure you wish to break the trust? You know I am young to have the full management of Ardara—the very thought overwhelms me!"

"Nonsense, child! You're as sharp as you can stare, and what's more, you love the place. Crosbie is an excellent agent, and he's had the running of the estate for years. Since Liscarrol died, he's looked after everything for me, so you needn't think I'm putting it all on your pretty shoulders. I had thought to wait till you were wed to wind up the trust, but there's no telling when that may be, so your twenty-first birthday is as good a time as any. Tomorrow I shall write to my lawyer to draw up the papers, just in case I suddenly go out of my senses during the next six months, or become otherwise incapacitated. I must also pen a letter to Jasper, too, informing him of my intention. And I do hope that you'll think kindly of this old pensioner, Rora, when you come into your own!"

This brought the young lady to her grandmother's side in a rush. She embraced Lady Liscarrol and gave her a smacking buss on the cheek. "Dearest Grandmother, how could I not? There are no words to thank you—indeed, you leave me bereft of speech altogether!"

"You've nothing to thank me for, lass. This place should be yours even now—but Liscarrol knew I loved Ardara and he couldn't bear to will the place away from me. Now, if you'll excuse me, I'll take these old bones to bed. The last time we had a ball, I had your grandfather at my side to support me; I was missing him prodigiously tonight. Goodnight, my dear." She pressed a withered finger on the crease in her granddaughter's brow. "Get some sleep and that headache will be gone by sunup. If not, we'll have Clodagh make a tisane for you in the morning." She rose and went to the door.

Watching her grandmother's uncharacteristically slow departure, Rora felt a terrible pang of guilt at her own duplicity. She was on the point of a secret meeting with the man whom her ladyship had intended for her other granddaughter, for Joan. And because of Briavel's odious, overbearing manner, Rora dared not fail him again, which her loyalty to her grandmother argued she ought to do.

This astonishing news about the ending of the trust almost completely overshadowed her intended tryst with Briavel, which, if the clock was right, was to take place in little more than half an hour. She toyed with the idea of telling him of her good fortune, but as she struggled into the same long-sleeved cotton dress she had worn at their last midnight meeting, she decided that she ought to wait, to see if he made her an offer before informing him that she would receive her inheritance in six months. Otherwise, she would never know if it was her self or her lands that he desired —if he did so. Who could be sure, with such a man?

After ascertaining that the house was silent at last, she took up the shawl and placed it over her head. Then she slipped quietly into the hallway and down the back stairs just as she had done before. Apparently her grandmother had sent the servants to bed already, for there were some stray wineglasses on the tables, and the saloon had been left in disorder.

Outside it was lighter than it had been two nights before. The moon was on the wane and no longer visible; besides, it was nearly sunrise. Rora's head still ached abominably and she cursed Briavel for making it impossible to refuse him tonight. If he was so misguided as to make her an offer, she would be hard put not to laugh in his face, because at present she could think of nothing worse than going through life chained to a monster of inhumanity. But if his proposal was of another nature—let him give her one of his insinuating glances, and she would take great pleasure in striking him! Her anger was exacerbated by her damp feet; she hadn't thought to put on sturdy shoes, and her slippers were entirely soaked through by the time she reached the folly.

Briavel was dressed as though for a journey and was so absorbed in his examination of his timepiece that he was unaware of her approach until she was almost at his side. "Ah, Miss Donellan," he greeted her, pocketing his watch. "I see that you took me at my word—most wise!"

"Lord Briavel, I wish you will tell me at once whatever you want to say, for I'm not in the mood for conversation this night—rather, this morning," Rora informed him darkly, sitting down upon the top step of the temple.

"Not quite yet," he demurred, taking the place beside her. "Tell me, did you enjoy the ball? Quite an elegant affair, and not unlike the last one I attended here. That was on the occasion of the betrothal party for your mother and my father, of course. I had a much better time at this one, I ought to add!"

"Yes, that is all very well, sir, but please to say your piece and then let me go." Rora turned imploring eyes upon him. "I am so very weary."

"So, too, am I—although I fear it will be many hours before I see a bed."

"It most certainly will *not* be many hours! I shan't remain much longer, sir, because soon the laborers and servants will be stirring. So if you mean to prate of your blighted youth again, you may spare your breath!" Rora had no idea why she was lashing out at him in such a way. She only knew that she'd had little enough sleep in recent evenings, and it was late, and he was smiling down at her in that alarming way of his. Her anger flared into white heat at his expression, for he must believe he could cozen her into quietude. "Be quick now, for I must go!" she said irritably.

"You are looking especially lovely this evening, ah, morning," he remarked as though he had not heard her entreaties. "I thought so earlier when I first saw you tonight. That pretty green gown became you well, as did those butterflies that looked as if they had just landed on your bright head and meant to take off again at any moment. But now you are even more beautiful, with your hair unbound and spilling about your shoulders."

She had forgotten that her hair was undressed. " 'Tis unfair of you, sir, when you promised me you'd not make remarks that might put me to the blush," she pointed out.

"What I meant by my promise was that I would not make any ungentlemanly remarks—I cannot help it if your sensibilities become unduly ruffled by my compliments. So far my words have been well within the bounds of gentlemanly behavior, my dear Miss Donellan, and I refuse to take them back, or apologize."

"I am not your dear Miss Donellan," she interjected rudely, turning her face away. How she wished he would let her go back to the house, to the warmth and comfort of her own bed. He seemed frighteningly close to making advances: no doubt he was on the verge of offering her a *carte blanche,* or some such thing, and she recalled rather belatedly that he was not a gentleman who had any respect or desire for the married state. Rora pulled her shawl tightly around her shoulders as though to shelter herself from the warmth of his burning gaze. She knew herself for a fool and, given half the chance, would tell this leering beast exactly what she thought of him and his libertine ways.

Briavel placed his hand on her arm. "Miss Donellan, I am leaving this place today."

His voice gave her no indication of his feelings and she hardly knew what to say. "Will—will you be gone for a long time?" she managed, hoping that her tone was as neutral as his had been.

"I don't know. Shall you mind?" His arm stole around her, and after pulling her closer to him, he dropped a soft kiss upon the top of her head. When she stiffened, he released his hold immediately. "Excuse me, I am forgetting my promise! I hope you will disregard my presumption, Miss Donellan."

"I'll do my best," she said icily. "Is that all you wished to say— that you are leaving? It hardly seems worth my effort in coming here." She jumped to her feet and moved away from him, now more than ever aware of her unprotected state and her folly in agreeing to meet him. If he truly intended leaving Kilkenny, he might venture anything, and she could be ruined.

Briavel followed her. "Rora!" he growled in exasperation, reaching for her shoulders and pulling her toward him with a grip of iron. He kissed her swiftly on the mouth, almost angrily, then pulled back. Looking down into her frightened face, he amended his tone, saying gently, "My dear, there is much I would like to say, but haven't enough time. Nor have I the right, although that wouldn't weigh with me if I thought—well, never mind that. The reason I asked you here is to beg a promise from you."

Hope surged into her breast, replacing the panic his rough kiss had caused. She whispered, "A promise?"

"Yes, that you will not think badly of me in future, no matter what you hear to my discredit—perhaps as soon as later today. I am sworn to secrecy and am unable to explain fully, but some future day I'll lay all before you, I swear it. Only I beg you not to think the worst."

Rora's mind was frozen with disappointment and she had no idea what he was trying to say to her, except that it was not what she wanted to hear. And she was unable to accept the little that she did understand, the fact of his leaving, probably for good. Any promise not to think badly of him would be quite meaningless; she was already thinking the very worst. Furthermore, she resented the feel of his hands on her body and furiously she flung herself away from him.

"Secrets!" she uttered scathingly. "I might have known! Everyone has secrets here, you, Joan—even Grandmother, I think—and I'm sick to death of them! This, sir, is one secret I'll be keeping to myself no longer: I hate you. I could *never* think any worse of you than I do at this moment, so you may go away tomorrow and do all manner of shocking things, for I swear I care not!" She stood panting with fury, all heaving bosom and flashing eyes.

Never had she looked more magnificent, or been more unapproachable, and Briavel looked up to the fading stars with a deep sigh. "Manville! I might have known, and after I was so forbearing as to refrain from abusing him to you—which I could very well have done—he serves me such a trick." He smiled wryly, recognizing that it would go ill with him if he tried to kiss Rora again. Angry as she was, she looked ready to spit and to sink her claws into his flesh at any moment. With a brief, ironic bow he told her that he hoped he would have the pleasure of conversing with her upon his return to Kilkenny, whenever that might be.

Rora laughed harshly, wishing she might weep instead. "You may hope, sir, but if you ever set foot upon this property again, I'll —I'll have you thrown off it! And what's more, I'll sue you!" She was uncertain of whether or not trespass was sufficient grounds for a lawsuit, but by now she was so enraged that she didn't care one whit.

His lordship was amused; his voice shook perceptibly as he asked by what authority she would have him thrown off Lady Liscarrol's property.

"If you must know," she said haughtily, "Grandmother has just informed me—not an hour ago—that she will wind up the trust on my twenty-first birthday! Come November, Ardara will be mine— mine alone—and you had best remember it before coming back here with your scheming, hoaxing, libertine ways!"

"Oh, I shouldn't think I'll be away so long as that, dear termagant," he remarked cryptically. "I must congratulate you on achieving your inheritance. I'm glad to hear it, if it makes you happy. But will you feel yourself tied to Ireland in the future, my lovely Rora? I pray it won't be so, for to hide such beauty and spirit away from the world—which is to say, my world—would be a sad crime."

"You needn't try to cozen me with your graceless proposals! I know what you have in your disgusting mind, and let me tell you, I will have none of it!"

"If you know what I have in my mind, you are remarkably astute, and what's more, you'd not be ripping up at me in so absurd a fashion. We might be better employed than with this silly quarrel —this is a thorny farewell indeed! Don't look such daggers, I beg you, or you'll put me in a quake." When moved forward to frown down at her, she backed away from him. "No, this is not at all the scene I envisioned, but the hour is advanced and I have little time to prove to you how false are the delusions you cherish about my character. Take comfort from the fact that you may abuse me to your heart's content later this day—when I shall no doubt deserve it better. Goodbye, my dear." He turned on his heel and in a moment had disappeared into the wood beyond.

Rora glared after him, and many more cutting and offensive remarks occurred to her as soon as he was out of sight. She was sorry that they hadn't come to her sooner. She pressed one palm to her aching head and again felt as though she could weep, something she hadn't done in so long she believed she had quite forgotten how. She knew she ought to thank the fates that Briavel hadn't attempted anything more than a kiss tonight. The unwelcome memory of his strong grip on her shoulders caused her to feel hot and uncomfortable, despite the cool breeze. She felt a foolish regret that he was gone, but she shoved this sentiment back into the recesses of her mind as she plunged through the lessening darkness toward the white house. The only thing she could do now was forget all about Briavel, who was unworthy of her notice anyway, and to concentrate upon her future as the mistress of Ardara. The sooner that man was gone from Ireland, the happier she would be. From the moment they had met, she had known him for a thorn in her flesh, and she couldn't believe that she had been so stupid as to expect him to marry her—or even want him to. Doubtless all he had in mind was to whisk her off to London and make her his mistress, with the probable intention of discarding her as he had the many others Hubert Manville had mentioned. As though she, Aurora Donellan, would consent to such an alliance— she would die first! Unwelcome words from Lord Byron's poem came unbidden to her memory: "Few earthly things found favor in his sight, save concubines and carnal companie." Those words aptly described Briavel, she thought savagely, choking on a sob that she refused to allow to escape her. At such a time tears were less than useless; she would not be so weak as to give way to them.

Some minutes later she gained entry to the house through an unlocked library door that opened onto the gardens, and she climbed the back stairs slowly, pulling herself up one step at a time, clutching the bannister rail as though it were a lifeline. By the time she tumbled into bed, her eyes were half closed, and just before falling into the deepest sleep of her life, Briavel's handsome, mocking face swam before her. She ought to be glad he was going away, but deep in the unexplored regions of her sore heart she already missed him.

CHAPTER XV

Much later that morning Rora woke feeling battered and bruised, not in body or limb, but in spirit. She knew a strong desire not to rise from her bed all day, but cowering beneath the bedclothes was not in her usual style. So when Mary came in with her morning chocolate and asked what gown she preferred, Rora answered perfectly naturally, as though this were any other day and her entire life had not been destroyed only hours ago.

"You may lay out my riding habit, Mary. I intend to call at the lodge to see how Tomsy Drennan's cold does, and then Mr. Newburgh and I shall ride out together. Has my grandmother risen yet?"

"That she hasn't, Miss Rora, and no wonder, for 'tis true the dear lady isn't in her first youth any longer. Miss Joan is altogether done up by the party. Sure, and she never moved a muscle when I went to stir her fire this morning. I couldn't bring myself to part the bed curtains for fear of disturbing the poor lass! Shall I tell them to lay your place for breakfast, miss?"

Rora sighed and nodded; best to begin the day as usual, but if she encountered that weasel Hubert Manville across the breakfast table, she'd not be responsible for her words or actions. She knew perfectly well that her troubles could be laid at her own doorstep: falling in love with Briavel had been a serious mistake. But if in this situation she needed a scapegoat, Manville was the perfect one. She disliked him, most particularly because his words about Briavel had been proved to be mostly true. His warnings had once annoyed her, but now the memory of them incensed her. Never again would she allow herself to be so taken in by an artful libertine like Gavin Hargrave!

Within half an hour she was dressed in her riding habit and making an effort to at least appear to enjoy her breakfast of ham, toast, and coffee placed before her in the solitude of the breakfast parlor. Purdon served her silently at first, as though aware of her mood, but he could not continue so. After informing her rather

gloomily that although two wineglasses and a plate had been broken last night, he judged that the ball had been a success.

Shaking his head dolefully he added, " 'Tis a pity we've had so
little entertaining since his lordship passed on, Miss Rora. Last
night was like the old days, when our own Lady Alanna was in the
house. Such a number of parties as there were then, and the balls,
and picnics by the Old Castle—they were so pleasant! And while I
regret the breakages, miss, permit me to say that I hope we've
seen the first of more activity of a social nature."

Rora smiled affectionately up at the butler. "I think you may be
right, Purdon, for I cannot doubt that we'll be having more parties
in future. Only wait till the hunting begins—why, the staff will be
fairly run off their feet!"

He answered her with a bow and the barest flicker of a smile
flitted across his countenance. "I'm very glad to hear it, miss."

After he left the room, Rora stared listlessly into her coffee cup.
Hunting season—why had she even thought of it, much less made
mention of it? Perhaps because Briavel had said he would return,
and before November; she took that to mean he would come back
to Kilkenny and Hargrave House for the cubbing season and the
hunting in the autumn. Why this should both excite and terrify her
she could not be sure. Their last conversation had left her with the
certainty that anything, everything, between them was at an end.
Sadly, this included the special, three-day-old friendship that had
been so real on her side, so false on his. She ought to have trusted
her instincts all those weeks ago, when they had first met at the
folly and he'd looked at her in that horrid, overly familiar fashion;
she had known him then for a rake, and a rake he always would be.
Marriage to such a man, even loving him as foolishly and without
reason as she did, could only make her life a misery, and the wisest
course would be to put him out of her life and her heart. She ought
to be grateful to him; he had made it very simple for her to forget
him, and by now was probably halfway to one of the ports—likely
Waterford—and on his way to England. And if he returned to
Kilkenny, she would run from him as she would have from an
adder—except that there were no longer any snakes in Ireland.
She would forgo hunting in the neighborhood altogether come
autumn, a great sacrifice, but she could take herself off to Dublin to
stay with her father, or perhaps one of Jasper's sisters would have
her to visit.

Her father—there was a comforting thought. She could return

to Dublin now, could be there within the space of two days if she began ordering her journey straightaway. She set down her piece of buttered toast, her pensive expression replaced by one of relief, and formed hasty plans. Lady Liscarrol had Joan to bear her company, so there was really nothing to tie Rora to Ardara if she wished to visit her papa, and after her ride with Peyton she would inform her grandmother of this intention. Then she would post a letter to Jasper telling him to expect her by the end of the week.

By the time she was riding toward the lodge to call upon the Drennans, Rora was feeling more optimistic. There was further cause for elation in that she had only thought of Briavel a dozen times since making up her mind to leave Kilkenny: a vast improvement over the hundred or so times she had thought of him between waking and breakfast. She prided herself on the fact that she was on the way to making a quick recovery from her infatuation with his lordship. One only needed a diversion, she continually reminded herself, and a return to Merrion Square for a short visit would answer perfectly.

Tomsy Drennan's cold had degenerated into little more than sneezes and coughs, and his loving grandparent could do nothing other than keep him still until he was fully recovered. The lad was skilled in plaiting willow baskets, and he proudly displayed his latest masterpiece to Miss, his wide face split by a simple, gleeful smile.

"Drennan is forever afther scolding me for coddling our Tomsy," the gatekeeper's wife informed Rora as she handed the young lady a refreshing glass of milk, her offer of tea having been declined. "But of all our childer or grandchilder, he's the most dear, his infirmity being none of his own fault, and he's the sweetest-tempered of any Drennan I e'er met." The good lady nodded her head several times and continued, "And such goings-on at the Big House last night. 'Twas a great party, sure, for we counted no less than twenty carriages passing through the lodge gates!"

"Yes, 'twas a large gathering," Rora agreed.

"Faith, I was afther bein' reminded of the grand ball his lordship —the old earl—gave for the Lady Alanna on the night of her— well, that same night when she run off with yer father, Miss Rora. We was but new-come to Ardara, having been farmers on one of Lord Liscarrol's other estates till Drennan aged so, and 'twas the first such ball I'd seen at a great house. His lordship, ever a decent man, sent wine 'round to us for the toasting of the couple, but then all of a sudden, all was in an uproar! Ah, well, sure and we opened the bottle the very next day and drank the healths of the bride and groom anyhow, for all that it was Mr. Donellan our lady married and him not bein' the gentleman we'd expected!"

Rora laughed. "How surprised everyone must have been that night! Our ball last evening was less eventful by far!"

After a few more minutes she decided that it was time to take her leave; Peyton would arrive soon for their ride. She mounted Falstaff from the block and was making her goodbyes to Mrs. Drennan when the other lady shaded her eyes and pointed in the direction of Ardara. "Look, miss! There must be a power o' trouble at the Big House, for if it isn't yer own groom riding fit to kill his horse, poor beast! From the look of them, I fear there's apt to be a worry."

Rora saw that Slaney was indeed galloping down the drive at a mad pace for one of his years. "Oh, I hope nothing is amiss—good day, Mrs. Drennan, and thank you for the milk," she said hurriedly. She wheeled her horse around and trotted off to meet the oncoming rider, her face a study in perplexity and concern.

Slaney had difficulty reining in; his horse circled Falstaff before he could bring it under control and shout to his mistress: "Miss Rora, hie yerself to the house—a fearsome thing has happened! There's the divil of an uproar and ye're wanted!"

"Good God—not Grandmother? 'Tis not her ladyship fallen ill?" she asked hoarsely, paling as she uttered the worst of her fears.

"Nay, miss, her ladyship's stout enough, I'm thinking. 'Tis Miss Joan—sure, and she's eloped! Run off with a gentleman and only just found missing! Do come now, Miss Rora," Slaney pleaded, wishing his mistress wouldn't sit there atop her horse like a statue.

But Rora was too shocked to move, for the truth had dawned on her. It had to be the truth: Briavel and Joan! He had been dressed for a journey last night at the folly—for his elopement, undoubtedly, she realized, and he must have spirited Joan away from Ardara not long after he left Rora. She wavered in the saddle and reached blindly for the pommel to steady herself. Oh, what a fool she had been! Briavel had been flirting with her all along only to cover up his affair with Joan—and how her cousin could have been so deceitful, Rora was unable to fathom.

She started Falstaff down the drive and left Slaney choking in her dust, her thoughts moving forward as quickly and surely as the strong animal galloping beneath her. She fervently prayed that Briavel's intention had been to marry Joan. Could it be that Mr. Manville's accusations about that deadful creature's habit of ruining young ladies was true? But Joan was not stupid; surely she wouldn't be taken in by false promises. Then Rora remembered how she herself had been taken in, had gone so far as to fall in love with Briavel and to even meet him alone at midnight on two occasions—it was the sort of behavior she would have scorned in another female. Oh, she ought to have seen the signs: the letter he had given Joan (lying, of course, when he denied having written it), the many whispered conversations between the pair, and most of all, Joan's recent unexplained trips to the rose garden. That must have been their meeting place all the time, and Briavel had lured Rora to the folly merely to screen his other meetings with her cousin.

What was more, only hours ago he had begged her not to think badly of him, had mentioned being sworn to secrecy about something he could not tell her—Joan had made similarly vague remarks yesterday, Rora recalled. But right now the only thing that mattered was hurrying to the house to comfort Lady Liscarrol, who must be prostrated by the discovery of Joan's flight.

Never had the approach to the house seemed so endlessly long, and when Rora drew up before the door, she dismounted so quickly that a waiting stableboy was unable to reach her in time to assist her down from Falstaff. Once they touched the ground, her legs wobbled such that she nearly lost her balance, and her chest felt queerly hollow. Her mind kept shouting that it couldn't possibly be true, and she dreaded learning that it was. Briavel—and her cousin. Were they laughing at her even now, as they traveled together to wherever they were going?

Upon entering the house, she turned a white and beseeching countenance on Purdon, who was mouthing something about the Great Parlor, so she went immediately to that room. Her grandmother was there sitting upright on a sofa, holding a letter and chuckling to herself.

Rora flung her hat and whip onto a marquetry table by the door and rushed toward Lady Liscarrol. "Grandmother! Oh, I'm so glad to see you're well—I was in such a worry!"

"And why should you be?" the old lady asked imperturbably.

"The shock of it!"

"Oh, pooh, child, I was never better in my life. And I must say that seldom have I enjoyed a joke more—but what Brendan will say to all this I can well imagine."

"They—they are married?" Rora asked breathlessly, feeling both relief and a great stab of pain and loss all in the same moment. But Briavel had never thought of her, had never been hers. She must forget all that had passed between them, or else die of this new disappointment.

"Yes—oh, yes! By special license, in Kilkenny, with Gavin and the parson's wife as witnesses, I should think. I can't be certain, though, because Joan wrote this before she left Ardara, and didn't know—"

"Gavin? But I don't understand! Was it not he who—"

"Briavel? Lord, Rora, I ne'er thought you a fool! 'Tis Sir Nicholas Tobin who's eloped with Joan, not but what I'm sure Gavin planned the whole. Joan writes that she can never be grateful enough to him—good God, child, you're not about to faint, are you? I keep no smelling salts at hand, you know, so I wish you won't."

"I *ought* to faint," Rora said with dangerously glittering eyes, "for I'm sure I never in my life had half so great an excuse for it! Are you telling me that Joan has eloped with Sir Nicholas Tobin, a man she's hardly met half a dozen times? And Briavel assisted them?" Rora sank down onto a parlor stool, murmuring more to herself than to her ladyship, "Then that must have been what he meant about not thinking the worse of him."

"Well, I don't know about that, but I do know that my granddaughter is a sly puss if ever there was one. Sir Nicholas is the gentleman she met last autumn, the very one my idiot of a son chased from Newburgh Hall after selling him a string of hunters. Joan could have come to me with this, and I would have supported her, but I imagine she didn't want to involve me in a scheme that would require my taking her side against her father's—not but what I've always done so. I've already sent a messenger to Newburgh Hall, telling Brendan and Peyton to come here at once, so we can expect to see them within the hour. That minx has left it to me to inform her father of the marriage, though of course I'm glad to do so." Rora could easily believe this, for the old black eyes were sparkling with mischief; Lady Liscarrol evidently relished the prospect of telling Sir Brendan of his daughter's elopement.

"You aren't angry with Joan, ma'am?"

"Gracious, no! I'd more than an inkling about her and Tobin, and nothing could please me more. Brendan will go off in an apoplexy —I hope he may do so in my sight! Now, please to run upstairs to change out of that habit and comb your hair, for you look positively demented! But before you go, take your letter from the mantel. The post bag has been brought from town and there's a note for you in Jasper's fist."

Rora rose unsteadily and went to the fine mantelpiece of Kilkenny marble. She took the letter, which had been propped up against a Dresden figure of Columbine. The painted porcelain features looked down at Rora mockingly, as did those of the companion piece, a masked Harlequin. Rora wished she could share the joke they and Lady Liscarrol were so enjoying.

In her bedroom she changed into a sprigged muslin gown and smoothed her curls, obediently but unthinkingly following her grandmother's instructions. She replied in monosyllables to Mary's murmurs of amazement at the elopement, her mind too busy to pay her abigail any heed. After the events of the past six or so hours, Rora felt that if any more shocking news was revealed to her, she would fall to the floor in a screaming fit. The facts had rearranged themselves in her exhausted mind, but despite the new knowledge that Joan was Sir Nicholas's bride, not Gavin Hargrave's, she was sure that all was at an end between the latter and herself. She had told him that she wished never to see him again, and while she was overwhelmingly thankful that he hadn't eloped with her cousin, she could not forgive him for his scheming duplicity—nor his dishonorable intentions toward herself. If he'd ever had a thought of offering for her, he would have done so before going away. That he had made no declaration seemed proof enough that he had been trifling with her all along. The ruthless kiss he'd snatched at parting carried no deeper meaning and had been prompted by a desire to discomfit her. His return to Kilkenny was an empty promise: he had come to Hargrave House only to help his friend, who was Joan's mysterious Englishman of last autumn. Now that he had united the couple, Gavin Hargrave, Viscount Briavel, had likely taken himself back to London and his mistresses, and in due time (perhaps a day or two) he would forget Miss Donellan's existence. He may have already done so.

Rora dismissed the maid and broke the seal on her father's letter, hoping that it would at least divert her attention from the events at hand.

What she read there caused her to abandon all thought of the comfort of a visit to Merrion Square: Jasper Donellan wrote that he had been invited to Londonderry to lecture to a learned society, the subject of his talk to be monastic life in Ireland during the Middle Ages. He would be gone from Dublin a week or more, but hoped to pay his daughter a visit in the country soon after his return. He hoped she was still enjoying herself, and looked forward to hearing all about the ball. In closing, he jokingly asked if all the gentlemen in Kilkenny were at the feet of the fair Rora, or had it been merely a false report?

Her father's playfulness could not cheer her; she sighed regretfully as she set the letter down, only a little heartened by the expectation of his visit to Kilkenny later in the summer. Perhaps by then she would have recovered from all these surprises and heartaches, and would again rejoice in that calm, pleasant life she had enjoyed at Ardara before Briavel had intruded upon it. Two of the persons in whose presence she had been most happy were gone, however. No longer would she and Joan giggle together over Hubert Manville, or share their past histories, nor could she look forward to seeing the heartless Gavin's tall, lean figure striding from the stables toward the house, a smile of warm greeting on his handsome face.

CHAPTER XVI

A little while later, commotion and raised voices below announced to Rora that her uncle and cousin had arrived from Newburgh Hall, and she knew she must go downstairs. It promised to be an ugly scene, for both Lady Liscarrol and her son were possessed of strong tempers. Rora suspected that both she and Peyton would be called upon more than once to restore peace between the combatants, and taking a deep breath, she turned the handle of her door and stepped out into the cool hallway. Had it only been hours ago that she had crept from her room on her way to the folly? It seemed like years since then. In the time that had passed, she had met Briavel in the early morning hours and had repulsed him; Joan had run away and been married to Sir Nicholas Tobin; and Rora had suffered from the unendurable (and erroneous) belief that Briavel had eloped with Joan. All in all, it had been a fatiguing sort of day, and it was not yet even time for luncheon.

Now that all the reasons for Joan's secrecy and apparent intimacy with the Viscount were clear, Rora could easily find it in her heart to excuse her cousin's reticence; she supposed that in the same case, so, too, would she have been reluctant to confide in others. Keeping Sir Brendan in the dark about the return of her Englishman had been Joan's chiefest motive, and this was understandable and forgivable.

Rora decided that the ordeal facing her downstairs might as well be viewed as less of a trial and more of a farce, for heaven knew there was little enough prospect for amusement in her future, with her cousin and Briavel both gone forever. By the time her slippered foot reached the bottom step of the grand staircase, a smile was teasing the corners of her wide mouth and the green eyes were sparkling with anticipation. Her uncle's reaction to the news would certainly be volatile, and no less so than her ladyship's triumph would be self-congratulatory. If only Jasper—or Briavel— were here to share in the joke, for then it would be all the richer.

In the Great Parlor four gentlemen had assembled themselves

in close proximity to the old woman: Mr. Manville, Sir Brendan, Peyton, and a dark-haired fellow whom Rora had no difficulty in recognizing as her eldest cousin, Symon Newburgh.

"Rora, my dear, I'm glad to see the color back in your cheeks," her grandmother approved. With the air of one hostessing a garden party, she said pleasantly, "You recall your cousin Symon, of course, for all it's been a few years since last you saw him. Come and sit by me, child."

On her way to her grandmother's sofa, Rora paused and shook hands with Symon, saying all that was proper and teasing him on his resemblance to Joan. Like his sister, he had a round, serious face, which in Joan was livened by the play of her dimples. His black head of hair was as smooth and neat as his sister's, but nothing in his physiognomy denoted his near relationship to his younger brother Peyton. Symon nodded rather speechlessly at Rora's bantering tone as she continued, "I am to felicitate you, am I not, Cousin? When is the date of *your* wedding?"

"Enough of weddings, Rora!" Lady Liscarrol said sharply, trying to frown down her irrepressible granddaughter. She was relieved to see the girl in such spirits, for half an hour ago the child had looked to be on the verge of collapse. "Symon's marriage is not what I wish to discuss right now." She turned to her son. "Brendan, I want you to prepare yourself for a very great shock." Pausing for effect, she waited a few seconds before saying carefully, "Joan eloped with Sir Nicholas Tobin in the wee hours of the morning, and they were wed earlier today in Kilkenny-town. I've already had a message from the Reverend Mr. Moreton confirming the marriage."

Sir Brendan stared at his parent in utter amazement; the elder of his sons made a strange, choking noise low in his throat, and the younger emitted a gleeful crow. Their father said disparagingly, "Tobin and Joan? Mother, you must be out of your senses! Sir Nicholas Tobin resides in England, and has not set foot in this neighborhood since he was staying at Newburgh Hall last autumn. Are you all about in your head, madam?"

"I hate to contradict you, Brendan, but Sir Nicholas has been installed at Hargrave House with Lord Briavel these six weeks or more. The pair of them are as thick as inkle weavers, and no doubt they'd been hatching their plot all winter. Our Joan is already Lady Tobin, despite your efforts last year to prevent that outcome, and is even now on her way to Dublin with her husband. After their stay there, they intend to travel on to England."

Sir Brendan's rage was beginning to show itself in his florid face and clenched fists. "You can't mean to say that presumptuous Englishman has been sneaking around the district—and has carried off my Joan?" Both this question and the next were thundered at her ladyship, who sat imperturbably calm before the storm of anger being played out in her parlor. "How could you allow such a thing, knowing my feelings as you must?" Pacing the floor, he added, "If you had but told me of Joan's disappearance sooner, I could have ridden after them—they could even now be overtaken—"

"What would be the good of it, Papa?" Peyton asked, a grin splitting his freckled countenance. "They were wed in Kilkenny, so even if you had caught up to them on the Dublin Road—"

"Shut your mouth, young cub!" was his father's blighting response.

Mr. Manville delicately cleared his throat. "If you'll permit me to say so, Sir Brendan, Tobin is a most respected gentleman—in fashionable circles."

As though aware for the first time that an outsider was present, Sir Brendan exploded again, "What is that man-milliner doing here?" He spun around to glare at Manville. "You are not a member of my family, sir, and what's more, you have no right to be here."

Drawing himself up, Manville said, "I may not be a connection of yours at the present time, but I have hopes of soon being—"

Lady Liscarrol broke in upon what threatened to be a *contretemps* of no short duration. "That's enough, Hubert! I warned you that you'd be very much in the way, but you wouldn't listen. Symon, stop goggling like an idiot and tug the bell. I could do with some refreshment, and so, I daresay, could the rest of you!"

"How can you be thinking of food at a time like this?" sputtered her son, but he closed his mouth quickly when a footman came into the parlor to receive her ladyship's instructions.

During the interval before food and drink arrived, Sir Brendan continued to pace the floor, grunting to himself. Symon Newburgh sat in stunned silence, apparently undone by his sister's shocking conduct. Mr. Manville tried in vain to catch Miss Donellan's eye to let her know he didn't consider Miss Newburgh's actions a reflection upon her, but the heiress was engaged in a whispered conver-

sation with Peyton, and he was unable to communicate his sentiments to her.

"You knew all about Joan and Tobin, I'll be bound—you wretch!"
Rora upbraided her cousin in low tones. "I ought never to speak to
you again!"

"Nay, you're too game for that! Besides, I dared not let on that I
knew Tobin, or that I suspected why he was here—we were all at
pains to keep Papa from discovering it, and the fewer people who
knew Sir Nicholas and Joan were acquainted, the easier it would
go for them. At first, even Gran wasn't sure he was the lover,
although I fancy she smoked it out long before this day. And all the
time you were thinking Jo and Briavel the pair! Didn't you ever
wonder why Tobin disappeared at Race Week? He had to leave the
neighborhood lest Papa learn of his presence here, and poor Nicholas was racking up at the Staff and Serpent in Ballyfore this long
while. Jo told me last night that he'd been back at Hargrave House
the past few days, hanging about and creeping around in the roses
at odd hours to speak to her—I never thought her such a romantic!
And to elope! I must say, that's a surprise; sure, and what a lark for
the three of them. Briavel was in the secret, you know. He's a great
gun."

The servants brought in a bottle of wine and some glasses, and
one footman carried a tray of food. Some time was spent in drawing up tables and distributing plates, and Rora had to admire her
grandmother's strategy in introducing a diversion, which she recognized as having been a masterly tactic. Lady Liscarrol dismissed
the servants and bade Peyton pour out the libation.

"We must toast the new-married couple," she said imperiously,
with a wicked glance at Sir Brendan's flushed face, as though she
dared him to gainsay her. "Joan has done well for herself. Faith, I
never thought *she'd* be the granddaughter to elope: 'tis in Rora's
blood, after all, for Alanna did it and so did Liscarrol's sister!"

"I cannot believe that Cousin Rora would ever do anything of a
clandestine nature, Aunt Hester," was Mr. Manville's comment.

"What do you know of her?" Peyton asked rudely. "Anyway,
your own mother eloped, so you oughtn't to cast stones!"

"Now, now, Hubert merely considers our Rora a pattern card of
respectability," her ladyship soothed her flame-haired grandson.
"No doubt he'd have said the same thing of Joan—yesterday!"
Then she turned abruptly to her son and said with some severity,
"You must accept the match your daughter has achieved,

Brendan, and you have only yourself to blame for the secrecy in which it was undertaken. I'm sure that between the two of us we can concoct an explanation for the privacy of her nuptials, one that will satisfy Symon's starchy future in-laws. In this district the true circumstances are already known, and the tale will spread before the cat has time to lick her ear, but none of our neighbors will think it anything other than another example of family eccentricity. The scandal will die down quickly, as did the ones about Hubert's mother and my own Alanna. But the Fitzgibbons, now, might look askance on a runaway match. Things will go better for you, Brendan, and for Symon, if you accept this marriage at the outset. Do you not agree, Symon? Your knowledge of the Fitzgibbons must be superior to mine, for you have been visiting them so recently."

Symon gulped and nodded. "They will be very shocked," he managed, with a pleading look directed toward his father. "So will Caroline."

"Humph," Sir Brendan replied succinctly, twirling the braided stem of his wineglass in one hand.

Rora hastened to add her entreaty to the rest. "Oh, Uncle Brendan, 'twould hurt Joan so if you failed to accept her marriage. I cannot understand why you considered Sir Nicholas unsuitable in the first place."

"Nor do I," said her grandmother tartly. "And if I had known that it was Sarah Tobin's grandson to whom you objected so strenuously, I'd have stepped in last autumn and championed Joan and her suitor. As it turned out, it did my old heart good to see these young people weaving rings 'round you with their plots and plans, Brendan. Your daughter's been secretly betrothed to Sir Nicholas since October; 'twas the first thing she wrote in her letter. Naturally I had guessed that Gavin's friend was the Englishman, and that's the reason I invited Joan to Ardara in the first place!"

All of the company stared at her, with the exception of Mr. Manville, who had little understanding or interest in the intricacies of the situation.

Peyton broke the silence. "Oh, Gran—you Trojan!"

"She's a schemer—I always said so," Rora added. "How you can sleep nights is beyond me, Grandmother!"

"Aunt Hester, it was certainly ill advised of you to countenance this secret betrothal," Manville said, frowning with distaste. "You ought to have warned Miss Newburgh's parent."

"Stuff! And I don't need you preaching propriety at me, Hubert Manville! This is Ireland, not England, and your fine notions don't serve here. My granddaughter is happy and that's my only consideration. Brendan can hire a housekeeper to look after him if he wishes, and if he's wise, he'll tell the Fitzgibbons that he made the match himself!"

By the time Sir Brendan and his sons departed, he had more or less agreed to this. When his mother wisely told him the extent of Sir Nicholas's fortune and property, he was considerably cheered, and said that as soon as he had Joan's direction, he would write to her.

Peyton drew Rora aside before leaving. "I'm powerfully sorry about the ride, Cousin, but I wouldn't have missed this for the world, would you? And Jo would have liked it beyond anything, I'll be bound! 'Tis a marvel how Gran manages our father—he's all blustering and blowing one minute, and yet she can twist him 'round her finger whenever she sets her mind to it. Well, I must return to the hall with him and my brother, but perhaps we can have that ramble tomorrow."

"You may count upon it," Rora agreed, holding out her hand to her cousin. "Only, you mustn't plague your papa, Peyton, if he seems a bit angry after this. He's suffered a shock today—and a disappointment—and 'twill likely take some time for him to accept the fact that Joan won't be returning to the hall." She waved him down the front steps and watched as the three horsemen disappeared down the drive. She was sorry to see her cousin go; he was her only friend now that Joan had left and Briavel too, not that he had been a true friend. And it did no good to think of him, halfway to London as he must be by now. She must rely upon her grandmother for company, and Peyton would not be a stranger, and soon, perhaps, Hubert Manville would leave them, and Rora could be as happy as she had been before she met that fiend Briavel.

When she returned to the Great Parlor, she discovered that Lady Liscarrol had left it, but Mr. Manville was still there, tossing back a full glass of her ladyship's excellent vintage. Rora must have startled him, for the gentleman choked and flushed; then he came forward to meet her. He led her to the sofa with an expression of discomfort on his face, and said that he had something of an important nature to discuss. She hardly knew whether to be thankful or alarmed; he had evidently bolstered his courage with the Liscarrol wine and was about to make his offer for her hand.

"My dear cousin, I know that you must be greatly overset by Miss Newburgh's shocking flight from this house," he said by way of preamble. "And while I hesitate to excite you further, there is a most particular question I feel I must ask you at this time—"

"On the contrary, Cousin Hubert, I am not at all overset," Rora interrupted him, barely controlling her desire to giggle at the caressing manner he had assumed. "I couldn't be happier about Joan's marriage, and how could I be shocked? You must not know me very well to think that, for my own parents made a runaway match, you ought to recall."

"Yes, as did mine—we have that in common! But although it would be most improper in me to disparage the characters of our parents, Cousin, I must say that their example is not one that should be followed: I know you will agree with me on that score."

"Should I do so?" Rora asked, cocking her head at him. "I fancy that there might be a gentleman, somewhere, who could induce me to run off with him." She narrowed her eyes, thinking of Briavel; she had been enough in love with him to have eloped with him, provided that it had been marriage he offered, and not another sort of relationship. "I fear I am not as respectable as you think me, Cousin Hubert," she informed him apologetically.

"You are funning—well do I know your lively sense of humor. It is one of the things that first awoke in me that—what I mean to say is, I knew within hours of making your acquaintance that you must be the gayest, cleverest, most beautiful lady in all of Ireland! A veritable prize, in fact!" Manville added, warming to his theme.

"'Tis kind of you to say so," she murmured, and waited patiently for his next words. Any attempt to forestall them would be useless. Not only was she resigned to hearing him out, she rather looked forward to it now.

She was not disappointed. "Dearest Cousin—I ought to say, dearest Rora!—would you do me the honor of exchanging our cousinship for a tie much nearer, more sublime? Would you consent to become my wife? For it cannot have escaped your notice that as the week has progressed, so, too, has my ardor, to the extent that I can scarcely conceal it any longer!" Mr. Manville dropped to his knees; they creaked audibly. He reached for Rora's hand, bringing it to his chest or, as she surmised, near the region where one presumed his heart to be. "Say you will marry me! It would make me the happiest man on earth!"

His was not the first proposal Rora had ever received, although this was certainly one of the most passionate. It had dawned upon her long ago that the more regard a gentleman had for a female, the more sensible he was likely to be in tendering his offer. That Manville was anxious to marry her, she was aware, but that it was due to an ardor so strong that it was impossible to conceal, she strongly doubted.

Pulling her hand away gently, she shook her head. "I'm sorry, Cousin Hubert, but I fear that we shouldn't suit at all. You would be wishing me at the devil within hours of the engagement, for you would be marrying me with expectations greater than I could ever fulfill."

"Never! You are an angel!"

"If you wish—but I think I ought to warn you that I must be considered a most ineligible bride: I have no money of my own, sir —not a penny to bless myself with, save my allowance from Papa. I live on his bounty and that of my grandmother, you see." This was perfectly true, she told herself in excuse. She wasn't lying to him, and however much she took a perverse pleasure in revealing her situation, she could not tell an untruth.

Manville was gazing up at her, a sickening expression of adoration on his face. "How can you think that your prospects would weigh with me, dearest Rora? And besides, this lovely estate—all of Ardara—will be yours one day!"

"Alas, who knows when that will be?" Rora wondered aloud, assuming an air of great concern. "Under the terms of my grandfather's will, Ardara remains in trust for me until such time as my grandmother—oh, I cannot bear to say it! During her lifetime," she amended primly, fluttering her lashes downward. Well, that was no lie, either. Lady Liscarrol had probably not yet had the opportunity to write to her lawyer, and Rora chose not to believe her grandmother's intentions to set aside the trust as fulfilled until that letter had been posted.

"You—you mean to say that you do not receive your inheritance upon attaining your majority?" Manville asked, bringing himself to his feet jerkily, and Rora realized that it was the most direct speech that he had ever addressed to her. She shook her head and he stared back at her, perplexed. "But I thought—only tell me, your twenty-first birthday is in November, is it not?"

"Yes, but what does that signify? Grandmother is only sixty-five," Rora said in a tone that implied sixty-five to be no great age. "She might live many years more—indeed, I hope she will. Her papa, you know, lived to be eighty!"

This news did not seem to please Mr. Manville, although he said he was glad to hear it. "You have no fortune of your own. No dowry? Forgive me for being so personal, but I have some right—"

"Every right!" Rora agreed warmly, smiling at him. "But that is something you must discuss with Papa. I expect he is prepared to settle a thousand or so pounds of his private fortune on me—unless, of course, he decides to increase his stables this year. I will certainly understand if you wish to withdraw your very flattering offer, Cousin, although I would be aggrieved. Still, as I said, we should not suit, and you see now how very right I am!"

Manville glared back at her, for she seemed to be quizzing him, as well as implying that he required money. "I see what it is!" he cried suddenly. "You think to have Briavel, don't you? Well, let me tell you, ma'am, he has no thought of marriage—to you or any other female with whom he has flirted. You mustn't pride yourself on having received his attentions!"

"I don't," she replied grimly. "But come, sir, there is no need to abuse him. I have been informed lately that 'tis the height of bad form for one gentleman to slander another in the presence of a female, or some such thing. His lordship did not serve you such an ill turn, and I have heard that there are much worse things he could have said of you than you have so readily told me of him!" She stood up and faced the gentleman squarely. "If you don't choose to take my word for it that I've no money, you may ask my grandmother. True, such an inquiry might anger her, and we all know what a Tartar she can be when in a passion, but that's your business, Cousin. Now, if you'll excuse me, I should see to some household matters—I must earn my keep here at Ardara! I trust we'll not see one another till dinnertime, and will bid you good afternoon."

She took herself off to the laundry, where she had nothing particular to attend to, but where she was tolerably certain that the head laundress would enter into a harangue about the failings of her staff. After an hour spent in hiding, Rora crept upstairs to her grandmother's sitting room, dreading to come upon Manville along the way. She only hoped he was as reluctant to see her as she would be to see him.

"So, I am blessed with two clever granddaughters!" was Lady Liscarrol's comment when she admitted Rora into her room, not even bothering to lift her eyes from the embroidery in her lap. "However did you contrive to be rid of Hubert so quickly? He says he made you an offer and you refused him, but what is there in that to send him to his room to pack his bags, I'd like to know?"

Noting from the twinkle in the black eyes that her grandmother was in a mellow mood, Rora gave a merry laugh and sank onto a footstool. "Well, I told him Ardara could not be mine during your lifetime—it wasn't a whisker, exactly, for the lawyer hasn't even been told you intend to break the trust, much less had time to draw up the necessary papers. That was enough to scare him off, especially when I added that I've no money of my own other than the allowance Papa gives me. I shall be well served if Cousin Hubert departs thinking me monstrously ill used by my relations!"

"Nay, I'm convinced he's no thought to spare for any but himself, because never in all my years did I meet such an encroaching, selfish toad of a fellow! I admit, I hoped for better. His mother was a sweet creature when I knew her, but I daresay she doted on him overmuch, which can be enough to make any child self-centered. Just so did your dear grandfather spoil our Alanna, though she grew out of it in time, and Jasper improved her out of all recognition. Were it not for your papa's influence, you'd be just as bad. Remember that, Rora, when you're a mother—do not be too indulgent!"

"I fear I may never be one, as I have just whistled my only prospect down the wind," Rora pointed out, with forced cheerfulness. "So Cousin Hubert is leaving us already? Dear me, I hope it won't be an awkward sort of dinner this evening. Ought I to come down?"

"Foolish girl—oh, you jest, do you? No need to worry about awkwardness—we have too much scandal to discuss, what with Joan's elopement. Hubert dotes on gossip, you know. Sure, and he can hardly wait to get back to England and spread his tales of all us Irish savages. Provided that he can make it past his front door to his club without being dunned to death, which I fancy he will be upon his return. Gavin hinted that Hubert is deep in debt and a gamester besides, and we've enough to deal with here without one of them around! I count myself kind in giving my nephew a pleasant, rural holiday before he finds himself ruined. Bail him out of his difficulties I will not do—if he needs assistance, let him go to his father's people! Gavin says they are an odious lot, and after meeting Hubert, I think it likely, do not you?"

Rora agreed absently, wishing that her grandmother hadn't mentioned Briavel's name quite so often. Her attempt to appear unconscious of it required too much of an effort not to be obvious. But although Lady Liscarrol peered sharply at the younger woman, she held her tongue. The look on Rora's face was enough to confirm her suspicions that her favorite grandchild was not at all indifferent to the viscount. But just as she had trusted Joan to take care of her own affairs, so must she trust that Rora would do the same. And whether or not the girl had conceived a *tendre* for Briavel, her ladyship knew it mattered not one bit unless Gavin felt similarly, and he was certainly too difficult to fathom for her to assume he did so. Who would have imagined that he would embroil himself in planning and assisting in his friend's elopement? After meeting Rora, he hadn't seemed displeased with her, and he had even gone so far as to favor her with his attentions, but he hadn't come forward with an offer either. Lady Liscarrol had made the opening moves and had set all the pawns in their places; in Joan's case the outcome had been just as she had hoped and expected. But Rora was Alanna's child, and the dearest of all her children or grandchildren, and looking at that lovely, thoughtful face, she prayed that she hadn't made a mistake in bringing the girl into Briavel's way. For who was to know if he would even remember her once he returned to England and the busy social season? Anyone so courted and highly sought, as her London sources indicated he was, might well regard dalliance with pretty Miss Donellan in the light of a pleasant flirtation only, and no more meaningful than any other he had enjoyed during his checkered past. And there was his father, to consider, for the Earl of Rothmore was unlikely to approve a match between his heir and the daughter of the very girl that had jilted him so cruelly. Her ladyship began to fear that for once she had mislaid her plans, but she expected that Rora would quickly recover; the girl was too lively in spirit to pine away, too proud to wallow in grief. She hoped that the child had also been too wise to let her heart be touched more than a little by that handsome young devil.

CHAPTER XVII

In the days following Hubert Manville's departure, life at Ardara Castle was calm and uneventful. It seemed particularly true after the abrupt cessation of activity surrounding Race Week. The ball, too, was past, and the excitement attendant upon Joan's elopement soon subsided. At first Rora reveled in the peace of her days, but soon she learned that it was accompanied by an all too busy mind, and she sought refuge from disturbing thoughts by turning to books and local society. By day she occupied herself with country visits and long rides with Peyton, and by night she read aloud to her grandmother from an interesting new novel, *Sense and Sensibility.*

The neighborhood interest in Joan Newburgh's runaway marriage was intense in the early days after it took place, but it blew over within a week, as Lady Liscarrol had prophesied, to be entirely eclipsed by the political news from England. The Prime Minister, Spencer Perceval, had been shot down in the lobby of the House of Commons. Rora's grandmother had the news from one of her London correspondents only a week after the fact, and a Tory precedence was anticipated by those in government circles.

Although Rora would not allow herself to pine for Briavel, who truly seemed lost to her, she wondered how he had received the news. She knew that he was occasionally active in political affairs, as was his father, who was reputed to have strong Tory sympathies. She found herself thinking of Briavel entirely too often, in fact, despite her desire to do otherwise. Her grandmother never mentioned his name in her presence, and had Rora not possessed the memories of conversations, dances, and meetings at the folly, she could almost have believed that he'd never been in Ireland at all. She knew beyond all doubt that he had come to Kilkenny for the sole purpose of helping Sir Nicholas and Joan. An admirable motive, to be sure, but now that the marriage was an accomplished thing, Briavel could have no intention of returning to Hargrave

House. Even his housekeeper was unsure of whether or not to keep the place in readiness for her master, as Rora learned from Mrs. Drennan at the keeper's lodge, for that good lady was a bosom-bow of Mrs. Cleary's.

As the days passed, Rora found it harder and harder to live with her disappointment, and she was surprised at how deeply her feelings had been touched. She had never had any serious hopes that Briavel would marry her, and the foolish ones that had persisted had been utterly groundless—she knew that now. But at times she would recall his expression and his anger the day she had been trapped at the folly by the rain; she had been so sure of him then, and so many other times. Even worse, she found herself missing him, and to compensate for this feeling of deprivation, she began to save up the incidents and occurrences of her days, little things to tell him that she believed he might find as amusing as she did. Not that she would ever be able to tell him of them, but she had to take her comfort where she could find it.

She missed Joan's company within the walls of Ardara, but Peyton had ever been her companion on horseback, and with him she spent every sunny day in the saddle. Spring was at the height of its flowering, and Rora's happier hours were experienced while roaming the countryside with her cousin, galloping across meadows and down lanes, jumping their horses over walls so overgrown with honeysuckle that the stones were hardly visible beneath the vines. At Ardara the rhododendrons bloomed profusely in shades of red and purple, and Rora took pleasure in strolling the flower gardens and the orchards, where the cherry trees spread their white-covered branches over her head. Yes, at times she could even imagine herself not entirely unhappy.

"We had a letter from Joan yesterday," Peyton informed her one day as they walked their mounts through a quiet hamlet on their way home from Clomantagh, where they'd visited Kilcolley Abbey. "She and Nicholas were about to make the crossing to England; he's anxious to make her known to his mother and sisters. Seems he has a lot of relations—the newly married couple will be making a progress the length and breadth of England! Jo says to tell you she'll be writing to you as soon as ever she may."

" 'Tis glad I'd be to have a letter from her. She seems happy?"

"Can you doubt it? I'm happy myself—Papa's calmed down a wee bit; he blusters about the elopement only twice a day now, instead of half a dozen times, so he must be getting used to it. He don't fancy Jo's living across the water above half, but a lass must follow her husband, and well he knows it."

"True," Rora agreed, her eyes fixed on the space between the points of Prince Hal's white ears. Perhaps she should be thankful that Briavel hadn't wished to marry her, because now she would never feel torn between Ireland and England, as Joan might be. But no, Joan was too sensible and too prosaic to feel homesick, and her loyalty was all for Sir Nicholas, as it had ever been. Joan never knew uncertainty: she was all decision and resolution, and Rora had always envied her that. Still, had Briavel shown himself willing to marry, she supposed she'd have been happy anywhere, as long as she was at his side.

"Papa's still hopeful I'll be marrying you one of these days, Cousin—even after Gran wrote him that she wouldn't countenance the match. Can you believe it?"

Knowing her Uncle Brendan, Rora said that she certainly could believe it. "Poor Peyton, couldn't you develop a *tendre* for some other female, so your father will stop plaguing your life? You must be so tired of hearing my name mentioned and my fortune praised that 'tis a wonder you can bear to be in my company so often!"

Peyton threw back his red head and laughed heartily at this, but adjured his cousin not to be a pea-goose. "You're the best fellow I know, Rora, 'tis a fact! Marcus Whitney can spend his time writing verses to your moss-green eyes, but I'd liefer have you for a friend than a—a goddess."

"Oh, dear, don't tell me he thinks so!"

"Aye, but his cousin Molly is coming for a visit next month, and he was acting the same way about her last summer, so—" His voice trailed off meaningfully. "A little dark beauty, Molly."

"Then I must hope that his affection reanimates toward her. Thank you for warning me that I'm about to lose a third suitor—Manville's and Briavel's defections were bad enough!" The words were said before Rora had a chance to think them through, or to realize their implications.

Peyton was regarding her in surprise, but he quickly averted his freckled face and appeared to be more interested in a bog across the road, over which a flock of birds hovered. In a moment he turned his head her way again. "I say, Rora, you aren't nursing a—a broken heart or anything of that nature, are you? That is, I don't mean to pry, but if you're thinking that Briavel wasn't—didn't—"

"Oh, Peyton!" Rora was unsure of whether to be vexed or

touched by his concern. "You know that all the time he was in the neighborhood, I thought him to be fixing his interest with your sister."

"You're a fool, then, Rora Donellan! Even Papa noticed, at the races, that Briavel was making up to you, as he called it, and in a rare rage it put him, wanting his lordship for Joan and you for me as he did."

"Well, Uncle Brendan was mistaken," she said coolly, "as has been proved by Briavel's continued absence from these parts. Do let us change the subject. This talk of my supposed conquests begins to bore me!"

He accepted this in good part and was happy to talk of horses for the rest of the ride, until they came to Briavel's acres. The shortcut to Ardara Castle required that the cousins cross Hargrave land and they did so without compunction. As Prince Hal's hooves flew neatly over the grass that belonged to Briavel, Rora thought ironically that her trespass on his property was so slight a one, and would go undetected; it was almost as nothing when compared to his more considerable trespass upon her heart. She and Peyton raced through a meadow and into the wood, coming out at the folly, now a painful sight, so much so that she hadn't visited it once since her final meeting with Briavel. She had avoided the place altogether, foolishly fearing to find some sign of her false lover's presence there—the imprint of his boot, perhaps, or a stray thread from his clothing.

When the two ladies of Ardara sat together after dinner that evening, Lady Liscarrol asked her granddaughter if she was ready to continue reading the history of Marianne and Elinor Dashwood.

She had interrupted a pensive reverie, not unusual these days. "Yes, of course," Rora answered, going to the sofa table whereupon the volume lay. There she spied several letters received in the post that day, and attempting an unconcern she was far from feeling, she asked her grandmother if she had received any interesting news.

"Quite a bit. Here, take your teacup before you sit down," Lady Liscarrol replied, handing Rora the delicate bit of porcelain. Pouring out her own cup, she went on, "Louisa Conolly wrote; she wishes us to purchase some chip-straw hats from her working girls at Cellbridge. Oh, and I had a letter from England—Lady Bessborough, my dear. Poor Harriet! So many sorrows for her lately! There has been Georgiana Devonshire's death—they were the most charming pair of sisters imaginable; none could rival the Spencer girls in their heyday. The Duke of Devonshire's passing last summer was sad too, and only two years after marrying his mistress, Lady Elizabeth Foster—she's Irish, you know—an old flirt of Liscarrol's. And now Harriet, who's ever down pin, just like dear Georgiana was, informs me that her daughter Caro Lamb is taking the *ton* by the ears with this poet fellow,—what's his name—"

"Lord Byron," Rora supplied, lifting her cup to her lips.

"Yes. The whole family is after Lady Caroline night and day to give him up. Lady Melbourne, William Lamb's mother—a dreadful creature—wishes Caro to leave England altogether. Harriet hopes to induce her daughter to come to Ireland, and I hope she may succeed, for to have them at Bessborough would be delightful, although the circumstances requiring the visit are distressing. It would be a rare treat to see the Ponsonbys and the Cavendishes again. Why, poor, deaf Hart is the duke now, and Lismore Castle, his property, is in Waterford—only a county away. If his aunt and favorite cousin are to be in Ireland, he might take it into his head to come, too—he's the finest match in England, excluding the royal brothers. Have you an ambition to be a duchess, child?" Lady Liscarrol asked with a smile.

Rora's eyes lowered to gaze upon the carpet, their expression hidden. "No, I have no such ambition, Grandmother." Her only plan was to go on as usual, to try to forget one recent ambition that was now hopeless.

" 'Tis just as well, for I don't fancy your wedding into that family. Oh, the scandals and the debts poor Georgiana incurred! But that's all ancient history, my dear, and I shan't be boring on about it."

"Was there any other news from England?" Rora asked, opening the book to the place where she had left off the previous evening.

"Why, yes, from another Irish friend: Emily Castlereagh wrote to tell me about the politics, but other than mentioning that the Tories are in the ascendant and Lord Liverpool is to be Minister, she says little that would interest you."

Rora concealed her disappointment by plunging into the novel, but even as she read aloud, some part of her mind was wondering when she would ever hear news of Briavel. Lady Liscarrol was tied to nearly all the hostesses of the *ton* by blood or marriage, and Briavel moved in those circles. Rora was suspicious that her grandmother might be shielding her from unpleasant news. Perhaps his lordship had already embarked upon a new flirtation or had set up a new mistress, and the older lady was trying to keep that fact from her. To know the truth would be preferable to senseless imaginings, yet Rora couldn't bear to raise the subject, and she was thankful that the Court news which filtered into Kilkenny was sketchy at best. Even in Dublin, where the London papers circulated, the gossip about Briavel that she both longed for and dreaded would be hard to come by.

When Peyton invited Rora to go trout fishing with him later in the week, she agreed to it halfheartedly, not much caring what she did. The oppressive heat of the day had engendered a lassitude that was difficult to shake off, but angling for brown trout beneath the cool shade of trees sounded more agreeable than any of her other prospects for the day. She returned from that excursion late in the afternoon, feeling wretched and rather cross, for Peyton had invited her to travel to Cork for Symon's nuptials in the Newburghs' company. The thought of attending a wedding just now was irksome enough, but to do so with her Uncle Brendan would be worse; she couldn't decide in what terms to couch her refusal, but she knew that she must do so. She regretted disappointing Peyton, but felt no desire to oblige him at her own expense.

Upon arriving back at Ardara, she sought refuge from her troubles in the library, but found Lady Liscarrol there before her.

"Come in, my girl, and tell me about your day," her ladyship invited. "Is Peyton with you? Did you fish the waters clean?"

"Hardly that," Rora answered, dropping to the floor to stroke the silky ears of the spaniel bitch resting at her grandmother's feet. "Peyton had better luck than I, carrying four trout back to the hall. I left my paltry pair at the lodge with Mrs. Drennan, not wishing to reveal my sorry showing to anyone within the gates of Ardara." She went on to tell her ladyship about the Newburghs' invitation and her own wish to decline it, and found the older woman in perfect sympathy with her.

"It wouldn't do at all, Rora, to go jolting your way to Cork in Brendan's company. You and Peyton would be hounded to death to wed one another, and besides, the Fitzgibbons sound like a horridly dull set of people. You'd be worse off than you are here."

"No, no, ma'am, how can you say that? I am perfectly happy here." At the basilisk stare from the wise old eyes, she amended,

"Oh, very well, I am a trifle *ennuyée*, but nothing to signify. No doubt it is the heat."

"No doubt," her ladyship agreed dryly. "I have a little news that might brighten your spirits, though—it certainly has mine, I don't hesitate to tell you. But enough preamble: Gavin has returned to Hargrave House, and with yet another visitor, if you can believe it!"

Rora was speechless, but she sat stiffly and ceased petting the somnolent spaniel.

Lady Liscarrol smiled at this reaction. "Yes, I was surprised, too, for all I knew he'd be back in time. He left a good deal of unfinished business; that must account for his return, don't you think?"

"I expect he did," Miss Donellan agreed hollowly. "How—how long has Lord Briavel been here?"

"He arrived last night. Mind you, I've not had a word from him; Clodagh heard it from the undergroom, who saw the carriage pass through Kilkenny last night—the groom happened to be at Kyteler's Inn when it passed by and he recognized the crest on the panel."

Rora could hardly swallow the rest of her tea, she was in such a state of excitement. All of her former lethargy had vanished, to be replaced by a breathless anxiety that was almost as difficult to bear. If Lady Liscarrol noticed this, she said nothing. Nevertheless, there was a pleased expression in the depths of her bright black eyes; they reflected the hope that had sprung into those of her granddaughter.

Mary, unaccustomed as she was to her mistress's recent fleeting and changeable moods, was even more surprised by Rora's sudden insistence to have three of her most becoming gowns freshened and pressed. Before finally retiring that evening, the young lady had been in a fever of activity, jumping up and down from her chair as though uncertain of whether she wished to stand or sit. After dinner, when her grandmother desired her to play the pianoforte, Rora could barely slow her fingers; as they rapidly crossed the keyboard, they moved apace with the frantic beating of her heart, till at last she had to close the instrument with apology and suggest that she take up *Sense and Sensibility* instead. But as she read of the troubles of the Dashwood sisters, the flow of words had to be checked with as much difficulty as had the notes of her sonata, and more than once Lady Liscarrol had to beg her granddaughter to reread a sentence, since it had emerged as such a jumble.

The next evening Rora was able to sit still, complete a sonata, and read through a paragraph perfectly intelligibly. There had still been no word from Hargrave House, nor had anyone called at Ardara. Rora had stayed home all the day long, attired in various of her freshly pressed gowns, not even venturing out on horseback, so certain had she been that Briavel would put in an appearance. She intended to do the same on the morrow, but her optimism was beginning to wear thin, and it threatened to be overcome by a growing sense of ill usage. Her hope that Briavel had returned for the purpose of making a proposal of marriage was dimming with every passing hour.

A new problem faced her, that of how to greet him when finally he did call, which he must surely do sooner or later, although clearly it would be done as a courtesy to the Countess of Liscarrol, and not from any particular desire to see her granddaughter. Reproaches for his insensitive behavior and his unkindness in leading her on came to Rora's mind, before she ultimately decided to adopt a cool civility toward him, and a frigid politeness. It would be as though nothing had ever passed between them. And if Briavel was so misguided as to suggest another midnight meeting, he would quickly learn that he could no longer take her acquiescence for granted. She was tired of being made to act the fool over him, and she wished she could inform him of the fact without losing any of the dignity which she was determined to preserve when—if—he came to her.

CHAPTER XVIII

In the morning Lady Liscarrol announced her intention of visiting a tenant who had succumbed to an internal ailment; she felt it her duty to call upon the invalid and to carry some calf's-foot jelly and a restorative cordial. Rora promptly offered to accompany her grandmother, masking her reluctance to go so far afield, but the old lady replied, with some asperity, that she was still the mistress of Ardara and as such could be trusted to look after the ills of those under her care.

Chastened by this retort, Rora uttered a disjointed apology, saying that she'd had no notion of offending.

"Never mind, child, you did no such thing. I confess I slept ill last night, and it's put me in bad skin, so you must forgive me my crotchets. 'Tis a sad fact that I'm becoming a crusty old woman! You remain here, Rora. Crosbie is coming to give me some reports, and 'twould be just as well did you receive him in my stead."

Rora's meeting with the agent was brief. Mr. Crosbie's reports were satisfactory, and she gave him the necessary orders about the matter of the thatching of a tenant's roof: if the man was unable to complete the job himself, then some of the estate laborers might be sent to assist him. She told the agent to do what he and the chief shepherd thought best about choosing the day for the start of sheep shearing and the village fair to be held in the summer.

After the interview, Rora sat in the estate room for some minutes more, gazing bleakly at the many ledgers that lined the bookshelves. Running Ardara was a difficult enough task as long as she had her grandmother at hand, as well as Crosbie to take control of matters beyond her ken. But both were elderly, and if something happened to one or the other of them, Rora would be cast adrift in a sea of uncertainty. She might well need a hand in the administration of her inheritance, as she realized for the first time how very young she was to gain control of her birthright. She was only just beginning to be conversant with estate matters, but the fact was that she was city-bred and until lately her exposure to Ardara had been minimal. She had no doubt of her ability to learn, but did she really want to devote her life to nothing but the running of her property? Neither could she bear to be an absentee landholder, turning the estate over to a middleman while she continued on with her father in the Dublin life she had already left behind. And suppose some question of grave importance cropped up—it would be nice to discuss the problem with a head more experienced and better trained than hers, one accustomed to running several establishments at once. Someone like Briavel would manage Ardara to admiration.

After straightening the papers and closing her ledger, Rora left the room, so preoccupied with her concerns about the estate and how to go about replacing Crosbie when he grew too old to continue in his work that she neglected to change into one of her fetching dresses, or even to put on a hat before wandering onto the terrace. She crossed the lawn toward the formal gardens, where she strolled aimlessly between the tall hedges, finding relief from the warmth of the day but not from her tortured ruminations. Coming to the bench where she and Briavel had once discussed the topic of matrimony, she sat down to admire the flowering borders along the path.

At the unexpected sound of footsteps on the walk, she lifted her head to see who was coming. It was not one of the gardeners, as she had at first supposed, but a strange gentleman, and she rose to meet him. His figure was unfamiliar, tall and spare. His gray hair and the stick he carried for reasons of necessity rather than fashion suggested that he was older than he looked from a distance. She rose and stood there, quite perplexed, as he approached her in his strange, limping gait, and she dropped a quick curtsy when he reached her.

"You must excuse me for breaking in upon your reverie, ma'am," the elderly gentleman said in a pleasant voice. "They told me at the house that you had come this way, and I was anxious to speak to you, if you are indeed Lady Liscarrol's granddaughter?"

Rora nodded assent, smiling back at him in her friendly way. His voice was mellow and kind, although at close range his features seemed rather harsh when he was not smiling. "I am Rora Donellan, but I fear my grandmother is not home at present. Will you not come back to the house to await her return, sir?"

"Thank you, my dear, but I prefer to look over the grounds, if you would be so kind as to act my guide. I ask this only because it is

better for me to walk than to sit, although my infirmities make me
a poor companion for a stroll."

Her ready sympathies were excited by his self-reproach. "I
should be happy to walk with you, sir." She wished he would
introduce himself to her, for she was at a loss as to his identity. She
guessed he was some acquaintance of her grandmother's who
happened to be passing through the district. He looked as if he
might be one of the senior Connollys of Castletown; or a Fitzger-
ald of Carton House, of the Duke of Leinster's family, but Rora
could not be sure, and dared not ask. "If you like, we might feed
the swans," she suggested.

The old gentleman commended this as a delightful plan, and
together they walked up to the rear terrace. In but a moment a
footman supplied Rora with a silver bowl filled to the rim with the
breads she had left untouched at breakfast, and she led the visitor
around to the front lawn and the ornamental lake. As they crossed
the field of waving bluebells, Rora's companion asked her certain
questions about Lady Liscarrol that proved him no stranger to
these parts.

"Have you visited Ardara in the past, sir?" she asked him as they
came to the water's edge.

"Indeed I have, but not for many years. It is as lovely as ever,
and possesses as charming a young lady now as it did then."

She turned her sweetest smile upon him, her attention diverted
from the several swans that glided up to meet them. "That would
have been my mother, but she has not lived at Ardara Castle for
twenty years, and died four years ago."

"I'm sorry for it; I remember her well. You favor her, as I had
heard her daughter did, but your eyes are the larger, and your hair
the darker."

"You forget to add that my mouth is much wider than hers, nor
am I as tall as she!"

"Dear me, I suppose you hear these comparisons all too often,"
he sympathized.

"Yes," Rora admitted. "I'm quite used to them. But really, sir, I
am nothing like her in disposition. In fact, I sometimes feel that—
well, I'm sure you have no wish to hear." She broke off a piece of
bread and tossed it in a graceful arc over the heads of the impatient swans.

"But I do wish to hear, Miss Donellan. And you must know that
strangers always make the best of confidants," he added with his

kind smile. "Tell me more of the differences between you and the Lady Alanna Morres."

She had to laugh at the truth of his observation about strangers. "What I was going to say is that I am more of a thinker than Mama was, and I fancy I get that from my father. He's a great scholar, you see, and while I am not as brilliant as he, I do believe I inherited something of his propensity for thoughtfulness. Of course, he is very jolly, too, and therefore not like most academics; he has a very active mind. Mama was more—frivolous, and not at all the sort of wife you would expect a learned man to have."

"Quite the opposite, I should think a man concerned with serious pursuits might require a certain levity in his wife."

"Yes, I fancy it was Mama's sense of humor that attracted Papa initially—his is so marked! My parents had such fun together. They were to be envied." She sighed, knowing hers a futile dream: that she and Briavel might share as rewarding a life together as her parents had, one filled with love and laughter and joy, enough of all three to make the bad times endurable. "Mama and Papa married hastily, but not blindly; each knew the faults of the other and accepted them. I suppose the failure to do so is why many other love matches fail to prosper."

"You are a very wise young lady, particularly in the ways of the human heart," the old gentleman said, accepting a bit of bread from Rora and throwing it to the birds. "Do you speak from experience? Surely so lovely a creature as yourself has been touched by Cupid's dart ere now?"

"Oh, I don't know my own heart as well as I do others!" Rora disclaimed, dimpling up at him. "That is why I am all of twenty and still on the shelf."

"It pleases you to jest, Miss Donellan, but I will not believe you a stranger to the promptings of the heart. I detect a trace of maidenly reserve beneath your protestations—quite proper!" His voice held a teasing note, but Rora blushed nonetheless, causing him to say quickly, "Forgive me, my dear! I am a foolish old man, full of fancies, and did not mean to discomfit you."

"No, never that. The fact of it is that you are entirely too perceptive, sir." Rora sighed again and shredded her bit of bread vigorously.

"We shall leave it at that, then. Tell me, are these graceful beauties capable of doing us some injury? I have never before seen such ferocity in swans!"

" 'Tis my fault that they are so importunate; I have neglected them shamefully these past few days. Swans are terribly rude birds anyway, although they are so pretty to watch. A pity that their manners do not match their looks!"

"They should follow your own excellent example in that respect," the old man said gallantly, dusting the crumbs from his hands with his handkerchief.

She thanked him for the pretty compliment, which pleased her. Before she had time to turn the subject or to raise another, the approach of a horse could be heard along the drive, and she looked up to see who might be coming to call.

That black steed was well known, and its arrival had long been anticipated, but from Rora's expression one might have supposed that it was a most unwelcome sight. She started, paled, and dropped the bread she had been clutching so tightly a moment before. Then she flushed and brushed at her skirt in an agitated fashion, although no crumbs clung to it. The rider had cantered past without a glance in her direction; she could not even be sure that he had noted her presence.

None of the changes in her face had been lost upon her companion. "Dear me, that young fellow seems to be in a tearing hurry," he observed, his thin lips twitching. "Had you not better return to the house, child?"

He offered her his arm; biting her underlip in hesitation, Miss Donellan laid trembling fingers upon it and walked slowly beside him toward the crest of the hill and toward the house. Of what the strange gentleman conversed as they went along, she never knew. Her heart was hammering against the wall of her chest and her mind was completely overwrought. She hoped that she did not appear stupid or rude, for she had a strong liking for this kind old man, whoever he might be.

Purdon met them at the door, taking the empty silver bowl from Rora's nerveless grasp. "Lord Briavel has arrived, Miss Rora—my lord. I have shown him into the Great Parlor."

She nodded curtly and looked at her companion, whom Purdon had addressed in such a way as to give some indication of his rank. Count on Purdon to know! Of course, the visitor could be a baron or a marquis, or anything in between, but he was clearly no stranger to the butler, who had beamed at the old gentleman. The unusually benign expression hinted at a strong familiarity between the two, for Purdon's smiles were reserved only for family members (those of whom he approved), or equally well-respected persons. But Rora had not time to ponder this oddity. As she and her companion crossed the threshold of the parlor, her throat was perfectly dry. Briavel stood at one of the long windows, his back to them, but he must have been aware of their entrance, for he turned around as soon as they were in the room. Rora clutched at the old gentleman's arm convulsively, but she was so intent upon the viscount that she quite missed the warm smile that he cast upon her.

Briavel looked the pair over for a moment, then said lazily, "Miss Donellan, early in our acquaintance I told you I didn't care if you chose to jilt as many gentlemen as you pleased, but I do think it incumbent upon me to warn you: my father has suffered that disappointment once before. Therefore, you will please me by not charming him overmuch, since he is known to be susceptible to the females of your family!"

Rora gazed at him in blank astonishment. "Your father?" Looking up at the tall gentleman at her side, she gasped, "This cannot be true! Are you indeed Lord Rothmore, sir?"

"I am. I beg you will forgive my little deception, but every bit of it was Gavin's idea—and you know how he can be," his lordship said apologetically. "It is easier to fall in with his wishes, even when one is convinced that they are wrong."

"Yes, I know that well," Rora agreed bitterly, casting a fulminating glance upon Briavel, who grinned back at her shamelessly.

Said that gentleman, "I thought it best to return to Ireland before you came into your inheritance, ma'am, since I was afraid you might make good your threat to have me thrown off the property. You see, there is some business that I was unable to complete at our last meeting. As you have no doubt learned since that evening—or was it morning?—I had a pressing engagement, and had to be on my way!"

"The rumor did come to my ears," she replied with thinly veiled sarcasm. Turning to the earl, she asked if he would like some refreshment.

For a moment the old gray eyes bore mercilessly into those of the younger man. At last Lord Rothmore said that a glass of wine would not go amiss with him, and that dear Liscarrol always did have the best cellars in Ireland. Rora was pleased to see that his desire for wine angered the son, who fairly glowered, but she was too busy seeing to the comfort of the older of her two callers to pay

Briavel any mind. "Here is a footstool, sir. I am persuaded that you'll be more comfortable if you rest your leg upon it," she said as she helped the earl into a chair.

"Many thanks, my dear. Is that a carriage I hear in the drive?"

It was; within moments Lady Liscarrol was in the room, handing her bonnet and gloves to Rora as she said briskly, "I hope I have missed nothing! Rothmore, do my eyes deceive me? No, do not get up; you've no need to do the pretty, and I can see you're comfortable. I hope that Rora has been looking after both of you properly. Purdon, another glass at once, and you may open a bottle of champagne as well. It ought to be cold enough; we've had it on ice these three days!" she added cryptically. Rora frowned in confusion, but their lordships both smiled at this remark of her grandmother's. "So, Rothmore, you are the mysterious guest Gavin brought with him this time! I suppose you've heard all about how he brought my granddaughter Joan and Sir Nicholas Tobin together?"

"Certainly, Hester. I don't doubt they fooled you for a moment, though, despite my boy's clever machinations."

"Oh, I enjoyed every bit of it. 'Twas better than a play! I couldn't be happier about the match, either, although my son Brendan was hopping mad! But he'll dower the girl, if I have anything to say to it, and properly, too. Joan will have my rubies for a bride-gift, besides. They'll never suit you, Rora, so I'm sure you won't mind that I'm giving 'em to your cousin. Emeralds are the jewel for you, my girl. See that you take care of it, Gavin!"

Briavel's mouth twitched. "I will."

Rora stared at him, but she encountered so warm and meaningful a look in return that she went weak in the knees and felt incapable of speech. It was as though she were a spectator, or like one in a dream; all her active powers seemed suspended.

"You're ahead of things, Hester," the earl told her ladyship ruefully. "Nothing has been settled yet—at least, not as far as your granddaughter is concerned, poor child. And as she has lately informed me that she doesn't yet know her own heart, I hope my boy can be as persuasive with her as he was when he informed me of his decision to marry Lady Alanna's daughter. You can imagine the reservations I had about such an alliance, but I assure you that when he was done talking, he had overcome all of them—or very nearly." Smiling across at Rora, he said, "My dear, I hope you will encourage Gavin to use his talents for oratory in the House of

Lords in the future. To waste eloquence like his in the face of a cause dear to him would be a shame!"

Rora colored faintly and dared not meet Briavel's eyes.

Lady Liscarrol was saying, "I cannot conceive of any drawback to an alliance between our houses, Rothmore, and I only wish Liscarrol had lived to see this day, for 'twas the wish of his heart to have the Morres and the Hargrave families united. Before Rora was out of leading strings he'd formed the intention of wedding her to your Gavin, but how could the match be achieved with the lad always in England, and you so cut up after that business with Alanna? As soon as I knew of his visit to Hargrave House, I doubled my efforts to get my granddaughter under my roof, I can tell you! And Joan, too, for I had a good notion who Sir Nicholas was."

"Oh, Grandmother!" cried Rora, mortified. "You meant me to wed Gavin—Lord Briavel—all along!"

"Of course she did," Briavel answered her. "But I confess, I balked at her plan—until after I had seen you, at all events. When I had done so, I made up my mind to wed the heiress of Ardara, not Rora Donellan. That desire came a little while later."

"Oh, dear, oh, my!" moaned the heiress. "I do wish Papa were here!"

This non sequitur apparently did not surprise her betrothed, if such he could be called, considering that he had never yet proposed. "Oh, I expect him to be here any time, and wrote days ago requesting his urgent presence. I cannot think why he hasn't arrived already, but you may rest assured that he approves the match, for I asked his permission to address you long ago."

Stunned, Rora asked faintly when he could have done so.

"When I went to Dublin—nearly two months ago. You see, my sweet, your father was the only person I knew who could provide Joan and Nicky with a place for their honeymoon."

"Is that why Papa went to Londonderry so suddenly? Do you mean to say he left Merrion Square in order that Joan and her husband could—could be alone there?"

"Yes, my clever one, that is perfectly correct! Moreover, he possessed experience in planning an elopement, and his assistance was invaluable to me. I consulted him during my visit, when Nicky and I went to Dublin—shortly after I so cruelly robbed you of the horse Troilus," he reminded her.

Miss Donellan's hand flew to her throat. "I remember, and then you spoke so particularly of Papa—that day on the terrace when you gave Joan her letter. I was so puzzled when you said I was as like him as I was Mama; I thought it odd at the time, given the fact that you and he had never met!"

"But we had! I don't know how I maintained my countenance when you spoke of not wishing to wed a man whom your father disliked! Only a short time before I had spent several days in his company; when I informed him of my growing regard for you, he advised me most straitly not to follow in his or Nicky's footsteps, thereby denying him the privilege and pleasure of giving you away."

"Oh, I can just hear him saying it, too." Rora laughed, sinking onto a chair, nearly overcome with mirth that was as surprising as it was impossible to stifle.

"If Gavin is going to make his proposal, Rothmore, I believe we had better leave the room," Lady Liscarrol declared, setting down her wineglass decisively and rising. The earl did the same, more slowly. After bestowing a kindly look upon Rora and winking broadly at his son, he followed in her ladyship's wake.

When their elders were gone, Rora looked up at Briavel. "If you were so desirous of wedding me, sir, why did you wait all these weeks before returning to Kilkenny—and two days and a half before coming to Ardara to pay your addresses?"

He advanced and pulled her out of her chair, his gray eyes alight with laughter. "And were you counting the minutes as well, my love? My reason was this: I could not speak to you until I had made all right with my father, and in addition, I wished him to meet you before I made my proposals. When I returned to England, his leg was troubling him, and we had to wait some weeks before making the crossing. After we finally arrived at Hargrave House, he was somewhat fatigued by our journey. I couldn't let him stir until he was rested, however much he and I were eager that he make your acquaintance."

"And if he had not approved of me, what then? Would you have gone away without a word—as you did the last time?" she wanted to know, frowning at him.

Standing quite close to her, he replied, "There was no fear of his not liking you. His old feeling for Lady Alanna is by now a memory only. It was I who harbored any resentment against your mother. Initially, I wished to wed you only as a sort of revenge, and because of the, ah, baser promptings of my nature. But you enchanted me, and by the time I had fallen in love with you, my darling, I dared not speak. Not only was my father a consideration, but I had my duty to Nicky and Joan, you know."

"You didn't trust me to keep their secret?" Her voice shook with the joy she felt at his words: he loved her!

"It was not my secret to tell." He put his arms around her and looked down into her face. "Time and again I begged Joan to tell you, but she only said it would do me more good in your eyes if I appeared unattainable. Was she right?"

"I don't know. Perhaps she was," Rora said softly, meeting his gaze. "And—and for what reason did you invite me to meet you in the folly, sir? Those baser promptings of your nature?"

"I wanted to see if you would come," he answered frankly, tightening his hold. "I was not at all sure of you, you know, thinking that you might prefer young Peyton Newburgh and his stable of horses, or heaven forbid, Hubert Manville. When you came to me at night, I knew I could safely leave you without speaking, without fear of any rival. I don't know how I knew, precisely; I fancy it was the expression in your eyes whenever we met. But I knew you were mine, as you always will be!"

He bent his head to press his lips to hers, first gently, then with increasing ardor. Rora hardly knew how it happened, but her arms crept around his neck and almost immediately she was returning his kisses with an enthusiasm that quite matched his.

In a moment he loosened his hold slightly. "Miss Donellan, you cannot refuse a gentleman whom you have encouraged in so shameless a fashion, to say nothing of having twice met him secretly by moonlight! May I therefore assume that my suit is acceptable to you? Will you do me the honor of becoming my wife, my own and only love?"

Her green eyes met his, wordlessly answering his question. It was not enough, so she reached up to smooth his dark hair with a gentle hand as she replied, "Oh, yes, Gavin, I will indeed! For I have loved you this age, for all I detested you at first, and have been so blue-deviled since you went away that I could hardly bear it. And even when I hated you, I think I must have cared for you, and have been half longing for you to hold me thus since first setting eyes on you!"

This reply evidently satisfied him, and his lips met hers again.

It was some while before an anxious clearing of the throat heralded the entrance of Lady Liscarrol and the Earl of Rothmore. What they saw in the Great Parlor assured them that Briavel had made his offer at last, and had been accepted by the blushing young lady who leaned so brazenly against him. The wineglasses were refilled and toasts were drunk all around, to the heiress of Ardara and her future happiness. Rora and Briavel were soon off in a corner discussing which of her horses should be conveyed to England after the marriage, and which should remain in Ireland for their return in autumn for the hunting. The older generation was heatedly debating the rival merits of long and short engagements with all the warmth of long-standing friendship.

Their argument was interrupted by Briavel, who lifted his head long enough to say, "My betrothed and I find that we do not approve of engagements at all, so I advise you to send your cards of invitation at once, Cousin Hester. Within two days of Mr. Donellan's arrival, I intend use the special license I've already procured to make his daughter my wife—or else will follow his good example and spirit her away from Ardara at midnight!"

After this threat, the older lady and the earl were never more glad to see anyone than they were Jasper Donellan, who arrived half an hour later with hugs and kisses and felicitations for the happy couple. He teased his daughter, his eyes twinkling, and immediately joined in the toasts and the wedding plans. Rora was thankful to see that Lord Rothmore greeted Jasper warmly, but then, no one could hold a grudge against her papa, not even Lady Alanna's onetime suitor, who seemed as pleased to renew his old rival's acquaintance as Jasper was to meet the earl again.

The newly engaged couple took the first opportunity to disappear from the room, and their relations were so involved in discussion that their exit was hardly acknowledged. Rora and Briavel went outdoors, hand in hand, walking slowly in the direction of the folly and the Old Castle, murmuring utter nonsense to one another and pausing frequently in their progress for the exchange of tangible proofs of their mutual regard and affection.